Road to Marrakech

Road to Marrakech

Olmond M. Hall

Writers Club Press
San Jose New York Lincoln Shanghai

Road to Marrakech

All Rights Reserved © 2001 by Olmond M. Hall

No part of this book may be reproduced or transmitted in any form or by any means, graphic, electronic, or mechanical, including photocopying, recording, taping, or by any information storage retrieval system, without the permission in writing from the publisher.

Writers Club Press
an imprint of iUniverse.com, Inc.

For information address:
iUniverse.com, Inc.
5220 S 16th, Ste. 200
Lincoln, NE 68512
www.iuniverse.com

This is a work of fiction. The characters, events and places portrayed in Road to Marrakech are fictional and any resemblance to real people, places or incidents is purely coincidental. Although the names of some of the cities and towns are real, the locations are not, nor the characters portrayed.

ISBN: 0-595-18127-9

Printed in the United States of America

Dedication

To Mary Ann
Road to Marrakech is dedicated to Mary Ann, my wife, for her untiring support and patience in editing, proofreading and most of all enthusiasm and encouragement and faith.
Words cannot express my love and gratitude to her.

To Shirley and Jim Pohlers
You were the first to read parts of the unedited, unproofed, and unspell-checked chapters. Special thanks for finding more mistakes than I want to think about.
Your excellent suggestions and enthusiasm gave me encouragement to continue.

To Bobbi & Rog Patterson
Special thanks to these friends who read, proofed and gave crucial editorial advice that was beyond the call of duty. As usual, the mistakes are all mine.

Chapter One

Jeff woke up in the swaying hammock, hot and sweaty. As hard as he tried he could not get back to sleep. The odor from the sweating sailors, sleeping and snoring was overpowering. He had been on this freighter for eight days and had not yet mastered the technique of getting in or out of the hammock. The odor reminded him of when he was a boy, going to the cotton gin in late July on a wagonload of cotton. He would lay in the hot sun, with no breeze, sweating, his Pa and the mules sweating. The smell of this hold was similar to that, especially when both mules farted simultaneously.

Jeff's hammock was the middle one, of three high, and three wide. The ropes were tied front and back to a hook in a three-inch steel bar that ran from wall to wall of the ship's hold.

This time he reached up with his right hand to grasp the rope that fastened the hammock to the hook and pulled himself up, swinging his legs over the side, with his left hand on the back wall to steady himself, then eased his feet to the deck. Just then the freighter changed course, and he fell flat on the steel deck. No one moved or said anything, just kept snoring and sweating. The hold was all the way forward below the water line, with no portholes. It was about 20 feet by 24 feet, with sailors stacked three high and three wide, sleeping 45 sailors. The hold was not full at any one time. The sailors were on duty 24 hours a day, leaving about 30 sleeping at night. Jeff and five other men were paying passengers. They did not work, but ate and slept with the crew, which made the fare cheap.

    Jeff made his way among the swaying hammocks, down the passageway toward the stairs to the deck. Arriving on deck, he walked over to the guardrail and sucked in as much fresh air as his lungs would hold. As he often did on the past seven mornings, he removed his pocket watch in the light of the bright full moon to read the time. It was three o'clock. He walked over to one of the cargo holds on the starboard side, which was covered with canvas. He took another piece of canvas, folded it and lay down. Lights shone in the distance. Maybe it was another ship. He saw what appeared to be some stationary lights on the port side. Taking a map out of his pocket and going under a dim light on the hull, he estimated they were east of the Canary Islands and west of the coast of Africa. His ocean journey was almost over. The estimated time of arrival in Casablanca was approximately two days.

Chapter Two

Jeff stretched out on the canvas, looking up at the bright stars, full moon, feeling the warm Atlantic breeze and thinking, *how in the hell, did a poor country boy from a farm in south Alabama get here?* He closed his eyes and went back to his childhood.

What a rotten time that was. The kids at school calling me names, such as clubfoot, sharecropper, preacher's boy, beggar, white trash and other names.

Jeff was born with a deformed left foot. The foot did not have any toes where they were supposed to be attached. Yes, they were poor; Jeff's daddy was a sharecropper and part-time preacher. He could barely remember his mama; she died when he was two years old. His grandmother helped his daddy, but then she died when he was about six years old. His only real friend was a boy his same age, who lived about a mile and a half down the road. Sometimes Jeff would spend the weekend at his house. He enjoyed going there because he was treated like one of the family and they never mentioned his clubfoot.

World War I ended when Jeff was eight years old. Soon afterward, his friend's daddy joined the Army and they moved away. Jeff was lonelier than ever after that and kept to himself. One day, he found an old harmonica that his daddy used to play. Jeff picked it up and began trying to play some of the church songs his daddy sang while preaching. The crops were better this year, and Jeff's daddy was preaching on the street corner in Andrea. His daddy, known as the preacher, would sing religious songs in his deep baritone voice, then preach a hellfire sermon and sing some Hardshell Baptist songs, while walking around with his hat taking up a collection. Jeff kept practicing and was becoming an accomplished harmonica player. One night, when he was on the front porch playing, he saw his daddy ease over to the window and begin to sing the song he was playing, Rock of Ages. Jeff was nine years old, and this was the first time he remembered his daddy putting his arm around him.

"Jeff," he said, "You play better than I, and I was a good harmonica player." Daddy always called him Jefferson, never Jeff; this was the first time he had called him by that name. Sometimes he would call him by his full name, Jefferson Davis. When he was mad, which was often, he would call him by his complete name Jefferson Davis Stewart.

"Let's practice some songs and you can come with me next Saturday to Andrea. We will have a grand time, singing, preaching and saving souls."

This was the best time he had ever had with his daddy. He played the harmonica while Daddy sang until after midnight. The moon was full, a pleasant summer evening with a cool breeze blowing; the music and singing must have carried a country mile.

Things between the two were good for about a year. He enjoyed playing the harmonica, and people began to notice him for how good his playing was rather than the old clubfoot. He had purchased some new shoes and put cotton cloth in the toe of the shoe for the clubfoot, so that the shoe didn't flop as he walked. That was much better than using old newspapers. With these shoes he learned to run and walk without much of a limp. People who did not know he had a clubfoot would not guess it was the foot that gave him the slight limp.

He remembered when the change came over Daddy. It was not long after he met the widow, Patsy Jo Bradley. Daddy began staying out most of the night and didn't feel like going to the field, especially when the sun got hot. Jeff noticed that things got even worse when Daddy would get up in the morning and take a drink of moonshine.

The cursing and beatings were worse, before and after school. When he wasn't in school, Jeff stayed in the field to keep away from his daddy. On Saturday, in Andrea, Daddy would preach behind Barry's Drug Store. After about a half hour his words were slurred and his singing off-key. People would pass them by, not stopping as they used to do. At night he would curse and knock Jeff around, because the collection was way off. They barely had enough to eat. The kids at school were merciless, kidding him about the street preaching and his foot. He had outgrown his shoes and didn't have enough money to buy new ones. All he could get were those black tennis shoes, made with rubber. They were hot, made his feet stink, and the clubfoot flopped around like a dead mackerel. He would get up early on Saturday mornings, go down in the woods and stay until noon when he knew his daddy had left to try to get enough in the collection hat for moonshine. It became so unbearable that he quit school in the seventh grade. They tried to farm, but couldn't make ends meet. Finally, Mr. Neal kicked them out, and the only place they could go was to Patsy Jo Bradley's house.

Patsy Jo lived near the textile mill in a run-down clapboard two-bedroom house. The outhouse was directly outside the room where Jeff slept, or tried to sleep. The odor was awful, especially in summer. The drinking, hollering, cursing and fighting continued almost every night. In the mornings Patsy Jo dragged herself out of bed went off to the textile mill. She was a big woman, with light red mousy hair turning grey. She wore a bright red lipstick that clashed with her hair and complexion. Patsy Jo's skin was pale pinkish with freckles. She had small, washed-out green eyes. Her stomach was rather large, as were her breasts. She wore no brassiere, which made her breasts hang down and rest on her stomach. Patsy Jo always wore dresses that were large and came down to the ankles. The dresses were bright colored, often clashing with her hair and lipstick. They looked as though they were made by Omar the Tentmaker.

Jeff could not find work in the small town of Andrea. One day after Patsy Jo stumbled off to the textile mill and before his daddy got drunk, Jeff said, "Daddy, I'm going to leave; I know I'm only a little over 13 years old, but I can't do nothing here. I will go to Mobile and play the harmonica on the streets and see if I can make enough to live on."

"You know, Jeff, I think I'll go with you."

"Daddy, we can't make any money when you are drunk; people don't like a drunkard preacher."

"Jeff, you are too young to go off, besides, if you do I will have the law put you in the reformatory school. We'll go together. I know I can't preach while I am drinking, so I will not get drunk when I preach and try to wean off the stuff."

For the next three years, it was cities like Mobile, Memphis, St. Louis, New Orleans, Houston, San Antonio and others. It was always hopping freight trains, sleeping in the hobo jungles, eating whatever and whenever they could get food.

Things got better in Houston. They had a room with a hot plate and were allowed use of the stove in the kitchen. They were taking in enough money to save some, but it seemed as if in the last two weeks there was no money left over. Coming home from street preaching one night, Jeff knew what happened to the money. As they entered Patsy Jo was sitting on the bed.

Jeff asked Mrs. Hartley, the landlady, if he could sleep on her sofa that night. She gave him a blanket, and as he lay there, knowing what would happen, he decided he would leave in the morning. Pasty Jo and Daddy came in at 2 AM and began arguing, cursing and hitting each other. The fight lasted about an hour. The next morning, when Jeff went up to the room, they were both out like lights, naked as a pair of jaybirds. *What a horrible sight to see.* He packed his few belongings, got a pencil and a piece of paper to write a note, then thought the better of it. *To hell with them.* "Goodbye, Mr. Robert E. Lee Stewart," he mumbled as he closed the door and headed for the freight yard.

He got to the freight yard just as a long freight train was slowly getting up steam. He didn't know where it was going and didn't care. He looked around to see if there were any railroad detectives or bulls. No one was in sight. As the train came by he saw an open door. He ran beside the train, threw his croaker sack of belongings in the car, and was ready to boost himself up, when a hand was extended to him. He grabbed it, and a strong arm pulled him into the car, where six other men were sitting. The man who pulled him in must have been about his daddy's age, but looked much younger. He was tall, had broad shoulders, dark hair and a mustache, with streaks of grey in both. His clothes, a plaid shirt, dark pants, high top brogan shoes, and a red bandana around his neck, were clean. The man reached out to shake hands saying, "My name is Jeff Davis; I am King of the Hoboes, Knights of the Road. Welcome aboard."

Jeff clasped his strong hand and said, "My name is also Jeff Davis; actually it's Jefferson Davis Stewart. Thank you for helping me aboard."

"Well, another Jeff Davis. So that we don't get confused, we will call you JD. Where are you going my young friend?"

"I don't rightly know," said JD, "wherever this train goes, if it looks good I'll stay."

"Well, me and a couple of the boys are going to New Orleans. Have you been there?"

"Yes, but it was a couple years back, and I was with my daddy, so I don't know much about it."

"What type of work do you do, JD?"

"Well, my daddy was a street preacher and I played the harmonica while he sang and preached and I took up the collection."

"Did your daddy pass on?"

"No, Sir, he's a drunkard and it got so bad I had to leave. All I know is how to play the harmonica, but I'm willing to learn anything."

"JD, maybe you can make it as a street entertainer. Let me hear you play."

JD took out the harmonica and began to play the church songs. Jeff and the other hoboes joined in singing.

"You are good, JD, but you need to learn some other songs, popular songs, that is. When we get to New Orleans we will go to the music store and see whether we can get some sheet music." JD explained that he couldn't read music, but if he heard it he would be able to play anything.

"JD, you will make a fine hobo. Would you like to join the 'Knights of the Road?'"

"I would, but I ain't got a penny and I can't eat until I can get on the street corner and play."

"Tell you what, JD," said the hobo known as Big Red, "I'll chip in a nickel of the twenty cent fee." The others put pennies and nickels in the pot, until they had forty cents. Jeff Davis threw in a dime, making the total fifty cents. "Now you have thirty cents left over until you find work. I'll make your card out and it will be official, you are JD Stewart 'Knight of the Road,' a hobo in good standing. However, let me explain the difference between a tramp and a hobo. A tramp will beg for food or whatever his needs are, is usually lazy and won't work. A hobo will work for his keep, but will not pay for transportation from one city to the next."

"JD, I am a bartender. I think I can get a job in the French Quarter tending bar. Stay with me in the hobo camp, and when we reach New Orleans I'll see that you get some type of job, OK?"

"Sure, Jeff. I'll do any type of work; I don't care what the job is."

The train slowed as it reached Harhan. JD looked out of the boxcar at the mighty Mississippi River, with jungle-like bushes going right into the water. There were openings where people had houseboats. He thought, *what would it be like living on a houseboat? They don't look too strong, but they had to be better than living on the farm in a clapboard house with the Grit newspaper nailed inside to keep the wind out. And it must be a hell of a lot better than the hobo jungle. I would love to live in a real house.*

The train moved slowly along the river where it crossed over the river into New Orleans at Highway 90. Jeff said, "Hey, JD, snap out of it, we will be getting off soon. The train's destination is Port Nickel, near the sugar mills, but that's too far from the city, so we'll have to be careful. The bulls are out watching for the hoboes to hit the tracks. When I give you the word, follow me. The train will be moving, but you jump as I do, with the direction of the train. If you stumble when your feet hit the dirt, ball your body up and roll. Get ready, here I go."

JD watched as Jeff jumped from the boxcar and hit the ground, running. *He sure made it look easy.* JD leaned out and with one hand holding to the door of the boxcar, leaped forward. When his feet hit the ground he felt himself going head first for the dirt. As Jeff had instructed, he rolled his body into a ball, or tried to. He hit the ground, tumbling head over heels. Jeff grabbed him about the time he stopped rolling, helping him to his feet.

"Can you run?"

"Yes," answered JD.

"Follow me. Just run like hell, two bulls are after us with baseball bats."

Jeff led the way through some thick bushes to the river, where they came upon a hobo camp with about a dozen hoboes sitting around a campfire boiling coffee. JD and Jeff pulled off their hats and jackets, placed them on a log and sat down on them. When the bulls ran into the little clearing, they saw fourteen of the toughest, dirtiest looking men, and quickly backed out of the clearing, disappearing into the bushes.

Jeff knew a couple of the hoboes, who gave them the low-down on the lay of the land, as they called it. No one bothered them here. Three or four of the hoboes had found work, doing odd jobs. One of them caught the six o'clock freight train down to Port Nickel where he worked in the sugar mill. At night he caught another freight train back.

Hawkeye, so named because he only had one good eye, saw more than most people did with two good eyes. Most of the hoboes had nicknames, which were reflections of the way they looked, dressed or behaved.

Hawkeye told Jeff that he worked at a tavern named, Le Havrey Saloon. He cleaned, washed dishes, and did other odd jobs. He said he would be leaving in a couple of days, so they would need someone to replace him and they also had an opening for a bartender.

The next day, Jeff and JD went to Le Havrey Saloon on Toulouse Street to meet the owner, Monsieur Jean Laveau. With Jeff's experience, it didn't take long for the two to reach an agreement. He would start to work the next evening at six o'clock. Jeff asked about the handyman's job for JD, saying he would be responsible for training him. Monsieur Laveau agreed and JD had his first paying job.

On the way back to the hobo jungle, they discussed Le Havrey Saloon (The Happy Bar), who's slogan was "Venir Dans Triste et Parti Havrey," which roughly translated to "Come in Sad, Leave Happy."

That night at the hobo camp they had beef stew prepared in a gallon lard can, with beans, potatoes and turnips cooked in with the cut up beef. As they sat there savoring the stew, Jeff said, "JD, you will start a new job tomorrow. Although, I will be there, you will have to learn fast. Remember, you must always do better than anyone else. Look for things to do instead of waiting for the boss to tell you. You will be under my management on the night shift from six PM until midnight. Tomorrow I will instruct you on your duties and I expect you to do them promptly and thoroughly. If you do a good job, you will be recommended for other jobs and you will never be without employment unless you want to be unemployed."

JD was awake before the sky was light and watched the sky as it turned pink and the sun was up enough to shine down on the mighty Mississippi River. What a beautiful sight; how peaceful the world was. He daydreamed about his new life and was determined to be a success.

After a full day of instructions on how to be the best handyman trainee in New Orleans, they arrived at Le Havrey Saloon at five PM. Jeff received his instructions from Monsieur Jean Laveau. In turn, he showed JD around, describing his duties. JD loved this job from the first minute as he went about washing the glasses, cleaning the bar, sweeping and mopping the floor, bringing ice to the ice well, and stocking the beer cooler with beer. He was busy the full six hours and on the way back to the hobo jungle, Jeff asked him whether he was tired and how he liked his job.

"I am tired happy. I believe this is the happiest day of my life. I want to get a good night's rest and go back."

"JD, my boy, you will be successful if you can keep that attitude. In the morning I will give you some more tips on how to work so that you will be happy and your employer will be happy. Let's stop at this market and get a chicken. We can fry it in the lard can and eat it before we go to sleep."

JD loved his work and as the days passed he became more useful, so that Monsieur Laveau offered to let him start at three o'clock and work until twelve with a pay raise. Three to six was not too busy and JD could use the extra money, so he jumped at the opportunity.

Just after this offer, he and Jeff got a room with a hot plate only three blocks from Le Havrey Saloon on Bourbon Street. Now he had time to play his harmonica.

He would arrive at the rooming house about twelve-thirty AM, sleep to about seven-thirty, get up fix something on the hot plate and go downstairs. The stairs went from the second floor to the street. JD would sit on the concrete banister and play new tunes he had heard on the radio at the saloon. His harmonica drifted over Bourbon Street in the morning hours and people would stop for a minute and listen. One morning, before the sun reached the street, JD laid his cap on the banister and was playing some of the songs he had heard the night before. People passing by stopped to listen and dropped some change into the cap. That morning when he counted the change it came to fifty-five cents. This was more than half of what he made working at the saloon for nine hours. So each morning he would go downstairs sit on the banister and play until about one o'clock.

After about three months Jeff told JD that he had a craving for travel.

"JD, you have a good job and you are doing well playing down on the street. I think you can manage the room on what you are making. I would like your company, but you will fare better if you remain here. What do you think about going with me or staying?"

"Jeff, you are better than my daddy, and I love you like a daddy, but I am living in a house and sleeping in a soft bed, and I love my job and New Orleans, so I think I'll stick around here. Will you write me and tell me where I can write you 'cause I will miss you?"

"Sure, JD. As I am leaving, you should start using your real name, Jeff. The name fits you, and I would be proud for the two of us to share the same name. Monsieur Laveau likes your work and has plans for you. Good-bye, dear friend."

To keep his mind off his departed friend, Jeff (JD) would play his harmonica on the street until one o'clock each day, then go to Le Havrey Saloon at two where he would clean and get things in order. One day, Jeff moved all the tables and chairs, swept and mopped the floor. When he put the tables and chairs back, he rearranged them so that two more tables and eight additional chairs could be added. It looked better than the old set-up, which was all over the floor in disarray. Monsieur Laveau liked the new look, especially since he could now seat eight more patrons, and complimented Jeff on the fine job he had done.

One afternoon Jeff approached Monsieur Laveau. "Monsieur, I have an idea how maybe you can increase your business. I am not a businessperson, but see what you think. Get three fellows with a piano, trumpet, and a saxophone, and let them play the blues. Leave the doors open so people walking down Toulouse can hear them. Maybe some of them will come in instead of passing by the saloon."

"Jeff, you may be right. I have thought about something like this since you rearranged the tables and chairs. I think it will work. Do you think you could get another table and four more chairs in without overcrowding the place?"

"Yes, Sir. You know the storage room behind that wall over there? Much of that stuff could be tossed out and we can move the good stuff to another place. Then we can take the wall down, put the musicians on one side and a small dance floor on the other side and maybe serve crab cakes and other snacks."

"That's a good idea, Jeff. You take charge of it and if it works out, you'll have a raise."

After a month Le Havrey Saloon had been remodeled and spruced up. The musicians, Mama Agnes, a seventy-year old black woman on the piano, Hotshot Hawkins, a sixty-eight-year old creole (a mix of African and French parentage) on the trumpet and Jiving Praslin, a sixty-six-year old Cajun on the saxophone, were practicing every day. The front doors remained open and people hearing the blues sound coming out of Le Havrey Saloon began drifting in. While the musicians were practicing, Jeff would stand in the doorway and play along on the harmonica. He was getting the blues down and dirty on the instrument. Monsieur Laveau asked Jeff to sit in with the band at night.

On opening night, Jeff made a contact that would steer his life in a different direction. A regular, who came in Le Havrey Saloon often, a Mr. Clio Conti, was having an afternoon beer and asked Jeff whether he had flowers for the tables.

"No, Sir, I hadn't thought of that," answered Jeff.

"Well, Jeff, I own a funeral home a few blocks over and we have many flowers remaining from a funeral this morning. If you would like, come over in about an hour and I'll give them to you."

When Jeff returned with the flowers, he put them in small vases on the tables. Mr. Conti told Jeff he was providing a service by removing the flowers, saving the funeral director the trouble of carrying them to the dump. Each day after that, Jeff would call Mr. Conti and get the leftover flowers. When Mr. Conti did not have any funerals, Jeff would check with other funeral homes, until he had about four or five funeral homes that regularly supplied him with flowers.

One afternoon things were quiet in Le Havrey Saloon, with only one couple sitting in the corner. They acted as if they were lovers or newlyweds. The man, who wore a white linen suit and a Palm Beach hat, came over to Jeff, where he was arranging flowers for the tables.

"My good fellow, would you make me a bouquet for my sweetheart?"

"Sure," Jeff answered. He found some poppies in assorted colors with contrasting centers. He selected one pink and one yellow, added a small white chrysanthemum and a piece of fern, tied them with a red ribbon, then delivered them over to the table. The man handed him two dollars for the bouquet.

This is a great profit, free flowers and less than a half of a cent for the ribbon.

The next afternoon Jeff approached Monsieur Laveau with an idea of selling bouquets at Le Havrey Saloon. He explained how he was getting the flowers free, that he only had to ride his bicycle to each of the funeral homes. He said that before setting the tables, he could make the bouquets, and display them for sale.

"Jeff, I don't think they will sell, but since you will be doing all the work on your time, and getting the flowers and ribbon, I think a twenty per cent commission for Le Havrey would be fair."

The next morning Jeff was up early and off to a bicycle shop, where he purchased two large baskets that were used for delivering groceries. He mounted one on the front and one in the rear. He arrived at Le Havrey about one o'clock, put the flowers up and started making bouquets. When he completed the task it was almost time for his shift. The bouquets looked beautiful. *I'll price them at two dollars each.*

No sales were made until about ten o'clock and only two were sold the entire night. Getting to his room about one AM, he was very tired and disappointed about the bouquets. He went to bed but could not sleep for trying to think of a way to make the bouquet business pay off. He awoke early, tired from the disappointment of the previous day and sleepless night, but as he rode his bicycle to the funeral homes, he had an idea. *I will tie two flowers with a ribbon around them and sell the bouquet for seventy-five cents.* He fixed the bouquets, placed them on a table with a new sign. As he went about his duties, his mind continued to think about the flowers. That night he took in three dollars, a little better.

The next day when Jeff arrived at Le Havrey, the door was closed with a wreath and a black ribbon on it. Monsieur Laveau had had a heart attack and passed away during the night. Monsieur Laveau's only son was an attorney, who did not want the saloon and informed the employees that Le Havrey Saloon was closed until a buyer could be found. They would have to deal with the new owner.

Jeff went back to his room to think. *Should he wait or not for a new owner to apply for a job?* While lying on the bed, staring at the ceiling, he had an idea of how to make a little money. *I will still keep in touch with the funeral homes. After creating some bouquets, I will go to the different bars and sell them.* Jeff fell asleep planning his new venture. The next morning, rested and alert, he took off on the bicycle for the funeral homes. He returned to his rooming house with the flowers, made some bouquets using two flowers tied with a ribbon. That afternoon, he proceeded to the produce department of a grocery store, where he picked up a couple of apple crates. After taking them apart, he reassembled them into a tray about twenty inches wide by about twelve inches deep. The tray was completed when he fashioned a rim 3/4 of an inch high and added a forty-eight inch long strap, which he fastened to each end of the tray. He put the strap around his neck, adjusting the length until the tray fit around his waist. Then he placed the bouquets on the tray. Jeff, the entrepreneur, was ready for his first night of business. That night Jeff dressed in his best pair of white duck pants, with a light blue shirt. He put on a pair of shoes, with cotton from a bed sheet, rolled up in the toe to keep it from flopping. Trying on the shoe and walking he had a slight limp, hardly noticeable. At seven o'clock, a little early for the type of customers he wanted, Jeff started off on his first night as a businessman. Going into a bar and strip saloon, he spoke with the owner,

Monsieur Angelico. Monsieur Angelico gave him permission to go among the customers to sell his bouquets but said he could not stay and associate or drink with the customers. Later, Jeff made a list of rules he would follow if the owner of an establishment would let him move quickly through, selling his bouquets.

That first night Jeff worked until one AM and sold only four bouquets at seventy-five cents each. Jeff did not pay for the flowers, and the ribbon was less than an eighth of a cent for all for the bouquets. He made a good profit, but not as much money as he had made at Le Havrey Saloon. He had to find a way to increase his income, so he went to work earlier and worked later, but with little improvement.

One day Jeff was discouraged and went down to the Mississippi River to do some fishing and think over his operation and how he could improve the situation. He had brought a sandwich for lunch and after eating he lay back and fell asleep. Waking at four o'clock he hopped on his bicycle and went to one of the funeral homes for flowers. They did not have any, so he went to another one. That one was also out. Finally, at his third stop they had some flowers, so he rushed home and began making bouquets. When he finished it was late, so he took his tray of bouquets and headed out to work without shaving, showering or changing clothes. He realized that he still had on his tennis shoes with the paper inside and the shoes were flip-flopping as he walked. He had made 15 bouquets, so he reduced his price to fifty cents each. His sales went well, and his spirits began to rise.

After he returned to his apartment, he counted his money. He had sold 11 of the 15 bouquets for a total of $7.50. After eating and taking a bath he lay in bed thinking back over every move and word he had spoken that night. The last time he looked at the clock, it was four AM. Jeff was up at seven, again making the rounds of the funeral homes and planning for the night.

That night he did not shave and again put on his old clothes, wore his tennis shoes and made sure they would flop, reminding himself to limp as the shoes flopped. He looked in the mirror on the dresser and liked the look. The night before when a customer who was high on booze and was with a younger woman asked, "Say, Buddy, how much for the flowers?"

Jeff answered. "Whatever you think your sweetheart is worth." The man removed two one-dollar bills from his wallet and placed them on the tray.

Jeff began to experiment with lines on people, letting them decide how much they would give for the bouquets. Most customers gave more than fifty cents. The later the evening became, and the more drinks the customers had, the higher the price they would pay. He became experienced enough that he could spot a married man out with a girlfriend or a prostitute and by using different lines he could extract the most money.

Chapter Three

A loud noise, and the rocking of the ship, brought Jeff out of his semi-sleep. He had been so deep in his thoughts that he did not realize the time or where the ship was. It was six-fifteen AM. When he got up, he saw that the sun was beginning to rise up from the horizon to the east. The ship had changed course, and some of the cargo had shifted. The sailors were scurrying to fasten the cargo on deck. Jeff overheard an officer telling the first mate that they were pulling into Agadir, Morocco to make some minor repairs and would be there until about nine PM. Going down into the hold to his hammock and removing his notes and maps, Jeff found that Agadir was approximately 125 miles southwest of Marrakech, approximately 260 miles southeast of Casablanca.

Walking over to the captain, Jeff asked, "How long will we be in Agadir and what is the new time of arrival in Casablanca?"

"Mr. Stewart, we expect to be in Agadir about twelve hours for repairs. We should be at the docks by eight and if everything goes right we should leave at nine tonight, with a stopover off the coast from Marrakech for unloading some cargo. We'll arrive in Casablanca about three days after leaving Agadir."

"Captain, if I proceed by bus or rent a vehicle could I pick the ship up off the coast of Marrakech and what time would the ship be there?"

"Mr. Stewart, I could not promise the exact time. The ship would be off the coast of Marrakech, so you would have to get someone to take you to the waterway that leads to the Atlantic, then hire a boat to carry you through the straights to the ship. I would not recommend this trip, for the ship may not be punctual. It is only 135 miles to Casablanca by road from Marrakech, about a four-hour trip. There is a four to five-hour trip from Agadir to Marrakech before entering Casablanca "Thank you, Captain, I'll stay with the ship. I'll go ashore to look around Agadir. Maybe I can get some information there."

As the New Orleans Trader was being towed into the inlet at Agadir, Jeff saw a long, wide, beautiful beach of white sand. Beyond the white beach was a row of beachside hotels and behind the hotels, hills and mountains. Going ashore, he found that most people came here for the warm winter weather, not for the architecture. Most of the buildings dated from the late 1800's or beyond.

As Jeff strolled along the narrow streets, the sounds and smells were very different from New Orleans. He knew the language was Arabic and French, but the French was the true French and not the Cajun French spoken in Louisiana and New Orleans. Jeff soon found that he could understand a little and be understood enough to manage in the Cajun French.

Before leaving on his mission, he had gone to the library to read about Morocco, Algeria and Tunisia and who controlled the countries, languages and customs.

Jeff found out that the Kasbah was on top of the hill, and rented a camel for a ride up the steep hill to the fortress-like 16th century Kasbah. A Kasbah is the native quarters of any village, town or city with a large Arab population, mostly found in Africa and other Middle East countries. Most Kasbahs have walls around them, for in the early times they were forts. As the Kasbah grew, the people were crowded into the same area. It had become a maze of narrow winding streets, living quarters, and people. The Kasbah is located in the Medina, the old city. Medina is also a Moslem holy city in Saudi Arabia, with a large square in the center. Medina is also a market place. Jeff was thankful that he had used the library before departing on this trip.

As Jeff rode the camel up to the Medina, he looked back down the hill at the beautiful view of the town and sandy beaches. As he arrived at the entrance to the Kasbah, the narrow street did not have a gate as it once had over a hundred years ago. The high rock walls that surrounded the Kasbah were about two feet thick and twelve feet high with broken glass set in cement on top. The streets were extremely narrow and winding with steps from level to level. No motorized vehicles, only donkeys with carts were allowed. Jeff found a stable where he left the camel and continued on foot. As he walked, the streets became narrower and the odor was very strange. There must have been a dozen different languages being spoken.

It was noon and he was getting hungry. He began looking for an eating establishment for lunch. Asking an Arab, in Cajun French where to dine, he received a cold stare that sent shivers up and down his spine. A soldier in an unusual looking uniform walked up and in English with an American accent, asked whether he could be of any assistance.

"Yes," replied Jeff. "I was looking for a place to eat lunch, do you know of any cafés near here?"

"My name is Tony Marro, originally from Queens, New York. This time of day a good many businesses in the Medina close from noon until two, however, some of the businesses that cater to the tourists are open. I am going to the Fosse Café which is open at this hour. A couple of Legionnaires will meet me there, and maybe some tourists and local people will be there."

"My name is Jeff Stewart. I am from New Orleans, Louisiana. What army are you in and what do those insignias mean, Tony?"

"I am a Sergeant in the French Foreign Legion, stationed at Goulimime, about 100 miles south of here, on the edge of the Sahara Desert. Three of us legionnaires are here on three-day passes which end today. Let's go to the Fosse Café, have a couple beers and get acquainted. I would like to know how in the hell you got to this God-forsaken place."

"OK, Tony, I also would like to hear how you arrived here in the French Foreign Legion, and maybe you can give me some information that may help me find someone."

Tony and Jeff walked through the narrow winding streets, past the small hole-in-the-wall type shops displaying their merchandise of mostly Arab clothing, copper items, wool, sheepskins, almonds and other nuts, baskets of dates and casks of olives. The air smelled of saffron, cumin, black pepper, ginger, cloves and oranges. Jeff felt as if he was in another world. Tony was filling him in on the languages and dialects. Mostly what was spoken in the Medina was Arabic, with many different Berber dialects, and the second language of Morocco, French. Tony turned into a doorway to the Fosse Café at the top of a flight of stairs. As they walked down the winding steps, about 15 to 20, the light was dim with an electric cord hanging from the ceiling and a twenty-five watt or less bulb. There were four of the electric cords with bulbs and small candles burning on each table. Musicians were playing cymbals, two-stringed instruments, and reed flutes, while belly dancers performed. Jeff and Tony found a small table in the corner where they could see everything. The patrons were mostly Arabian and French. Some were smoking water pipes. A water pipe is a round bowl of water with a tube running from a clay bowl of tobacco drawn through the water. Tony pointed to an Arab sitting on a blanket with a water pipe and said there may be hashish in the tobacco. The Arab was the owner of the Fosse Café and was getting a haircut, if you could call the shaving of the head a haircut. The barber gave the owner a shave and trimmed his moustache. He put a fez on and came by their table. Tony introduced the owner, a Monsieur LeBlanc, who noted that Jeff had a Cajun accent and asked whether he was from New Orleans in America.

"Yes, Monsieur, I am from New Orleans. I have lived there for eleven years."

"I have a cousin, once removed, who lives in New Orleans."

"What do you mean once removed, Monsieur?"

"He was a fils of one of my tante fille. Can you explain Sergeant?"

"Yes, Monsieur. Jeff, he was the son of his aunt's daughter, which would be his second cousin."

"His moth uh mota, I don't know to say it in English. In French it is Mére name was Laveau."

"You mean his mother's name was Laveau. Yes, I knew a Monsieur Jean Laveau. I worked for him until he passed away. You know, disparu?"

"Oui, that is he. When did Monsieur Jean Laveau disparu?"

"It must have been ten years ago, about 1929."

"Monsieur Stewart, I must go back to mon business. If I can be of any assistance to you while in mon city, moi content to give you help."

After Monsieur left the table, Jeff asked Tony how he got into the French Foreign Legion.

"It is a long story, Jeff. But, I'll make it shorter than it really is. I was born in Queens, New York, just after my mother and father arrived from Capri on the Isle of Capri, Italy where Papa was a tailor. He became a tailor in New York, but it was hard to support a wife and four kids. I have an older brother and two older sisters. In my early teens my older brother was selling numbers to help out the family, and I pestered him until I got a job selling numbers. I did some boxing because I was strong and had a mean streak. I collected money for the numbers bosses. I was arrested at the age of 18 for assault and battery and went to jail for two years. Six months after getting out, I was again arrested and sent back to jail for two more years. After one year I was released on parole, but I couldn't stay out of trouble. I was fingered in an armed robbery and knew that I would be sent back for breaking my parole, plus the new armed robbery charge. Facing a long prison sentence, I stuck up the mob's gambling room and beat it down to pier 13, where I caught the first ship out as a lowly deck hand. I did not know where the ship was headed until three days out to sea. The first stop would be Algiers, Algeria. There were several guys in the same situation as myself, and they had heard of the Foreign Legion, who did not inquire into the background of the person who wanted to enlist. When the ship docked in Algiers two other guys and I jumped the ship and headed for the Medina section. We were in luck for at a café we entered, several Legionnaires were drinking and began to fight. When it was over, my two buddies and I were the only ones standing; four Legionaries were out cold on the floor. We got some bar rags and wet their faces until they came to. We apologized, set them up for a round of drinks and asked them how to enlist in the French Foreign Legion. They told us that they were on their first leave since entering the Legion and had to report back to the garrison that afternoon and we could accompany them. We didn't know at the time, but they received a small bonus, I think fifty francs, or about thirty-seven cents, for getting new recruits. At five that evening we got on a bus to Sidi bel Abbes south of Algiers. That was five years ago. I was discharged six months ago but reenlisted for another five years.

"The French Foreign Legion makes a volunteer eligible for French citizenship. I became a French citizen four years ago, and I have enough leave accumulated to take a trip back to New York. I hope my papers will be in order to leave in about three months."

While Tony was telling his story, they had a Berber meal, which was mostly sheep and lamb. Jeff was not too fond of the meal, but knew that he had to get used to eating the food here.

"Incidentally, Tony, the name of this café is Fosse. What does it mean?"

"Fosse means hole. You notice we came down the steps to this hole."

"Jeff, you have not said what you are doing in this part of the world. What brings you here?"

Jeff filled Tony in on his early childhood and how he became a private detective. He said he was looking for a wealthy man's daughter, who was reported seen in Marrakech and last spotted in Casablanca. After the meal and a few more beers, two of Tony's Legionnaire friends came in, ready to go back to Goulimime. "Jeff, in ten days I will be transferred to an outpost near Meknes, some eighty miles east of Rabat.

The garrison is about ten miles southeast on the edge of the Sahara. While you are in Casablanca, or if you get near Meknes, I would be happy to see you. If you wish to tell me whom you are looking for, I will keep my eyes and ears opened."

"Tony, I am looking for a young lady, twenty-six years of age, five feet five inches tall weighing one hundred and ten pounds. She has blond hair and blue eyes and is a very attractive young woman." Jeff removed from his wallet a small photo of a beautiful young woman. He carefully unwrapped the photo from a cellophane wrapper, being careful not to ruin it. The two-inch by three-inch photo was taken up close to reveal the upper body and head. He handed the photo to Tony.

"The last notice we had, she was using the name Catherine. That may be only one of several names she uses. Her real name is Mary Alice Bakker, but I am uncertain of the name she is now using. She used the name Catherine on a couple of occasions. Mary Alice Bakker is from New Orleans and was last seen with a caucasian male, medium height and weight, about 160 pounds. He has brown eyes, a medium complexion and black hair. The belief is that the young woman was with the man willingly. Mary Alice was dining with the man at a fine restaurant in the French Quarter in New Orleans just before her disappearance."

"If you will tell me how to get in touch with you while you are in Morocco and if I see or hear of anyone that might resemble her, I'll get to you some way. If you can't pick up a trail in Marrakech or Casablanca you could try Rabat and Fez. Some of the royal families have palaces in and around Rabat and Fez. As rumors go, they have American and European women in their harem."

"Just what is a harem and what is it used for?"

"Harems are what you may call an apartment, reserved for the wives and concubines of men."

"Gee, Tony, I guess I have a lot to learn. What the hell is a concubine and how is it used?"

"Ha, you do have a lot to learn. A concubine is a female who cohabits with a man without marriage. In the Moslem world a man can have as many wives and concubines as he can afford. Some of the more wealthy Moslem men will see a beautiful female and if she is not willing to be a concubine or take money, they will have her kidnapped. They prefer blond American and European women who are educated. All wealthy Moslems are not like this, but a good many sons of royalty and oil rich families that live in the lap of luxury practice this life style."

"I should be in Casablanca in three days and will be at the Hotel Zouaves on the Boulevard du Zouaves. I'll be in and out of the hotel; maybe gone a day or two while I check out Marrakech, but if I am out, leave me a message. Give me your address and if I get near your city I'll stop by. Take this photo with you; I have several copies on the ship. Maybe some of your friends might have seen her. I don't have a photo of the last person she was seen with."

"You will be able to find me at the French Foreign Legion Garrison ten miles southeast of Meknes. Jeff, we must go, the bus leaves for Goulimine in thirty minutes and it takes fifteen minutes to get out of the Kasbah. Good-bye friend, until we meet again."

Jeff left the Fosse Café, said bonjour to Monsieur LeBlanc, made his way up the stairs, and stepped into the crowded street. The heat made the stench from the throng of people, waste-water running down the street, and freshly slaughtered sheep, lambs and goats hanging in the marketplace, seem even more putrid than before. This is another thing he had to get use to. Jeff made his way back to the camel stall. Riding down the hill to board the ship, he saw the most glorious sunset that he had ever seen. He was riding the camel west and below were the white and tan stucco and rock buildings bordering silver white beaches. The turquoise blue waters of the Atlantic Ocean glistened with the blazing orange sun setting on the horizon. Off to the left, he saw the shipyard where the New Orleans Trader was being repaired and the harbor leading out to the Atlantic. He reached for his watch fob to see the time and learned his first lesson of the crowded streets of the Medina. Yes, they too, have pickpockets in Agadir. He quickly reached for his wallet, and was relieved to find it still there. He pulled it out and opened it, everything was in order. Jeff asked the stable owner the time and was told it was seven. He had about an hour or more to kill before he had to be back on board and he could surely pass up the chow they served on the ship. Near the pier was a building in the forks of two streets, which advertised food, juice, fruit, bread and meats. The place was not too crowded. The young lady behind the counter was a very pretty girl in her early twenties. Jeff asked, in Cajun, for a quarter loaf of bread, cheese, orange juice and some figs.

"Oui, you are English, no?" she asked. He detected an English accent in her speech.

"No, I am an American. I am a passenger on a ship leaving within the hour."

While she was getting his order, Jeff watched her. *Was she French or Arab? I don't think she is Arabian. What a beautiful olive complexion and soft brown eyes she has. She's not wearing the clothes of the Moslem women, such as a veil or the white headdress and flowing white dress. I don't know the names of the garments, but I will find out.*

The building was round and open, a counter extended three-quarters of the way around it, with stools for customers. The waitress served his order.

"Thank you, and what is your name?"

"My name is Babette, what is yours?"

"I am Jeff. May I ask you a question Babette?"

"Hokey dookey."

"Are you French?"

"My papa is French. He was in the Foreign Legion and married my mother. He was stationed at Fort Tifemit just over the Kerdousm Pass. My mother is of the Ammelen tribe, and she still practices Islam. I am part French and part Ammelen, are you all American?"

"Well, yes, but I grew up in a rural part of the United States and went to New Orleans at sixteen. My grandparents came from England to America."

Jeff had finished his meal and asked the time. *Damn*, he thought, *I should buy another watch.*

"It is eight o'clock Jeff, you are in a hurry?"

"Yes, Babette, I must get back to the ship; it is leaving shortly. I am on my way to Casablanca, but I'll come back this way again, for I would like to spend some time with you. May I have your home address, in the event you aren't working? I could write to you if that would be all right."

"Oui, Jeff, I would love that. Please write and come back. Here is the address of where I live. I will be waiting to hear from you."

I wish that I could have met her earlier in the day, but then I would not have met Tony who may be a valuable contact.

When Jeff arrived at the New Orleans Trader, he was told they would be ready to sail in less than an hour. He went down to the seawall, looked at the last rays of light beyond the horizon. At eight-forty Jeff boarded the New Orleans Trader and reported to the first mate that he was aboard. The hammock and sleeping quarters did not seem like a place to finish his adventure so he decided to stay on deck. He found a place on the starboard side by lying on some folded canvas.

At nine-ten the New Orleans Trader was towed out of the shipyard, down to the channel to the Atlantic and the captain set the course due north. Being on the starboard side he could see the dim lights of Agadir fading in the background. His thoughts went back to Babette and how it would be with Babette on those white beaches with the full moon shining.

Chapter Four

As he watched the lights fade, Jeff's mind suddenly flashed back to New Orleans and his first girlfriend. His flower business was prospering, as he continued to expand into restaurants as well as the better class cocktail lounges.

One of the finer restaurants was Café du Lafitte on Toulouse, owned and managed by Monsieur Jean Laboutte. He remembered the first time he approached Monsieur Laboutte about selling his bouquets. Monsieur was an elegant looking gentleman, with white hair, moustache and goatee, always dressed in a tuxedo. They instantly took a liking to each other and Monsieur Laboutte gave him permission to sell his bouquets in the Café du Lafitte, with a few ground rules. He also allowed Jeff to use a small room next to the kitchen to store some of his flowers and to create his bouquets.

The first night Jeff arrived at the Café du Lafitte he was introduced to Nicole, one of the waitresses assisting the headwaiter. Nicole was a beautiful brunette with an olive complexion, large soft brown eyes and a beautiful body. He had no experience with the opposite sex, except in selling his bouquets. On a personal basis with women, he was painfully shy, became tongue tied and blushed. He felt inferior because of his limited education, and had been spending his free time at the library, reading as much as he could, English, math, Creole and Cajun history and romance stories.

He started reading about the Cajuns and Creoles while he was with Le Havrey Saloon and Monsieur Jean Laveau. Monsieur was a Creole. A New Orleans Creole is a descendant of early French and Spanish settlers, "born in the colony," not in Europe. They dominated the New Orleans cultural and social life for more than a hundred years before the "Americans" arrived in any number. Until the Civil War, the French Creoles educated their children in France, and spoke only the French language. Creole men shunned manual labor as uncivilized. According to most dictionaries, Creole comes from the Spanish "criollo." Over time, this went from denoting a person born of Spanish parents overseas, to a person born similarly of French parents. Yet Creole can also mean a mix of African-American and white parentage, or even undiluted African-Americans.

Cajun's ancestors were exiled from New Arcadia (Nova Scotia) by the British in 1765. In one of the nation's largest mass migrations, more than 10,000 found a permanent home in Louisiana. The word "Cajun" is a corruption of "Arcadian." They were hunters, trappers and fishermen, farmers, and boat builders who worked hard weekdays and spent weekends celebrating life. Lacking formal education, they lived close to the land, intermarried, and proudly retained their customs, their religion and their own provincial form of the French language. They liked their food hot and spicy.

By learning the history of the Cajuns and Creoles, combined with reading detective stories and romance magazines, Jeff increased his knowledge of the world around him. He purchased True Romance, True Detective, Crime and other magazines of this type. Then he tried practicing what he was reading in speaking to women until he began feeling more comfortable around them. Just when he reached this stage he met Nicole, and everything he had practiced was forgotten. He blushed and stuttered and couldn't say much. That night he laid thinking of her and how upset he was with himself for losing an opportunity to talk to her. Jeff was determined to find a way to talk to Nicole. Several nights later when he was in the room creating his bouquets, a light tap sounded at the door. Opening the door, he found Nicole standing there. He was so shocked, and tongue-tied he could not speak.

"Hi, Jeff," Nicole said in a soft slightly Creole accent, "May I come in?"

"Uh, oh, uh y-yes."

"Jeff, I have a favor to ask of you; I need some help."

As he looked at her in all of her beauty, she looked like a lost young girl.

Nicole continued without waiting for an answer. "Jeff, I know you get around to most of the restaurants, nightclubs, and bars, and I am trying to find someone to help me. Would you?"

"Uh, yes, Nicole. I'll try my best to help you, what would you like me to do?"

"I am trying to find a man about twenty-five years of age. He's six feet tall, and weighs about one hundred-eighty pounds, has dark hair and brown eyes. He has a small scar on his right cheek, and sometimes he gets up in crowds and sings Cajun songs. His name is Pepe."

Jeff thought that she wanted him to find her boyfriend, but she looked so forlorn and lost he decided he would try to help her. He did not believe he had a chance with her, anyway.

"Sure, Nicole, I'll see what I can find out and let you know."

"Jeff, I sure appreciate your help. Would you like to have a cafe au lait before you start out?"

"Yes, thank you."

While he was waiting for the cafe au lait, he wondered what would happen if he found Pepe.

As he made his rounds that night he did not see anyone that looked like Nicole's friend. When he returned to the Café du Lafitte, Nicole was busy and he did not have the opportunity to speak with her that night. Later, after he was in bed, his thoughts went to Nicole. *Did I really try to find her friend?*

He was studying a mail order course, "How To Become a Detective." In one chapter it stated that to be a good detective you have to put all personal feelings aside and do the very best you could to solve a case. He knew he had let his personal feelings interfere with looking for Pepe. He did not ask one person if they knew Pepe, nor did he look very hard. He was afraid he might find him. *I promise from this night on, I will put aside my personal feelings and become the best detective in New Orleans.*

The next night when he saw Nicole, he told her that he had not found out anything but would keep trying.

"Oh, Jeff, you are nice to help. I can't thank you enough. Maybe we could get together sometime when we are off duty."

Jeff left the Café du Lafitte walking on air. Nicole was easy to talk to.

This being a Saturday night, more people patronized the restaurants and bars. He would start asking at the bars on North Front Street near the Mississippi River. This was a good distance from the Café du Lafitte and a place where Nicole would probably not look.

A few minutes after eight, he went into the de Devant Saloon. Business was slow in de Devant and he knew the bartender and waitress. Jeff made a decision to do something out of the ordinary. When he first started selling bouquets, he vowed that he would not drink in the establishments where he sold his wares. The de Devant was a saloon that catered to the sailors, dockworkers and foreign transits that arrived on freighters. It was dimly lit, with a long curved bar that seated twenty people. There were ten tables and a small dance floor with a jukebox. Signs were displayed around the saloon advertising different beers, rums, whiskeys, cigarettes, chewing tobacco and other items. The sawdust on the floor had not been raked for several days. The bartender, a clean-up man and a waitress were Creoles, and another waitress, a Cajun, made up the staff. It was a rough place. Even with Jeff being known as the "flower man," he had to be careful, because some of the patrons did not know him and he would be considered an outsider. The waitress, Clio, worked the tables and would be in the position to see and know the regulars. Jeff seated himself in a booth near the door and motioned for Clio, who came over to serve him. He ordered a Regal

Beer and when it was served, Jeff said, "Clio, I am looking for a fellow name Pepe. Do you know him?"

"I know two Pepes who come in. Do you mean the short fat Pepe or the tall, good looking Pepe?"

"The tall one that you say he is good looking, I'll go with him, but he has a small scar on his right cheek."

"I know you Jeff, as the flower man, what do you want to see him about?"

"Well, Clio, I have a friend who asked me to find him, it is not the police or the law, just a friend looking to talk with him."

"He and a friend come in most every night about nine o'clock, although, they were not in last night."

"Thanks Clio, bring me another Regal please."

Jeff decided that he would take the time to wait and see if Pepe and his friend would show. While he was sipping his Regal, the bartender came over to the table.

"Hi, Jeff, what's the occasion for the personal visit, a night off?"

"No, Albert, I am trying to find a friend of a friend of mine as a favor, a tall, nice looking guy named Pepe. I think he may be her boyfriend."

"You mean his wife, or is it really his girlfriend?"

"I don't really know Albert, the friend is a girl at one of the restaurants I go into and she asked me to find him for her."

"Jeff, you're a good guy and I like you, but the patrons who visit here are my business and I do not want it known that we tell what is happening here, so please no trouble."

"I will speak with him and explain who is looking for him and if he has a reasonable excuse for not wanting to be found, then I'll drop it. I'll let you know the results."

"OK, Jeff, I'll nod my head and look toward him when he comes in."

About an hour passed with people coming and going, the bar becoming more crowded. Albert came down to the end of the bar and was wiping it, looked over and nodded his head slightly and looked at a couple of guys sitting in a booth near the corner.

Jeff walked over to the booth where a tall, nice looking young fellow and a real tough barrel of a man were sitting. The big man's beard had about four days growth and he was dressed as a dockworker.

"Hi, Pepe, how are you tonight?"

"Hey, Flower Man, I didn't know you knew my name. What is the occasion?"

"May I sit down and buy you guys a beer and have a little talk?"

"OK with me," answered Pepe.

The bearded one just grunted, nodding his head in the affirmative.

Pepe slid over inside of the booth and Jeff sat down. The bearded guy gave him a dirty look and said, "You a cop or something?"

Pepe spoke up, "No, Pug, he's not cop, he's the guy who sells the flowers in the clubs and bars around."

Jeff looked over at Pug, extended his hand and said, "My name is Jeff and I usually sell flowers, but I am off tonight. Someone asked me to find Pepe for her."

Pepe looked suspicious and said, "Hey, man, what are you trying to pull here. It's not my ex is it?"

"I don't know Pepe, a nice looking young lady, a waitress at the Café du Lafitte asked me to find you."

"What's her name?" asked Pepe.

"Her name is Nicole. I didn't ask her last name."

Gee, I should have gotten her last name. I must never forget to get all the facts if I am going to be a detective.

Pepe looked relieved and said, "Thank God. That's my sister who I haven't seen in seven or eight years. I left home, up in Leesville about eight years ago and I have not seen my mother, father or Nicole since then. Tell me how is she and how are Father and Mother?"

"I don't know. I have only known Nicole for a couple weeks. She is so nice and beautiful that I never inquired into her past." *Another mistake.*

"I did not know you were her brother. She only asked me to find you. Where can she get in touch with you?"

"What are her days off? I would like to see her, but this is not the type of place I want her to be in. Find out when and where we can meet and I will be there. Are you still selling flowers?"

"Yes, Pepe, I am. I'll see Nicole later tonight and I'll come back here tomorrow night with a place she can meet you."

Jeff left the de Devant Saloon and hurried back to the Café du Lafitte. He went into the restaurant by the back door to his little storage room. He looked around outside the room and spotted Henri, a waiter, and asked him to relay a message to Nicole to come by the storage room, that he had an important message for her.

He was arranging his bouquets and preparing to go out for the late crowds, which was the best selling time, when a knock came on the door. He opened it and there stood Nicole. *Gee, this was the prettiest woman that he had ever seen in his entire life.*

"Come in, Nicole." Just saying her name gave him a thrill.

"Did you hear anything about Pepe, Jeff?"

"Yes, I met your brother and he is well and wants to see you. He asked me to make arrangements so you two could meet. He does not want you to meet him at the place I found him."

"Oh, Jeff, you are so nice. Where can we meet? I can arrange to be off tomorrow."

"How would meeting each other outside of the French Quarter be? I know a nice restaurant on Canal Street that would be perfect. If Pepe can be there, why not meet at the Morris Restaurant, say, two o'clock tomorrow afternoon. That will give both of you time to spend together and you will still be able to be at the Café du Lafitte by six o'clock and will not have to miss work."

The real reason he had selected the two PM time, was because he didn't want her to be off the next night; he wanted to see her as often as possible.

"Yes, please see if Pepe can meet us at the restaurant at two. Are you going to see him again tonight?"

"I don't know if he will still be there, but I am ready to leave now and will go back there to see if I can set up the meeting. I will try to get back here before the café closes and have an answer for you."

"Jeff, if you can't get back, I have an efficiency at 212 Iberville, upstairs on the third floor, number 313. I will be up early waiting for you. Why not come by at seven and I'll make breakfast and we can make plans for meeting Pepe?"

His head was light, and he felt that he was walking on air. *Gee, a person like this wants to make breakfast for me.*

"OK, Nicole, I'll be there at seven with whatever I can set up. I'll go now and hope that Pepe will still be at the bar. See you in the morning."

Jeff picked up his tray and bouquets and hurried back to the de Devant Saloon, to see if Pepe was still there. Either way he would have breakfast with Nicole.

As he entered the saloon, a customer who wanted to buy a bouquet stopped him. The person was quite drunk and kept fishing for his money, as Jeff scanned the room. *Damn, won't this man ever find his money?*

At last, the man handed Jeff a couple of bills, which was more than the asking price. Jeff went to the back of the saloon, before he spotted Pepe.

"Pepe, I talked with Nicole and she wants to see you very much. How would two tomorrow afternoon at the Morris Restaurant on Canal Street do?"

"That's fine, I'll be there. I am very anxious to see her. Thanks, Jeff."

"Pepe, please come alone and don't disappoint her."

"I'll be alone and I promise that I will be there."

Jeff worked until twelve forty-five and went by the Café du Lafitte to put his tray in the storage room and clue Nicole in on the appointment.

By the time he arrived at the café, it was five past one and he didn't see Nicole. His heart skipped a couple beats, fearing that he had missed her.

As he was going down the hallway in back of the kitchen, he heard his name called and he knew the voice. His heart was now beating faster. He turned as Nicole ran up to him and threw her arms around him and said, "I thought that I had missed you, I was serving in one of the private dining rooms and they were late leaving. Have you any news?"

With her arms still around him and the sweet smell of her perfume, he could barely breathe. He sucked in some fresh air and managed to answer, "Yes, we will meet him at two o'clock tomorrow afternoon at the Morris Restaurant."

I would like to ask her out for some coffee, but I am afraid she would turn me down and I sure don't want to jeopardize any friendship I have made.

While his mind was racing for a solution, he was startled when Nicole said, "Jeff let's go get a cup of coffee at Pierre's Coffee House."

What a time to be asked out when he had his work clothes on.

From past experience, he found that by having a day or two growth of beard, dressing in old worn and slightly dirty clothes, his flowers sales were much better. He guessed people felt sorry for him. By now, he'd made enough money that he had some nice clothes and even custom made shoes for his clubfoot. He did not want to embarrass her in these clothes.

"Uh, gee, Nicole I have on these old clothes and haven't shaved for a couple of days. You don't have to invite me for coffee; I'll take you out when I am dressed better. In fact, I won't be dressed like this tomorrow."

"Jeff, don't be silly, you look fine, and I am excited about seeing my brother for the first time in almost eight years. Please let's go."

"OK, if you don't mind being seen with me like this, we'll go for coffee." He was glad that Pierre's stayed open 24 hours a day. As they strolled along Royal Street about four block to Pierre's, she held his hand and skipped along, happy as a little girl on her way to a circus.

I really don't care if she is paying attention to me because I found her brother. Maybe some day she will like me for myself.

After the coffee was served, Nicole told Jeff of her life in Leesville, Louisiana, about 100 miles northwest of New Orleans, on the edge of the Kisatchie National Forest. Her grandfather came from New Arcadia, Nova Scotia, in the middle 1800's and settled where some other relatives had settled earlier. When the government created a National Forest, which is now Kisatchie National Forest, the people who settled there were given title to their land under a grandfather clause. The family was hunters, fishermen and farmers. All of her family lived in an area within ten miles of each other and only a few left the area. Pepe, the oldest of six, (Nicole was the youngest) got into trouble in Leesville and left home to keep from embarrassing the family. They had not heard from him since he left. Nicole said that she left home six months ago to find Pepe, coming to New Orleans, as it was a large city and she thought maybe he came here to get lost. She was saving money to hire a detective, but just could not save much. She wanted to find Pepe and tell him that the trouble he got into was not serious, and that the charges had been dropped after one of the other boys told what happened. She was hoping Pepe would come home with her.

Jeff did not like what he heard, that would mean he would not see her anymore. They drank coffee and talked as the time flew by. It was three in the morning when they left Pierre's for the short walk to her place on Iberville Street.

When they arrived at her house, Jeff was a little apprehensive about what to do. On the front steps he took her hand and said, "Nicole, I have enjoyed myself more that you will ever know. I'll be here at seven in the morning." She was looking into Jeff's eyes, while standing on her tiptoes for she was some six inches shorter than he. Jeff bent over, intending to kiss her on the forehead, but she put her arms tightly around his neck and pulled him down until their lips met. His head was spinning. *Surely I must be in heaven.* This was his first kiss on the lips.

He walked to his place, the happiest man alive. He was so lightheaded his feet barely touched the sidewalk.

When he finally got to bed, he tossed and turned, thinking of Nicole and kept looking at the clock. After dozing off and on, he got up at five and took a hot bath, shaved and put on his shirt and trousers and his custom made shoes. He loved the shoes, for he could walk better and without a limp. He estimated the walk to Nicole's would take fifteen minutes. Sitting, looking at the clock, it seemed as if it took an hour for the clock to show six forty-five. Finally, he got up and started for Nicole's place. He had to slow himself down for he was almost running. Still, he arrived at five minutes to seven and knocked on number 313.

The door opened and there stool Nicole dressed in a stunning light beige dress, her black hair and her soft brown eyes stood out against the soft color. The smell of her perfume overwhelmed him when she came over and kissed him. Jeff looked at her, took her face in his hands and gently kissed her and they held the kiss a long time. Then they just stood there with their arms wrapped around each other enjoying the closeness and warmth of each other's body.

After breakfast they decided to walk down to the Mississippi River. Holding hands they walked and talked. Jeff told Nicole of his life's struggles and dreams, of how he longed for a family who was loving and caring. They spent several hours sitting on a bench and watching the ships go past and talking until it was time to leave for the Morris Restaurant to meet Pepe.

Chapter Five

They arrived at the Morris Restaurant at one forty-five and saw Pepe seated at a table near the back corner.

Nicole and Pepe saw each other about the same time and ran to each other and hugged and hugged. Nicole was crying and saying repeatedly, "Oh, my brother, my brother, my big brother."

After being seated, Pepe looked at Nicole and said, "The last time I saw you, you were a little ten year old scrawny tomboy kid. Now look at you, you're a grown up beautiful woman."

Jeff said, "Look, you have lots to talk about, so I'll leave you alone and meet you at four at your place, Nicole."

"No, Jeff, stay. We can all get to know each other."

"No, you two have some catching up to do. I'll see you at four. Have a good lunch and a good talk."

Jeff went back to his apartment and lay on the sofa, mulling over the last few days and trying to get his life organized. He would do anything to be near Nicole and have a relationship with her. After an hour he got up, washed his face and started for Nicole's place. Nicole and Pepe were already there, waiting for him.

Nicole said, "I will call Monsieur Laboutte and ask permission to have the night off. Can you take the night off Jeff?"

"No, Nicole, Saturday night is my best night, but I'll tell you what. When the cafés close and I have finished, we can go the ERWA Guild and have a party. You and Pepe can be my guests."

"What type of a gig is this?" asked Pepe.

"ERWA stands for Entertainers and Restaurant Workers Association. All entertainers and restaurant workers who are eligible can join. It is a private club and on Sunday mornings after two AM, when most of the workers are off, they gather there to socialize. Some of the entertainers get up and perform their act; food and drinks are served and there is dancing. The ERWA considers me an entrepreneur in the restaurant and entertainment field, therefore I was eligible to join."

"Please, Pepe, let's go. We can be with each other and you can get to know Jeff. I need to work, for I want to send a message to Mama and Papa that you are well and looking good."

"OK, it's a date. Jeff, can I bring my girlfriend? I'd like Nicole to meet her."

"Sure, why don't we meet here at about two AM and we can all go together in a taxi. Now I need to get dressed and go to the café to get my bouquets ready."

Nicole and Jeff kissed and he left for his place to dress in his shabby clothes.

Things went extremely well that night, sales were up, and he was happy and jolly with all the customers. Maybe the happiness he found with Nicole was the answer he had been looking for.

At one o'clock he arrived at his apartment, took a bath, shaved and put on his blue suit, white shirt, red tie and his custom-made black shoes. While dressing, he was wishing he knew how to dance. At a bar he frequented, they had a "dime-a-dance" floor and he often thought about getting some tickets and telling the girl he didn't know how to dance. Maybe she would teach him. But he never got up the nerve to try it. Maybe Pepe can dance with each of the girls.

When he arrived at Nicole's apartment she was ready, but Pepe and his girlfriend had not gotten there yet. Nicole brought out glasses and a bottle of wine, and poured a glass for each of them. They toasted each other and had there first sip when Pepe and his girl, a very pretty brunette whom he introduced as Alma Riley, entered.

Nicole poured two more glasses of wine and everyone toasted one another. They finished their wine, went downstairs to Iberville Street and got a taxi to the ERWA Club located on Lake Pontchartrain. Jeff was greeted warmly when they arrived, and as they were escorted to their table, a good many people spoke greetings to Jeff.

"Jeff, you are a popular person here. Do you come every Sunday?" asked Pepe.

"This is about the only entertainment I have, mostly working or studying takes the rest of my time."

"What are you studying?" asked Alma.

"I am studying general courses to further my education and also a home study course on how to become a detective."

"You do not have a Louisiana accent, where are you from?"

"Well, I was born in South Alabama, but left there when I was about eight years old and have lived throughout the south. I have been in New Orleans the last four years."

Nicole did not like the turn of events. *I wish Pepe would dance with Alma. Maybe I should ask Jeff to dance, if I can get a word in. Gosh, am I jealous of Alma paying this much attention to Jeff?*

Pepe came to the rescue and asked Alma to dance. After they left, Nicole leaned over and asked Jeff whether he would dance with her. Jeff turned red and said, "I would love to dance with you Nicole, but I have never danced before."

"I'll tell you what we will do. Let's go out on the terrace where we can still hear the music and I'll teach you."

Just holding her will be nice, even if we don't dance.

They went out on the terrace overlooking Lake Pontchartrain, with the full moon shining on the lake. The band was playing a slow love song and Nicole said, "I'll lead, you just follow me and don't worry about stepping on my feet. Holding Nicole in his arms and the sweet smell from her hair and body was intoxicating. He knew for sure at this moment he was in love, but how could he tell her.

After a while, Jeff began to feel the rhythm and the beat. *Why haven't I tried dancing before, it's fun? Hell, I had no one to dance with and I was afraid my clubfoot would make it awkward.*

They kept dancing, going back to the table every so often to rest. Alma and Pepe were dancing and did not miss them, and Jeff certainly did not miss Alma and Pepe.

They were still dancing when the sun came up over Lake Pontchartrain. His head was spinning when he kissed Nicole then whispered in ear, "Nicole, I love you."

It seemed like hours before Nicole replied, "I love you too, Jeff." They hugged and kissed, feeling relief that their admissions of love for each other had not been spurned. They were relaxed and happy just being together.

At seven AM they all took a taxi to Morris Restaurant for breakfast. Afterward, Pepe and Alma departed, with Pepe telling Nicole that he would see her at the Café Du Lafitte soon.

Jeff dropped Nicole off at her apartment and went home, but he couldn't sleep. Something was troubling him. *Why had Pepe not given Nicole or me his address or a phone number where he could be reached? It didn't seem right. I must try to find an answer. Maybe my detective course is about to pay off.*

Early Monday morning Jeff was at the Jefferson Parish Courthouse looking up records for the name of Pepe Grevy, Nicole's and Pepe's surname. He wasn't sure of the correct spelling, whether it would be, Grevy or Grévy, but he would look for both. After searching marriage and tax records, he was now looking at arrest records when he spotted the name

Pierre Lyle Grevy, age 23, POB, Fullerton, La. Pierre had been arrested for gambling, running numbers, and selling whiskey. There were two more arrests, both for prostitution, and pimping.

For the numbers charge, he was sentenced to ninety days in the stockade; for the selling of illegal alcohol, he served one year in state prison. After getting out of prison, he and a person named Bernie "The Pug" Russell were arrested for operating a house of prostitution, selling illegal alcohol and stolen property. They each served one year in the state prison.

Jeff wrote down the addresses on all of the records, and caught a streetcar back to his apartment. He put on some old clothes, stuffing newspapers in the toe of the shoe that he wore on his clubfoot. He slicked his hair down with Brilliantine, went out in the back yard and picked up some black dirt which he smudged on his face and hands, and headed for an address near the river, close to de Devant Saloon. Arriving on North Peters Street he looked for the address of one of the houses on his list.

When he knocked on the door, a large middle-aged woman opened it.

"What can I do fer you, Honey?"

"I am looking for Pepe. He said he had some work for me delivering goods."

"Hell, man, Pepe ain't been here fer nearly a year. When he tell you that and give you this address?"

"I just got out of the state pen, and I'm not sure, but I think it was about ten months ago when Pepe got out. He gave me this address the day he left the pen."

"Well, he and a big ugly guy came here and stayed with some of my girls a couple days. Then, the asshole took two of my girls and split, and I got word he set up a house over on North Front Street."

"Miss, could you gimme the address, cauz I need to see him real bad. I need help, I ain't got no money and I ain't had nothing to eat since yesterday morning."

"Oh, I don't know the number, but tell you what Honey, you come on in and I'll git you something to eat. My name's Grace, what's yours?"

"Everybody calls me JD," replied Jeff, reverting back to his hobo name.

"Well, JD, you wash up, and being you just got out of the pen, I'll bet you could use a woman."

"Thank you ma'am, but I just want something to eat. When I get on my feet, I will come back for the other offer."

"Suit yerself, Honey, it ain't going to cost you any money. I figger it will bring me business later. You go to the bathroom and wash up while I fix you something."

Jeff did not want to wash up too much, but he lightly wet his face and wiped it on an already soiled towel, put water on his hair and combed it back, then went into the kitchen. On the table was a plate with some eggs, grits and a cup of coffee. Two ladies of the house were sitting there eating with very little on, small loosely fitted bright-colored kimonos, breasts almost bare. They moved around so that Jeff was sitting between them. Lil, the peroxide blond said, "Say, Honey, you look down and out?"

"Yes, ma'am, I am and that's a fact. I am trying to find Pepe. He told me when he left the pen to look him up and he would help me get started. I don't know nobody else."

"Tell you what, you look like a decent fellow, and I know what it's like to be down on your luck. One time I was down in the gutter and a nice man helped me. So I'll try to return the favor. Roxanne, here, her boyfriend, Axel, my boyfriend, LeRoy and I all live together. I guess we can let you sleep on the sofa for a few days until you find Pepe. We'll ask around for you. In this business, we meet all kinds of people, and they tell us many things."

Roxanne, who was a Creole, mostly white with a trace of Negro heritage, said, "Sure JD, we will help you. We don't get home until sometime in the early hours and our boyfriends are bartenders and they don't get home till late, so you can get plenty of rest. Maybe we can have some news for you in the morning."

Jeff didn't want to miss working or seeing Nicole, but this might help him find out about Pepe.

"Look, JD," said Roxanne, "it is almost four o'clock and we will be getting busy pretty soon, so let's go around to our place and I'll introduce you to Axel and LeRoy because they leave at five for work."

Jeff and Roxanne left the house and walked the five blocks to a rundown house and went in. Roxanne introduced JD and told his story.

LeRoy said, "Well, Friend, I'll see whether I can find out where you can contact him, but I ain't going to talk to him; he has a mean temper and we've had our words."

"That goes for me too, Buddy. He comes in but the other bartender takes care of him. Take the sofa and get some rest. We'll be back about two, after the bars close."

Jeff looked the place over but did not see a telephone and the nearest place that he observed that would have a one was the de Devant Saloon. *Well, that knocks the hell out of that idea. I want to call Nicole but don't dare risk going to the de Devant; maybe Pepe or Pug would be there. I'll have to sweat it out and hope Nicole won't be too mad at me.*

Stretching out on the sofa, he realized just how tired he was. He must have drifted off to sleep, because he was awakened by loud noises and banging at the front door. After much fumbling with the key and a lot cursing the door finally opened and in came his four drunken hosts, laughing and talking loudly.

"Hi, JD," Roxanne mumbled, slurring her words, "I got some news and Axel's got some news. You tell him Axel."

"OK, Sweetie. Look, JD, this guy comes in about twelve o'clock, almost drunk, and after ordering straight whiskey, he asked if I knew where he could get laid. I played it cool and told him I didn't know any place unless he was recommended, you know the cops.

"'Well, do you know Pepe?' he asked.

"'Yes, I know Pepe, but he ain't here. How do I know you know him?'

"'Well,' the gent says, 'we done a little job tonight and he didn't want me to go to his girls. He said you fellows knew some good girls.'

"'If you were on a job with him, why in the hell wouldn't he let you go to his house?'

"'Well you see, the last time I was there, about a week ago, I got into a fight with my ex-girlfriend and he said she still works there and he didn't want any trouble.'

"'Pepe does not live at the house?' I asked him.

"'No, he lives with his girlfriend someplace else. I always call at his house or meet him at the de Devant,' he says.

"'Look, Mac, what's your name? Give me Pepe's phone number and I'll check it out. I have to be careful you know,' I told him.

"'My name's Willie, but most people call me WJ. I'll call the number and you can talk to him.'

"'Look, WJ, if you want a piece of ass, you give me the number. I ain't takin' no chances on bein' busted.'

"'OK, the number is JE-4837, but hand me the phone when he answers. I don't want him to know I gave the number out.'

"So I went over to the phone and called this number and when Pepe answered, I quickly handed the phone to WJ, who said, 'Hey Pepe, it's me. The bartender won't give me any girls unless you vouch for me, here he is.'"

"I took the phone and said, 'this is Axel. I got a guy here who says his name is WJ. He wants to get laid but I don't know who in the hell he is. You know him?'

"Pepe says, 'Yeah, I know him, he works for me sometimes. He's a little hot headed around his ex-girlfriend, but otherwise an OK guy. Go ahead and fix him up. I'll be responsible.'

"'OK, Pepe,' I said.

"I gave him Grace's address and told him to ask to be fixed him up with Roxanne. You didn't mind, did you?"

"Shit, no, I didn't mind. Money is money," said Roxanne. "He came in and asked for me. He was about shot and wanted a drink first, so I got Grace to bring him a couple. After a couple of drinks and him slobbering over me, I asked him if Pepe still lived on North Rampart Street. 'No,' he said, 'I only know he lives on Lake Pontchartrain.'

"I asked him, 'you mean near the dock on Lake Drive in the blue house?'

"'How you know he lives on Lake Drive?' he asked me.

"'Me and several of the girls went out there to a party one time. It was dark but I thought it was a blue house, across from the docks.'

"'Hell, you musta been drunk, thinking yellow was blue.'

"Well, JD, that's all I could get and he didn't know the number."

"Gee, thanks Roxanne. I'll go by today and see him, if I can find it."

LeRoy said, "Go up to St. Charles Street, catch the Pontchartrain Street Car and get off at the docks. It's quite a ways out but you should be able to find it."

Roxanne said, "By the way, here's a buck. You may be gone when we get up. Good luck."

"Gee, thanks. I'll never forget you."

As hard as he tried he could not go back to sleep, so he got up quietly, and went home.

Once there, he took a long hot bath, changed into some clean clothes and headed for 212 Iberville Street, room 313.

On the way to Nicole's house he was thinking, *What if she is mad and won't see me. I can't tell her what I found out up to now, and I don't want to lie to her.*

As he neared the house he was so nervous he had to stop and sit on the low wall in front of the St. Louis Cathedral, until he collected his thoughts.

I'll tell her I was working on a case and can't talk about it and I was in no position to call her.

As he started up the stairs to room 313, he met Nicole coming down. She began running and tripped on the stairs. Jeff caught her before she tumbled down. She fell into his arms and started crying.

"Oh, Jeff, where have you been? I haven't been able to sleep at all. I was just going to your place to see if you were home, maybe sick. I was afraid that you didn't want to see me when you didn't show up at the Café du Lafitte."

As Jeff held Nicole close in his arms he said, "No I'm not sick, but I am tired because I've had very little sleep. I have been on a case looking for someone and I could not contact you as I was not near a telephone."

They went up the stairs to Nicole's apartment holding each other as though they were afraid the other would disappear. Upon entering the apartment, Jeff stopped and put his arms around Nicole and kissed her deeply. His head was throbbing, he felt dizzy, and his heart was beating so rapidly he thought he might faint. *What is happening to me? I want her in the worst way, but I have never been with a woman before. When I hear other fellows talk about being with women or going to prostitutes, it sounds so easy. But where do I start; what should I do? I don't want to make Nicole mad and lose her.*

Jeff slid his hand under her blouse in the back. Her bare skin felt like silk as he tenderly massaged her back. He turned sideways, so she would not feel his erection.

Nicole's heart was pounding with passion. She knew Jeff was shy. *I don't want him to think I am loose, but I want him to be my first one.*

They hugged and kissed and caressed each other. Jeff didn't remember who did what first. But they began removing each other's clothes until they were standing in the room kissing and hugging, completely nude. They walked over to the bed. Nicole got in first and Jeff stood gazing down at her laying there without a stitch. His mind was almost numb seeing this beautiful woman with her perfect breasts, slender body, flat belly, and long slender legs. Her light olive complexion was flawless and he noticed her pubic hair was the same coal black color as the hair on her head.

Nicole looked up at Jeff standing beside the bed, admiring his strong body, flat stomach, muscular arms, and chest. Her eyes got down no further than his penis, which was large and erect. She wanted it desperately. *Would it be painful the first time?* she wondered.

Before she could think any further, Jeff was in bed and they were in each other's arms. Nature seemed to take its course and after the lovemaking they lay exhausted holding each other.

Jeff and Nicole woke up about one o'clock that afternoon and made love again. Afterwards, Jeff took a bath while Nicole dozed. She knew she had to get up and prepare for work, but dreaded the hours she and Jeff would be apart.

"Nicole, I have to go get my flowers and make the bouquets for tonight. I did not sell any bouquets last night, and I need the money. I'll see you later at the café and after we get off work we can be together."

Jeff walked on air all the way to his place, dressed and went to pick up the flowers at the funeral homes, then to the room at the café to make the bouquets for the night's business.

At six o'clock, Jeff was finished making the bouquets, when a knock came at the door. Opening the door, Nicole rushed in and put her arms around him and said, "Jeff, look who's here; it's Pepe. As I was leaving the house, Pepe came by and escorted me to work. He wants us to have dinner tonight with him and Alma."

"Sure, Pepe, we would love to have dinner with you and Alma. Where do you want us to meet you, at Morris Restaurant?"

"No, Jeff, we have reservations at the Iberia Restaurant and Bar, the treat is on me. I have a proposition for you, Jeff."

"What do you have in mind?"

"Wait until dinner, Jeff. It will make you some big money, OK?"

"Sounds good Pepe, what do I have to do?"

"Not much, but we will talk about it tonight."

Jeff gathered his bouquet tray and left to make his rounds, wondering what type of a deal Pepe had in mind. *Oh well, I will find out tonight.*

The night was uneventful until he went into his old stomping grounds, Le Havrey Saloon, now owned by a Cajun, Doodles Conti. Jeff had helped Doodles when he first purchased the saloon and they became good friends. Tonight, Doodles asked him to come back about ten PM, saying he had something to talk to him about.

At ten after ten, when Jeff arrived at the Le Havrey Saloon, the place was packed with patrons. He sold several bouquets, before spotting Doodles.

"Hello, Jeff. Come on back to the office; I have a deal for you."

Gee, thought Jeff, *two deals in one night, this must be my lucky day.*

Entering Doodles' office, Jeff noticed two men in business suits, sitting on a sofa, talking.

Doodles introduced them as Mr. Art McGraw and Mr. Aaron Bluestein. After shaking hands Aaron said to Jeff, "I understand you want to be a detective?"

"Yes, I am taking a mail order course from American Law School in Chicago, but I have a very limited practical experience."

"Maybe we can help you. You get into most of the restaurants, bars and nightclubs, especially in the Vieux Carre or the French Quarter. Occasionally, we need to find people and obtain important information, and for this service we will pay well."

"Mr. Bluestein, I would like to make some money and get experience, but I will not break the law. What type of business are you in?"

Mr. Bluestein gave Jeff his business card, which read, State of Louisiana, Drug and Alcohol Division. Aaron L. Bluestein, Special Agent, the address and telephone number.

"So, Mr. Bluestein, you want me to be a snitch, is that correct?"

Mr. McGraw spoke up, "No, Jeff, you would not be a snitch, you will work as an undercover agent on assignment. Assignments will be limited at first, but as you gain experience, you will get more jobs and your pay will increase. Your duties will be to find people and report to us, or to gain information from people that will not talk to a known law officer. You will go about your daily life as you are now. There is a risk for doing this and you are required to take a course and pass a background check. The course can be studied the same as you study your mail order, but in addition, you will have a four hour a week classroom lesson every Saturday morning."

Art McGraw continued, "You will be paid a salary after you've completed the course and passed the test. Until then, we will pay you by the job. We have already investigated some of your background and find you acceptable, so unless something pops up that would bar you, there should be no problem. Do you have any type of a record Jeff?"

"No, Sir, and I am very interested."

"Well, we have something we can try and see how it works. Do you know a Pepe Grevy?"

Jeff was reluctant to involve Nicole, but figured they would find out sooner or later and wonder why he had lied to them, so he said, "Well, yes and no. I just recently located him for my girlfriend, who is his sister. They have not seen each other for several years. In fact, my girlfriend and I are going to dinner with him and his girlfriend after we get off work tonight. But, I really do not know him on a personal basis."

"This is a coincidence. We need to know some of his background, his friends and hangers-on and from where the bulk of his income is derived."

Bluestein said, "We can meet tomorrow and see what you have found out. However, the only place we can meet you in the French Quarter is here. Leave a message at this number; memorize it and do not keep it on you." He handed Jeff a small sheet of paper, with the phone number and an address scrawled on it. "Check with Doodles for messages and only call us from a telephone where you can't be overheard."

McGraw added, "See if you can get to know him, but don't ask too many questions. Come to that address tomorrow morning at nine and we will talk." He pointed at the paper Jeff still held in his hand.

"Remember, you must not tell anyone, not even your girlfriend, of our relationship, understand?"

"Yes, Sir, see you tomorrow."

Jeff left Le Havrey Saloon thinking of the turn of events. *Was this the right thing to do? Hell, I can get the training I need and pick up some extra money? Now I can afford to ask Nicole to marry me, if she will have me. I will pop the question tonight before we go to the Iberia Restaurant. I hope she never finds out that I'm spying on her brother for the police.*

He was so nervous worrying about Nicole turning him down, that he passed right by a couple of clubs. Realizing what he had done, Jeff returned to the clubs, but his heart wasn't on selling bouquets. He decided to try to find the house were Pepe lived. Catching the streetcar, he rode out to Lake Pontchartrain and found the yellow house on Lake Drive. He observed the house with several cars parked in front. They would be parked only a few minutes, before the occupants would drive off. Jeff went across the street and posted himself behind a large oak tree where he could see, but not easily be seen. For the next hour he counted seven cars coming and going and the occupant of the car would go to the front door, knock once and turn the doorbell one turn. The door would open, and articles would change hands. He could not see either person clearly enough to identify them.

Catching the last streetcar of the night, Jeff returned to his apartment, bathed, shaved and put on his dress clothes and headed to Iberville Street.

Nicole answered his knock, dressed in a plain black sleeveless dress. She was so gorgeous he became tongue-tied and could hardly speak.

Kissing each other, and holding her close, so she could see his face, Jeff stammered in her ear, "Nicole, I love you more than I can express. I want you for my wife. Will you marry me?"

"Oh yes, yes Jeff, I will. I love you more than life itself."

They sat down holding hands and began discussing plans for their wedding and their life together, when a knock came on the door.

Nicole went to the door. "Hello Pepe. Hello Alma, come in. We have something wonderful to tell you. Pepe, Jeff and I are getting married next month, or as soon as I write Mama and tell her. I want to go home to be married. Will you come home for the wedding?"

"Yes, I wouldn't miss it for anything, maybe Alma can come too." Looking at Alma he said, "Maybe we can make this a double wedding, what you think Alma?"

"Gee, I would love to Pepe, but, uh, I don't know about next month. I'll have to check with my dad. I, uh, think he has a family reunion planned for next month."

"OK, Alma, check with your dad. I'm working on a deal that should be finished next week. Afterwards we'll get together and plan the date, maybe in six or eight weeks. But right now, we need to get to the Iberia Restaurant or we'll be late for our reservation."

Pepe's car was a beautiful black Cadillac. He opened the door for Alma and walked around the car to enter. Jeff opened the back door on the right side and Nicole got in. Before Jeff could enter, a large sedan came speeding around the corner and opened gunfire on them. Jeff dived to the sidewalk and rolled almost under the car. The gunfire lasted only seconds, but seemed like an hour to Jeff. Finally, it was quiet and he picked himself up to see how the others were. *Oh my God.* Nicole was lying lifeless, completely covered with blood. In his heart he knew even before he felt her pulse that she was not alive. He had enough presence of mind to look in the front seat and saw that Alma was in the same condition. The left front door was open and he could see Pepe lying on the street, looking as if he had been cut in half with a machine gun.

Someone must have phoned the police, as police cars and policemen were everywhere. When the ambulance arrived, the medics checked on Nicole, Alma and Pepe; they were all pronounced dead.

Jeff was in shock, his head was pounding, he was short of breath, his heart was beating so hard it seemed as if it would burst through his chest. *This must be a dream; it cannot happen to me, the love of my life can't be gone.* Feeling faint, he sat down on the curb to collect himself when a shabbily dressed man approached, sat down beside him and asked, "Are you all right, my man? Can I be of help?"

Jeff answered, "I guess I'm all right. I need some water."

The shabbily dressed man returned in a few minutes and handed Jeff a paper cup full of water. "Here, Jeff, drink this and pull yourself together." Shocked that bum knew him, he swallowed some of the water and felt better.

"Thank you, Mister, do I know you?"

"Yes, Jeff, I am Art McGraw. Remember me?"

"Of course, but the way you are dressed and with what has just happened, I didn't get the connection. I can't believe they are gone. Do you know what happened?"

"Look, Jeff," Art said, "let's go to your place so we can talk and get you calmed down."

After getting to his apartment, Jeff made a stiff drink of Jim Beam, with about two tablespoons of water, and took a big gulp. The bourbon burned as it went down and hit the pit of his stomach. His stomach churned and everything wanted to come up. He took a second smaller sip, and it seemed to settle down.

Art said, "Jeff, are you OK, do you have any snacks around?"

"Yes, I have some roasted pecans in the cabinet, but I need another drink."

"OK, let me fix you the drink and get the pecans. You just sit back and try to calm down."

After a few roasted pecans and another sip of Jim Beam the realization of what had happened hit him. It was not a dream and it was real.

Art said, "Jeff, tell me everything that happened, every little detail, from the time you met the first one of the group, until the incident. Don't leave out anything, even if you think that it is not important."

"Well, Art, nothing really happened. I went to Nicole's apartment. She answered the door wearing a very pretty sleeveless black dress; she was so beautiful. We kissed, and I asked her to marry me. She said yes. We had just begun to talk about how our life together would be when Pepe and Alma came in. Nicole told him of our marriage plans and asked him if he would come to Leesville next month for the wedding. He said yes and suggested to his girlfriend, Alma, that they make it a double wedding. Art, she did seem a little hesitant in her answer, as though she was thinking up an excuse. Then she said something about a family reunion that her father was planning for next month. Pepe said they'd discuss it later. He was in a hurry to get to the Iberia Restaurant, so we wouldn't be late for our reservation. But, everyone seemed happy; I know Nicole and I were.

"Then, we went down to the car. Pepe opened the door for Alma and was walking around the car to enter. I had opened the back door on the right side so Nicole could get in. Before I could enter, a sedan came speeding around the corner and started firing at us. I dived to the sidewalk and rolled almost under the car. I don't know how long the gunfire lasted; it seemed like an eternity. When it stopped, I picked myself up to see how the others were. Nicole was lying lifeless with blood everywhere. I knew she was dead. Then I looked in the front seat and saw Alma in the same condition. Pepe was lying in the street. He looked like he'd been cut in two.

"Before long, there were police everywhere. When the ambulance arrived, the medics said they were all dead."

Jeff was lost deep in thought, trying to reconstruct the scene, looking confused.

"What's wrong, Jeff, did you think of something?" "You know, Art, when you go down to the river bank to fish, you hear sounds, like birds singing and frogs croaking. Well, tonight when we got to the car, there was no one was in sight, no noise, everything was too quiet, eerily quiet. Then suddenly the car's headlights shone around the corner, followed by the roar of the engine and then the sound of gunfire. Pepe was running around the car shouting, 'Get down, get down,' and something like, 'God damn hug.'"

"Think, Jeff, what could he have meant? Did you ever hear Pepe mention a name like hug or anything similar before?"

"Art, I really can't think too well after what has happened. I just lost the only girl I'll ever love. My mind is not working right now," said Jeff, on the verge of tears.

"OK, Jeff, but I will give you a little advice. What happened tonight, you will never forget, you will remember Nicole always, but time heals and life must go on. To be a good detective or private investigator, you must put even the most personal matters aside. If you don't, it could cost you your own life. I know you are thinking, life isn't worth living, but it is. In the case we are working on, we need information. Take another drink and go to bed. Try to get some sleep. In the morning eat a hearty breakfast, bathe, put on fresh clothes and make your mind up that if you truly love Nicole, you will find her killer. Be at the Beinville Park sitting on a bench on the south side at ten-thirty, just use caution from this moment forward."

After Art left the apartment, Jeff poured another large portion of Jim Beam into his glass. He drank it without water, and then crawled into bed.

He awoke with a throbbing headache, which the vision of the night before made worse. He looked at the clock and saw it was nine o'clock. Remembering his appointment with Art, he dragged himself out of bed, took a bath, shaved and dressed. On the way to Beinville Park he stopped off at the Royal Cafe for breakfast. He was not hungry but forced himself to eat, and after consuming two eggs, with grits, country sausage, toast and coffee he felt better physically, but mentally he was drained. On the way to Beinville Park he relived the painful experience of the night before. It was going to be difficult to get past the awful tragedy of last night. As he entered the park he stopped, looked up and some of the faith he'd had as a youngster, before his daddy became a drunken preacher, stirred his soul. Kneeling down in the middle of the sidewalk in Beinville Park, he looked up and prayed. *Dear Lord, this poor sinner in front of you is confessing his sins and asks for your forgiveness. Please help me become a better person than I have been. Take care of Nicole and Pepe for I believe he would have changed if his life had not been taken at this early age. If it is in your will please help me to be a stronger person and be at peace. Thank you, Lord. Amen.*

He instantly felt at peace with the world, but still the sadness of Nicole's death lay heavy in his heart. He purchased a newspaper from a paperboy and sat down on a bench to read about last night's events. Deep in concentration, he heard a low voice, saying, "Good morning Jeff, keep reading and don't look around."

He recognized Art's voice. Out of the corner of his eye he saw Art, sitting at the opposite end of the bench, dressed in a blue business suit with a brief case at his feet, reading a newspaper.

In a low voice Art said, "Did you remember anything of last night that you haven't told me?"

"Yes, one thing is that word, hug, that Pepe called out. It could have been, Pug, a guy who worked for Pepe."

"OK, good. I will lay a section of my paper down and leave; you lay a section of your paper on top of mine. A few minutes after I leave pick up both sections and walk away. As you walk, look in my section and remove the folded note. Be careful not to lose the key, which is inside. Throw the paper in the trashcan; go to the restroom and into a stall. After you have read the note, tear in into small pieces and flush it down the toilet."

Art laid his paper down and left the park. Jeff placed the first section of his paper on top of Art's and read for a couple of minutes more, then got up and took both sections of the paper with him. After removing the note and key, he put them in his pocket, and then threw the papers in a trash bin. The restroom was empty and he quickly entered the stall furthest from the door before he removed the note. He placed the key in his pocket and began to read.

"Call Nicole's and Pepe's family at Prodomes Grocery Store in Fullerton, La. The number is JE-3579. Ask them to have Mr. or Mrs. Grevy call you back, that you have an important message. I know this will be hard for you, but you must do it. When one of them calls you back, inform them of who you are and your relationship with Nicole and of the deaths of their daughter and son. Get the address where to ship the bodies. You will escort the bodies to Leesville, as there is no funeral home in Fullerton. While there, keep your eyes and ears open and remember everything down to the slightest detail.

"When you finish reading this note, go to the post office, and using your key, take the envelope out of box number 873. Further instructions are there. This will be your box, so keep the key in a safe place and only on you when you are going to use it."

When he finished reading, Jeff tore the note into tiny pieces and flushed them down the toilet, headed out of the park and caught a streetcar to the post office. In box 873 was an envelope containing enough money to pay for the funeral and his expenses to Leesville. The part that he dreaded most was the call to Mr. and Mrs. Grevy. Jeff went to the Greyhound Bus Station where there were public phones and he could sit and wait for a return call.

After placing the call he picked up a magazine, sat down for the long wait and started reading. Some thirty minutes later he looked over the top page of the magazine and noticed a man in a straw hat, blue pants, black and white shoes, carrying a suitcase that was tied with rope. The man was looking at him out of the corner of his eye. Jeff got up and slowly walked down the aisle to a hallway. Pausing briefly, he reached down as if he had found something on the floor. As he did, he glanced back and saw Straw Hat had gotten up to follow him. Jeff went into a stall in the restroom and sat down on the stool. Under the partition he saw the black and white shoes.

A few minutes later, he flushed the toilet and came out, but Straw Hat was not around. As Jeff entered the hallway, there he was leaning against the wall in the main lobby. Jeff went out the side door, stepped between two empty Greyhound buses, stooped down looking under the bus and waited. As he expected, the black and white shoes were quickly approaching. As Straw Hat came around the corner of the bus, Jeff stood up, catching him in the belly with a hard right. The wind went out of Straw Hat and he fell to the concrete parking lot. Before Straw Hat could get his breath, Jeff pulled him up by the shirt, shoved him against the bus and gave him another one in the gut. You could hear his breath gush out and he went limp on the concrete again. Putting his hands under Straw Hat's armpits, he pulled him around to an alley about fifteen feet away. Dropping Straw Hat, who was out but gasping for breath, he untied the rope from the suitcase and opened it. Inside the suitcase was a sawed off double-barreled shotgun. Taking the gun, he checked to see if it was loaded. It was. He took Straw Hat, pulled him up next to the wall in the alley, making sure that no one was around. In a few minutes, Straw Hat began to breathe easier and looked up to find his double-barreled shotgun in his face.

"Look, Buster, I am upset. The love of my life has just been killed and now I find you with a shotgun, following me. I am only going to ask you one time, and if I don't get an answer that sounds like the truth, I am using both shells in this gun on you." Placing the double-barrel under Straw Hat's chin he said, "The truth or bye-bye, let's have it."

Jeff pushed the barrel harder into his flesh, and Straw Hat said, "Please, don't pull the trigger, I was just trying to make a little extra money. I was hired to follow you and if you contacted the cops, I was supposed to wound you. They don't want you dead, only to scare you so they could find out what you know."

"OK, Straw Hat let me have your billfold."

Taking the billfold, Jeff asked, "What's your name?"

"My name is Billy Ray Bartow."

"So why does this ID show that your name is John D. Foster?"

"Oh, well, you see mister, that's the one I found when I was in the bus station."

Pushing the gun hard against Straw Hat's throat, Jeff said, "This is your last chance. I want to know what your name is and you'd better be able to prove it, cauz I don't buy that crap about finding the billfold. You stole it."

"William Ray Forsite is my real name. I'm from Leesville," he said pulling out his own billfold. "A fellow named Pug was in Leesville and hired me to come down and help him with Pepe. After Pepe was killed he wanted me to wound you."

"What did he want you to do with Pepe?"

"I went to school with Pepe, so Pug thought I could get close to him and get information he wanted, like where he got his booze from, who was the head of the numbers racket and the inside on the whorehouses that Pepe owned and other stuff. Please, Mister, I just want to go back to Leesville."

"O.K. Billy Ray, I believe part of what you are saying. If I see you get on the first bus to Leesville, I won't shoot you, but I will wait in the bus station until I'm sure you are on the bus. Stand up."

When Billy Ray was on his feet Jeff said, "Go in the station and get a ticket for Leesville. Move!"

Billy Ray started slowly walking to the door of the station from the alley when Jeff raised the shotgun in the air and fired two shots. Billy Ray almost ran through the wall.

Jeff hurriedly put the shotgun in the suitcase, ran around behind the buses and dumped the suitcase in the trashcan and slowly walked around to the front door and entered. Almost everyone else, except Billy Ray, went out the side door to see what happened. A cop ran over to find out what the shots were about.

Jeff walked over to the counter and asked what time the next bus left for Leesville and was told in an hour. Jeff didn't know whether the Grevy's had called back, so he called the store again and owner told him they had been notified and should be there in about 30 minutes or so. *Fine, I have to stay to see Billy Ray off, anyway.* Walking over to Billy Ray, Jeff said, "I didn't see you purchase a ticket yet; what are you waiting for?"

"To be honest, I don't have enough money. I wasn't going to get paid until after I wounded you."

"The ticket is $2.50. Here is three dollars, now get the ticket. The bus leaves in fifty minutes. I will be in Leesville in a few days. Where can I find you? And if you lie I'll go the police station and file a complaint, and let them find you."

"Go to the Leesville Pool Room. I worked there at one time, and maybe I can get my job back. If not, they will tell you where I am. I don't want any more trouble, Mister."

The telephone rang and Jeff answered. It was Mr. Grevy. Jeff told him the sad news of the deaths of his son and daughter, but not how it happened. He told him of his relationship with Nicole and said he would escort the bodies to the Leesville Funeral Home. He would give them the details when he arrived in Leesville.

He sat down on a bus bench to wait for Billy Ray's departure thinking, *how can I tell Nicole's and Pepe's parents the cause of their children's death?. About thirty minutes later, when they announced the boarding call for passengers to going to Leesville, Billy Ray took a window seat near the rear of the bus.*

Chapter Six

Jeff was startled by the whirring noise of the cranes restacking the cargo on deck. He had to shake himself to get fully awake and get his bearings. He had fallen asleep on deck near a bulkhead on some folded canvas covering. Thinking back and reliving the Nicole episode had upset him greatly, remembering how he had found love and lost it. His head was splitting. He realized he did not have breakfast or dinner; he had to have some coffee. He headed to the officers' mess where he and the other paying passengers dined. The steward served him eggs with home fries and hot coffee. While eating, Jeff asked the steward, "Do you know the estimated time of arrival in Casablanca?"

"Yes, sir, Mr. Jeff, we are near the harbor and should be at the dock in about an hour."

He ate his eggs and potatoes and washed them down with more coffee. He still had to pack up his belongings and get ready to debark the New Orleans Trader. He went down in the hull and packed, checking his papers to make sure he had all of the documents that he would need to go ashore. Taking his suitcase, he went up on the deck of the New Orleans Trader. As the ship sailed slowly into the harbor, Jeff saw a sign that he couldn't believe. There on a large building was a red and white sign with about three foot letters that read, "Coca Cola," and under that, "The pause that refreshes," in English. French wording gave more information on America's favorite drink. Looking south as the ship came into the channel he saw the Atlantic waves crashing over the rocks, but just below the ugly sea crashing on the rock was a beautiful beach with pure white sand. To the north of the channel were factory buildings lining the shore back as far as he could see. The odor coming from this section became almost unbearable the nearer the ship got to the docks. The sailors were so busy that there was no one to ask about this strange land.

He walked over to the rail, making sure he was in a safe place out of the way of the cranes. One of the paying passengers came up beside him. The passenger went by the name of Tom Brown. Jeff judged that they were about the same age. Tom had stayed to himself for most of the trip, rarely speaking to anyone. His accent sounded European, something besides French or English.

"Good morning, Mr. Stewart, a beautiful morning to be in this great city."

"Yes, Mr. Brown, it is. Are familiar with Casablanca?"

"Ah, yes, I lived here for a few years before I went to America. I've been in New Orleans for about three years. I have come home to visit my father and mother who are getting old. They want me to take them back to the place of their birth. I have been observing you since the ship sailed. Are you an officer of the law in America?"

"No, Mr. Brown, I'm only an adventurous American, out to see the world."

"Have you any experience doing any type of undercover or detective work?"

I can't tell him I'm a private detective or know anything about that type of work, because I don't know who in the hell he is or the purpose of asking this question, but I will play along to see what he knows.

"No, Mr. Brown, I have no experience in that field. I am a small businessman in New Orleans, who has had lots of experience with people and I travel for adventure when I have the money and opportunity. I have a friend who came to Africa and joined the Foreign Legion and I wanted to see what he has been writing about in this strange land. I thought I would be getting off the ship in a jungle. The only thing I knew about Africa was Tarzan and the sandy desert my friend Tony has written me about in his letters. Here, I see Casablanca is a very large city and I am eager to explore this country."

"Where is your friend stationed, Mr. Stewart?"

"The last letter I received from him, he was stationed in Goulimime somewhere southeast of Casablanca, but he was supposed to transfer to an outpost near Meknes. I will look the country over and see if I can find him."

"Maybe I can help you see Morocco, have a little adventure and make your expense. Are you interested Mr. Stewart?"

"Sure, if it's legal and won't delay me too long. What do you have in mind Mr. Brown?"

"Where are you staying while in Casablanca?"

"At de Zouaves Hotel on Boulevard du Zouaves."

"We are about to dock. I will try to get a room at de Zouaves, or if not, at a hotel nearby. Good-bye, my friend. I hope to see you later tonight or early in the morning and we'll talk."

The ship docked and the few passengers departed. Jeff took his suitcase and went down the gangplank to the immigration office. The scent was similar to Agadir except for the rotten odor from the factories to the north.

The immigration officials were courteous and he was passed through very quickly. Making his way to the International Money Exchange, he exchanged five hundred dollars in international money orders for Moroccan francs. *How in the hell can I carry this much money? At 75 francs per dollar this will give me 37,500 francs, a bushel basketful of money.* Jeff went back to the exchange and changed some of the francs for larger bills. Six 5,000 franc bills, six 500 franc bills and the rest in smaller bills. The first thing he would do was shop for a waist belt to conceal his money, and a new watch to replace the one which had been stolen in Agadir. After converting his money he strolled out to a line of horses and carriages for a ride to de Zouaves Hotel. Before they could pull away, Mr. Brown appeared and asked if he could share the carriage to the de Zouaves.

"Sure," Jeff replied. "Mr. Brown, what is the strange odor that we smell?"

"Casablanca has a good number of leather and tanning factories. What we now smell is from the tanning of leather, mostly camel skins. Morocco ships fine camel leather all over the world, but we will be out of the factory district shortly."

The carriage passed some small shops displaying goods, clothing and other items made out of fabric and camel leather. As the horses trotted along the cobblestone streets, their hooves made clippity-clop sounds along with other horses and other strange sounds. As the street widened, the stores and buildings became taller and more modern. The street sign told him they were on General d'Amade Avenue. Mr. Brown made a lively tourist guide telling him of the buildings and some history of Casablanca. The carriage turned onto Boulevard du Zouaves, a very wide four lane boulevard with palm trees between the street and sidewalk on each side of the street, and a double row of palms trees in the center median strip. It was much larger and more beautiful than Canal Street in New Orleans.

The carriage pulled up to a large six story white stone building on the corner of Boulevard du Zouaves and du Avenue de la Gare. The hotel was an impressive building. Each of the top five floors had balconies giving an excellent view of Casablanca. Entering the hotel he noticed the decor, camel leather sofas and chairs, a walnut hand-carved counter, with the check-in desk managed by an elegantly dressed gentleman. The first thing that entered Jeff's mind was the price. The hotel was comparable to the St. Charles Hotel on Canal Street in New Orleans, only de Zouave was more luxurious. He knew that a deluxe room in the St. Charles was ten dollars a night. *The rate here must be at least fifteen dollars. That would come to 1125 francs, much more that my expense account allows. Oh, well, live it up for one night and move to a less expensive place tomorrow.*

As the carriage driver was handing the luggage to the doorman, Jeff turned to Mr. Brown and said, "Mr. Brown, do you have any idea what the room rates are here?"

"No, when I was here three years ago the base room was 375 francs and the deluxe room was 525 francs. I do not know what the price of the suite was."

Jeff was quickly calculating, *375 francs at 75 francs for a dollar would come to five dollars. Wow, a deluxe room for 525 francs would be, hmm, seven dollars.*

At the reservation desk he gave his name and the clerk asked what kind of room he would like.

"What type of room is the corner room that faces the boulevard and the avenue about the third or fourth floor?"

"Well, Monsieur Stewart, we have a room on the fourth floor corner, front, as you say in English. The rate on our luxury semi-suite would be 600 francs."

"I'll take that room for two days, maybe longer. I'll let you know."

Mr. Brown asked if they had a vacancy next door; if so he would like to have it. "Oui, Monsieur, we have room 406 available. It is 525 francs."

"Oui, that would be satisfactory."

"Porter, deliver Mr. Stewart to room 400L and Mr. Brown in 406. Monsieurs, here are some complementary drink and hors'doeuvre coupons for Le Cabaret du Zouaves.

Arriving in room 400L, Jeff took a look at the large room. It contained a double bed, a secretary desk and chair, a sofa, club chair and a coffee table. The walls were adorned with paintings and etchings of local artisans. Jeff spent several minutes just admiring his surroundings. He had never seen anything quite so elegant before.

Soon after he unpacked his belongings, the telephone on the nightstand began to ring. When Jeff answered, the voice of Mr. Brown said, "Friend, Jeff, let's go to Le Cabaret and use our complementary coupons."

"Sure, Tom, give me ten minutes to freshen up. Come by and we'll see what is happening in Casablanca."

When he answered the knock on the door, he said, "I'm ready Tom, shall we go?"

"I would like to speak with you before we go down, may I come in?"

"Sure, Tom. Come on in."

"Jeff, that is what I wanted to speak with you about, the name, Tom Brown. As I told you I left Casablanca three years ago. However, I was in trouble with the police, or I thought so. As soon as I checked in, I called my father. When I told him my name is now Tom Brown, he wanted to know why I changed it. Explaining the trouble with the police, I thought it would be best to change my name and leave Morocco. My father said that I am not in trouble with the police. The IMO (Independent Morocco Organization) was disbanded when the underground Vichy movement was organized. Some of the people in the IMO joined this movement, others dropped out.

"The Vichy movement is strong, so be careful with whom you speak. I had talked with my father before I left New Orleans, but did not tell him the name I was using. He contacted some of the former IMO members, then the police. My name is clear. My real name is Giovanni Malfa or Gino. Yes, your thoughts are correct, an Italian in French Morocco who lives in America."

"Tom, or Gino, how did your family get to Morocco?" asked Jeff.

"Our family is from the Isle de Capri, an island in the Gulf of Naples. My father was an appointed government official, similar to a mayor for the Isle. My father did not believe in Fascism and after two years of planning left Capri for Casablanca, with my mother, and sister, who is two years younger than I. I was in the Italian army, stationed at Foggia, training for the invasion of Ethiopia. Mussolini invaded Ethiopia in the spring of 1935, when I was 23. The second day, I was wounded and captured by the Ethiopians. I was sent to a field hospital near the town of Keren, in the northern part of Ethiopia. My wounds were not bad, but I faked the pain and was not guarded too carefully. One night, another soldier and I slipped past the guards and headed north. We crossed over into Sudan about eight the next morning. The Sudanese turned us over to the Germans who were allies of Italy. The Germans assigned us kitchen duty until we could meet up with the Italian army. The German army pushed north through southern Egypt, into the Sahara Desert. We went with the kitchen personnel to a small desert village, where a German depot was located, to get food supplies. My friend and I slipped away from the two German soldiers and made our way to a desert tribe of Arabians, camped north of the town. The tribe was waiting for a caravan going to Tunis in Tunisia. We were three weeks crossing the desert, walking and riding camels, where sometimes the heat was 160 degrees. After reaching Tunis we purchased some civilian clothing. We, as you say in America, hopped a train, riding in a boxcar to Algiers and then to Morocco. Finally united with my family, I secured employment. I did not care for Fascism and Nazism, so I joined the Independent Morocco Organization."

"Gino, you are quite an adventurer. I could learn a great deal from you."

"Jeff, I have told you about my life. How about you filling me in on yours?"

"My life is not as exciting as yours, and I don't have to keep it from anyone. Let's go down to Le Cabaret and I'll fill you in on my dull existence."

Gino and Jeff rode the cage down to the lobby, then walked to the north end of the lobby where the bright lights invited them into Le Cabaret du Zouaves. The maitre dé seated them at a table near the orchestra and dance floor, and called the garcon over for service.

"Jeff would you like to have the French national drink?"

"Yes, and what is this national drink?"

The garcon appeared and Gino ordered two cognacs. When the waiter delivered the drinks, Jeff picked up the glass, held it up toward Gino and said, "Salute my friend." Touching Jeff's glass, Gino replied, "Salute." Jeff turned the glass up, downing the drink in one large swallow. He lost his breath; tears came into his eyes as the cognac burned its way down his guts to his stomach. When the cognac hit bottom, he thought his stomach would turn inside out and he would vomit here in this fancy cabaret. Gino slapped him on the back and gave him some water. In a few minutes he began to feel better, except his stomach was woozy and eyes were still tearing some.

"You OK, Jeff, do you want to leave?"

"No, I'll be OK in a minute. Hell, I have never had cognac like this before, I've always chugged it down."

Gino motioned for the waiter and said, "Bring some tonic water and a lime. Oh yes, and bring some cold escargot."

"Jeff, this is not New Orleans, where the cognac is only fresh weak wine. This is the true cognac, and you must sip it. Another cognac drink is a highball, just pour the cognac over ice when you can get it and put some carbonated water in the glass. You can also add a little absinthe and lime juice, but sip the drink and smell the aroma. That is the way to drink the real cognac. Here's the escargot; eat it as you sip. The escargot absorbs the cognac and releases it slowly back to the stomach with your body juices. If you eat the escargot, you will not feel bad tomorrow but you will feel good tonight."

"Thanks Gino. I feel better already."

Jeff began telling Gino his life story, except for the part about working undercover for the police and the real reason he was in Casablanca. He still wasn't sure of him.

The room was beginning to fill and the band struck up the French National Anthem, the Marseillaise, and about half of the people stood up and started singing. Gino was on his feet singing as loud as he could. When the anthem was finished those standing cheered and applauded and toasted France.

"Gino, what was that all about?"

"Germany has taken Poland and some of the other middle European countries and is threatening France. The Vichy is getting stronger. They are the anti-France group and have set up a puppet government underground in some other countries. They are here in Morocco, Algeria and Tunisia and are supported by the Nazis."

"Are you playing a part in this movement Gino?"

"No, but I believe the Italian government is wrong and I will try to help free Italy of Mussolini's rule. I may look into the Free French Movement. Would you like to come along on a new adventure?"

"No thank you. I don't want to get into any political business, not in a foreign government's movement. I am on a holiday and will try to find some fun and hope to have some excitement along the way."

"Look, Jeff, you could escort my mother and father to Italy. This would not be politically motivated, just see that they arrive on the Isle de Capri safely and you can have fun."

"Gino, your father left Italy in an unfavorable environment. What makes you think the environment has changed? Isn't Mussolini still the head of the government; have you checked to see if it is safe? I don't understand why you and your sister don't escort them?"

"First, my sister doesn't want to go back. She is in the movement here. Second, I am a deserter from the Italian Army."

"Gino, if your father has to be smuggled into Italy, then it would not be safe for him to live there. Also, if I did it, and got caught, I would be charged as a smuggler and maybe get life in prison or death in a foreign country. Sorry, Gino, I won't do it. You should advise your father and mother not try to go back under these conditions."

While Gino and Jeff were having their discussion, Jeff had been making eye contact with a striking brunette at the bar. Excusing himself, he motioned for the waiter.

"Monsieur, see that brunette at the bar, the third from the end? Do you know what she is drinking?"

"Oui, Monsieur, she is drinking a vodka martini."

"Ok, give her a vodka martini and add it to my check."

While Gino was in the washroom, Jeff was trying to piece together his conversation to determine what his motive was, and if he was what he said he was, or whether he was an agent of one of these crazy governments. *Oh to hell with it.* He made eye contact with the brunette again after the drink was delivered. She raised her glass in his direction, nodded her head at him and smiled.

Jeff motioned for the waiter and asked him to ask the brunette if she would join him at another table, and if so to select one for them.

Gino returned as the waiter left to carry his message to the brunette.

"Jeff, would you like to see some more of Casablanca's night life?"

Jeff delayed his answer, with an eye on the brunette. When the waiter leaned over and spoke into the brunette's ear, she looked over, tipped her glass and nodded, yes.

"Gino, I have made a connection with the brunette at the bar. I'll have a drink with her and see where it goes. I'll see you around, maybe tomorrow."

The brunette eased off the bar stool, graceful as a dancer and followed the waiter. Jeff left Gino and walked over to the table as she was being seated.

"Bonsoir, mademoiselle. You compris English?"

"Oui. My name is Claudette Meteron, and you are?"

"My name is Jeff Stewart and I am an American with a limited amount of French. May I have a seat?"

"Oui. I mean yes. Jeff, it is a pleasure to meet you. What is your pleasure in our great city?"

"Oh, I have a small business in America. I am here on a vacation for adventure."

"Jeff, are you in any way connected to the gentleman at your table?"

"No. I met the gentleman on the ship as a passenger and by coincidence, he checked into the same hotel as I. We rode in the same carriage from the ship to the de Zouaves Hotel.

"Waiter, bring us another vodka martini and a cognac with ice and absinthe with a twist of lime. Do you know the gentleman, Claudette?"

"I am familiar with him from the past, maybe three or four years ago. His name is Bruno LaTorre and he is a mean, cruel person. He deserted from the Italian Army while in Tunis. He lured white European girls to an Arabic mob who traded them much like cattle, to tribesmen, oil sheiks or to anyone who would pay the price. The last I heard of Bruno he was sent on a mission to America to see if he could get some American girls for the Arabic mob. How can I be sure you are not one of his partners?"

Jeff's mind rushed swiftly trying to find a way to convince the brunette that he was not connected to Gino, or Bruno, or whoever the hell this guy was, and yet not give away why he was on this trip.

"I can only tell you who I am, a small businessman from the United States. I know very little French, and nothing about Morocco until I arrived in Agadir a few days ago, when the ship stopped there for repairs. I just arrived in Casablanca this morning. I thought Africa was all jungle and wild animals until then. I am sure you will find that I am not bright enough to be connected with anyone of his talents."

"I believe you Jeff, but heed my warning. Do not have much to do with him. Do you dance, Jeff?"

"Yes. Not well, but I do try. Shall we?"

Making their way to the dance floor, Jeff noticed that the cabaret was almost full. There were many soldiers in a variety of different military uniforms; Italian, French, German and a couple he could not identify. Putting his arms around Claudette, they glided around the dance floor to the smooth rhythm of the orchestra. She was a good dancer and so smooth that his clubfoot did not once make him stumble. Having his shoes special made had helped him to dance well. The big problem still was running at full speed. *Ha, maybe I won't have to run at full speed to catch Claudette.* The song ended and another slow number began. Claudette snuggled up close to Jeff and the smell of her hair and perfume was getting to him. As they finished this number Jeff held her close, not tight, but close and she seemed to feel right in his arms.

Back at the table Jeff said, "Thank you for the dance. You are an excellent dancer, do you dance professionally?"

"Not at this time. I did in Paris at de Folie Revue and a couple shows here in Casablanca, but my interest is in travel and I interned with the Moroccan Tourist Bureau for six months. The past six months I have been a tourist consultant."

"What a coincidence. I am also in the tourist business."

"Tell me about your business. Is it in New York?"

"No, not New York. Claudette, would you care to have another drink and then dinner? We can discuss our mutual careers. As you're a tourist consultant, I'll rely on you to pick the restaurant. Someplace secluded, where we can talk."

"I am not on duty as a consultant tonight, but as you are a stranger to Casablanca, I will give you a tour for your pleasure and mine. I know a place that is small, quaint, private and the food is delicious."

Jeff paid the check, giving the waiter a generous tip. He might need him for information later.

At the front of de Zouaves Hotel, Claudette chose the second horse drawn carriage in the line. The two white part-Arabian horses, stood stately by, their black camel leather harnesses adorned by shiny silver brads and tips. The carriage was white, trimmed in gold and black with white camel leather seats. The driver mounted the carriage driver's seat by stepping on the step, then on the wheel. Speaking through a tube coming down to the passenger coach, the driver said something in French, and Claudette answered in French. About the only thing that Jeff could make out was a beach, the words Dar Si Sald, Ain Diab Plage was someplace on the beach.

"Jeff, if your business is not in New York, where is it located?"

"It is in New Orleans, Louisiana. I have been in New Orleans for about ten years and I am in the flower business. I am letting two people run it on a profit-sharing basis and I started the tour business a few months ago. It is a tour and guide service that takes tourists around New Orleans into the French Quarter nightclubs, restaurants, and other attractions around the city. I am new in this field, but learning. My business is small, but growing. I came here to visit a friend in the Foreign Legion and see what the atmosphere would be for a vacationer on a tour in a foreign country. I thought I might pick up some ideas for foreign tourists who visit New Orleans. I probably should have waited until I had more funds, so I could spend more time."

"It is nice that we are in the same type of business. Here in Casablanca we can go on tours and in places where tourists visit. Show your business card and they will treat you like royalty. If it's not gratis, they will charge you a very low price."

"That may be a problem. The ship ran into rough weather and some of the cargo was swamped with water and I lost most of my baggage, including my business cards. All I had left was this casual suit, a couple of shirts and some underclothes. I did not have enough time when the ship went into Agadir to replace my things. The only good thing I have left is these shoes. I was born without toes on my left foot and I have special shoes made. That is why I have a slight limp. I should not have gone out tonight and waited until I have replaced my clothing and business cards. However, Gino, or as you call him, Bruno, insisted we go for a drink. Now I am happy I did for I have met you. Maybe we should call this off tonight and make a date after I have replaced the items I lost."

"Oh, no, Jeff, we will use my business cards for I am well known. Tonight you are my guest. I did not notice any limp when you walked and you dance very well. Are you, I think it is called in English, self-conscious, of your foot?"

"Yes, somewhat. I was teased in school about it and I have tried to walk, run and dance as well as everyone else, but it seems as if people are always looking at my foot. Let's change the subject to more pleasant things."

The carriage had good springs and was comfortable to ride in. Claudette nestled in his arms. He put his face on her hair and moved slowly around to her face. Almost as if on cue, they found each other's lips. It was a long, passionate kiss that left them both breathless. The rest of the trip was spent kissing until the carriage tuned into a driveway. Claudette straightened her clothing and turned on a dim battery-operated light to repair her makeup.

As the carriage stopped Jeff asked, "Where are we?"

"We are at the Club Dar Si Sald on the beach of Ain Diab."

Chapter Seven

Jeff opened one eye and looked around. It was not pitch black, dim light was coming from the outside.

Oh, yes, he was no longer down in the hull of the New Orleans Trader, but in a nice soft, comfortable bed in de Zouaves Hotel.

Oh, yes, that Claudette was some woman. A beautiful woman who looked a little like Nicole in stature, complexion, hair color and eyes. Claudette was not only beautiful but had an outgoing personality, witty and never met a stranger. Nicole was also beautiful, but with a different personality, quiet, a little shy, almost timid.

He had to find a place to purchase some clothing, special shoes and have some new business cards made. It was all because of Art McGraw that he had gotten started in the tour guide business.

He thought back to the time of Nicole's death. He had hated going to work at night, but had to make a living. One day Art McGraw, Special Agent of the Drug and Alcohol Division, asked him to take three couples on a tour of nightclubs in the French Quarter. They were suspected of selling drugs and wanted a good cover to make contact with prospective customers. Putting on his Sears, Roebuck suit, shirt and tie, he took the couple to some nightclubs and to an elegant Cajun restaurant where they feasted on lobster and had several drinks. At the end of the evening they paid him handsomely, for the fee was set by McGraw. The Drug and Alcohol Division owned the tour service. Jeff did a good job and was placed as manager of the tour service. He found a girl who wanted to work and he taught her how to sell flowers, while he did some detective and tour guide work. The experience of undercover work helped his career as a detective to accelerate rapidly.

The most satisfying work he did was closing the case on the deaths of Pepe and Nicole. He had a tour client who wanted to go to the better nightclubs and restaurants. He picked up Mr. James T. Tucker at the St. Charles Hotel on Canal Street. From there they went to Crondalete Avenue, a fashionable section of New Orleans, where they picked up his date, Miss Yulanda Sessoms, who was dressed in the latest fashions. They went to Philippe's for cocktails and dinner. Spending some two hours and consuming a large number of cocktails, Mr. Tucker asked to go slumming to some of the blues hot spots. He said he had heard of a place named Blues of the Night, on Bourbon Street.

About thirty minutes after arriving at Blues of the Night, a rough looking man, dressed in an expensive suit came over to Mr. Tucker. They spoke briefly, and then the man went into the back. When Mr. Tucker excused himself to use the restroom, Jeff noticed he went into a room next door to the restroom. A flash came to Jeff; *the rough looking man did not look the part of the expensive suit. Visually putting him in some everyday clothes and a beard, the man was none other than Bernie,"The Pug" Russell.*

But who was James T. Tucker?

About ten minutes passed and four shots rang out from the room next to the restroom. No one had enough nerve to go into the room. When the police arrived and went into the room, they found Mr. James T. Tucker dead on the floor with four bullet holes within a six-inch circle of his heart. Blood had splattered everywhere, but there was no sign of the well-dressed rough looking character. He must have left through a window.

Yulanda Sessoms was hysterical and asked to be taken home. However, the police had arrived and sealed off the Blues of the Night, and no one was permitted to leave.

Questioning Miss Sessoms, the police asked her about James T. Tucker.

She replied, "I was introduced to Mr. Tucker by a friend, June Bonner and her friend Jim Steel. I don't know anything other than that June said he was from Atlanta."

The police allowed Miss Sessoms to leave after giving her address and telephone number.

Jeff asked her, "Miss Sessoms, have you ever seen the man who spoke with Mr. Tucker at our table tonight?"

"I think so. He looked familiar but I can't place him."

"May I call you Yulanda?"

"Yes, please. You have been kind and helpful."

"Yulanda, would you like to stop off for a cup of coffee to settle your nerves before going home?"

"Yes, that would be nice, thank you."

Jeff was not far from the Morris Restaurant on Canal Street. After being seated and ordering coffee, Jeff said, "Yulanda, this must have been a terrible experience for you. Do you feel better?"

"Yes, I have never been through anything such as this. I don't know if I can settle down."

"Maybe talking about it will help. Tell me under what circumstances you met Mr. Tucker?"

"I met June a few months ago at a party given by a friend of mine, Sue Franklin. We would run into each other occasionally, and June was a likeable person. I didn't care too much for her friends. They seemed to be a rough group, course and foul-mouthed. I did go out with a decent, well-dressed guy by the name of Pepe. Not long afterwards, I read in the newspaper that Pepe was killed. That was a shock to me and now this."

"Think hard Yolanda, did you ever see the fellow who spoke to Mr. Tucker before, maybe with Pepe? Waiter bring us some coffee."

"There was a big bearded man who seemed to turn up almost every place we went, but he sort of stayed in the background. Pepe once said he was his right hand man. Yes, put some cheap clothing and a beard on him and it might be the same man."

They finished their coffee in silence, each lost in their own thoughts.

"Yulanda, are you ready to go home?"

"Yes, thank you."

After letting Yulanda off at her home, he went to the de Devant Saloon, getting there just before closing time. He asked Clio, who was cleaning the last table, "Clio, do you know where I can find Pug? I hear he has a new house but I don't have the address."

"Look, Honey, you don't have to pay for it. I'll be finished here in five minutes and we can go to my place."

"No, Clio, that's not what I am looking for. However, I will take your offer up some other time."

"Promise? OK, he had Pepe's old house, but he sold that and purchased a house three doors down. I don't know the number."

Jeff left the de Devant Saloon and took off for Lake Pontchartrain in the '33 Ford he had recently purchased. It was only a fifteen-minute drive from the saloon. Going down the street to Pepe's old house, counting off three houses, he rang the doorbell. A plump, brassy blond answered the door and said, "Hi, Honey what you like?"

"I would like you, where is your room?"

"Follow me, Honey, the price is $2.00 before we start."

Going into the room, he closed the door and locked it. The brassy blond said, "What you do that for, ain't nobody coming in here?" "That's right, Honey, and no one is going out either, that is alive, unless I get some answers."

"Git outta here," she said as she walked over to the wall beside the bed.

Jeff spotted the button for the buzzer and grabbed her before she could press it. Putting his right hand over her mouth and his left arm around her and stood behind her, with his left hand on her throat and put a little squeeze with his thumb on her windpipe.

"Look, Honey, one little peep out of you and you will never utter another word. Now when I release you, don't make a sound except to answer my questions in a low voice. If you understand, and will do as I say, nod your head, yes."

The brassy blond nodded her head up and down so fast it looked as if it would fall off.

Jeff relaxed his hand on her throat, but did not remove it.

"Honey, I want some straight answers and I don't have the time to play games. Your life is on the line, not some beating, as Pug would give you, but your life. Now tell me which room Pug is in and the type of lock on the door and who is in the room with him."

"Look Mister, don't hurt me. I wouldn't give my life for Pug's, it's a fact. I'll gladly help you nail the bastard. I have had all of the beatings I can take from him. He is upstairs in the last room on the right. He converted the last two rooms into one and the last door is the entrance. It has a sliding bolt lock besides the regular lock and his girlfriend is in there with him."

"OK, if you want to get rid of Pug, you can help. Let's go up to the door and you knock and tell him you have an emergency downstairs. Tell him a drunk is beating up one of the girls and threatened to call the police. When I go in the door I want you and the rest of the girls to go into a room and stay there, is this understood?"

"Yes, Sir, I'll see to it. Are you ready?"

"Lead the way."

They walked quietly up the stairs, Jeff sliding along the stair banister and the wall until they reached the last door. He nodded his head.

"Pug...Pug, come quick! A man is downstairs beating up Carol and threatening to call the police!"

He could hear feet hitting the floor and the unlocking of the door. Just as he opened the door, Jeff jumped in, kicked him in the balls and as Pug bent over in agony, Jeff interlocked his fingers and made a big fist and came up with an uppercut. Pug was out like a light.

"OK, Honey, go downstairs and get everyone in a room and stay there until I tell you to come out. To make sure, tell everyone that if any one sticks his or her head out of the door, I'll blow it off. If anyone uses the phone I'll be back to settle the score. Now git!"

Pug lay there in his underwear. Jeff tried to grab him under the arms and pull him back into the room. The man weighed over two hundred fifty pounds, and Jeff couldn't budge him.

Looking inside, he saw a girl about a hundred ten pounds looking as if the world had collapsed. Her eyes bugged out and she was as white as a bed sheet.

"Miss, you go over to the chair in the corner and sit there." Taking a bed sheet he tied Pug's hands in front of him. Just as he was coming to, he opened his beady eyes and saw Jeff.

Taking the tied hands, he pulled and ordered Pug to his feet. Pug struggled to get his two hundred fifty-odd pounds of flesh up off the floor. Jeff pushed him into a chair. Looking around, he spotted a claw hammer that Pug had used to hang some pictures. He picked up the hammer and a picture and slammed the picture over Pug's head. The picture flew out and the frame landed around Pug's neck.

"Now, Mr. Russell, that was only a picture frame. If you don't answer my questions or if I think you are lying, I will put this claw hammer first over your head, then next in your balls. Remember how it feels being hit in the balls. I'll keep hitting you there each time you come to, until I get at the truth. I am not a cop and I don't have to play by their rules. Are you ready for the first question? Nod your head yes or no and speak only to answer the question."

"The first question is, who is the girl sitting over there?"

Pug looked over at her with a pained expression and said, "She is my girlfriend; we are going to be married."

"Then you love her very much?"

"Yes, I do."

"OK. If your answers are not truthful, I will not only hit you over the head and in the balls with a hammer, but I'll take her and put her tits in the washing machine wringer, understood?"

"Yes."

"Not, yes. It's yes, Sir."

"Yes, Sir."

"First, I know you are not smart enough to run a organization such as this, so who ordered you to kill Pepe and Nicole?"

"Please, Jeff, I didn't mean to kill Nicole."

"You bastard! Dead is dead, whether you made a mistake or not. I may make a mistake and kill your beloved over there. Now, answer the question, who ordered you to kill Pepe?"

"It was Andre Gallier. He promised me that I could have the house here and be part of his organization and he would protect me."

"Is this the Andre Gallier of the Parish Commissioners who is a friend of the ex-Governor that has also been accused of taking kickbacks?"

"Yes, Sir."

"Did Andre Gallier also order you to kill James T. Tucker?"

"Yes."

"For what reason?"

"Tucker was from the capitol city of Baton Rouge. I think some type of undercover agent, and Andre wanted him dead."

"Andre is not here to protect you and will probably deny he ever knew you. You may be spared the electric chair, I can't say what is going to happen to you, but to save your life and maybe get your girlfriend out of trouble, it would do you good to cooperate with the authorities."

"Jeff, I need a doctor, my balls are killing me. Call the police and have them get a doctor for me."

Jeff went over to the phone and gave the operator a number; it was the private number for Art Mcgraw.

"Hello Art, I have Bernie, "The Pug," Russell here at his house. He has confessed to the murders of Pepe and Nicole, and possibly a state investigator tonight. He has named the head boss of the syndicate who ordered all the killings as Parish Commissioner Andre Gallier. I have Pug's girlfriend and the working girls of his house who may be witnesses. Give me five minutes before you or someone arrives here. I don't want to be here and blow my cover."

Jeff went downstairs and ordered all of the girls to report to Pug's room at once, then he went back and checked Pug's arms and hands, to make sure they were secure. When all of the personnel showed up, he told them, "Pug has confessed to killing Pepe and Nicole and named the head of the syndicate. The police are on the way. To keep out of trouble, stay in this room until they arrive."

Jeff walked out of the room, closed and locked the door, placing the keys about two feet in front of it and left the premises. His Ford was about two blocks away when he heard the police sirens on the way to pick up Pug.

Chapter Eight

Jeff picked his watch up from the night stand and saw that it was nine PM. *Let's see, the time is seven hours earlier in New Orleans than here, that would make it two PM there.* He needed to call and report to his client. Picking up the phone, he placed a person-to-person call to Marshall Bakker in New Orleans at Franklin 3-4464. As soon as he placed the call, he called the hotel desk and asked them to send up a pot of coffee.

He walked over to the window where he had an excellent view of Boulevard du Zouaves and du Avenue de la Gare. The white stone buildings held the colorful signs, like the blue Cinzano sign with the white neon letters, and the red and white Zopp sign. As he was admiring the signs a knock came on the door. It was the coffee. Damn, he was glad to get it. He had only had about two swallows when he heard a funny ringing sound. He realized that it was the telephone.

"Hello, this is Jeff Stewart speaking."

"Jeff, Marsh Bakker. I have been waiting for your call. Where have you been? You are overdue in Casablanca."

"Yes, Sir. The ship had engine trouble and docked in Agadir for repairs. I just arrived at the hotel early yesterday morning, which would have been sometime about midnight your time. I met someone last night, at the hotel cabaret, who may know where I can begin looking."

"Jeff, I've had some terrible news. Day before yesterday I had a call from the Préfecture of Police in Casablanca. They found Mary Alice, dead. She was murdered. She is at the Police Morgue and they need someone to identify her body and make shipping arrangements back to the United States. Do this for me, then spend some time there and see if you can find the bastard who killed her. Do you need money to ship the body back?"

"Mr. Bakker, I don't know how much it will cost to ship the body, but I'll find out and call you back in the morning; don't forget there is a seven-hour difference in the time."

"I don't care what the time is. As soon as you find out the procedure and cost call me back, no matter what time it is here."

"Sure, I'll get right on it. I'm sorry about your daughter. Good-bye Mr. Bakker."

Jeff took a quick bath, shaved and put on fresh clothing. Downstairs, he caught a taxi, the first motorized vehicle he had been in since getting to Morocco. He told the driver to take him to police headquarters. The man gave him a blank stare. Finally, with his little bit of Cajun French and gestures, he made the driver understand. The taxi could hardly pull away from the curb, but gained power when they were under way. He noticed a tank, similar to a hot water heater on the side of the taxi and on most of the other vehicles. Later, he found out it was a charcoal burner, that made gas to power the automobiles. The gas wasn't powerful but did move the taxi along pretty well once it got started.

The policier, or detective in charge of the Bakker case, Pierre de La Salla, filled Jeff in on the information he had. The body was a female of about twenty-five to twenty-eight years of age, five feet two inches tall, weighing approximately one hundred ten pounds, with naturally brown hair, that had been bleached blond. Jeff mentally compared the photo he had of Mary Alice Bakker to the description of the victim.

"Monsieur de La Salla, was there any identification on the body?"

"No, only a scrap of paper that said, 'my son do not forget your mama.' The note was written in French."

"How did you get her father's name and telephone number?"

"The blouse she was wearing, had a label sewn on it that read, 'Maison Blanc Department Store, New Orleans, La. Made especially for Mary Alice Bakker.' We called Maison Blanc Department Store and they gave us a telephone number. It was a Mr. Marshall Bakker. We gave Mr. Bakker a description of the victim in the morgue and he identified her as his daughter."

"Monsieur, did the shoes fit the victim?"

"We will have to confer with the doctor who performed the autopsy. Let's go to the morgue."

Dr. Moroe Burgress came in the room and escorted them to the morgue. Jeff took the photo of Mary Alice Bakker and compared it to the corpse. Even with the swollen body, almost anyone could tell this was a different girl. Jeff asked the doctor about her shoes. Opening a bag with all the worldly goods that the victim had, he pulled out a shoe.

"Doctor, what size feet does the victim have, if you discount the swelling due to death?"

"I would say she would wear a size five shoe," answered the doctor.

"This shoe is a size six, that would fit the victim now. If so, this would not be her shoe. Where was the shoe manufactured?"

Going over the shoe very carefully, they found stamped in the shoe on the sole near the heel, "Made in USA."

Jeff asked the detective Monsieur de La Salla, "Sir, could the shoe have been planted with this body?"

"Yes, I suppose it could."

"Dr. Burgress, can you tell us whether this woman ever gave birth?"

"Yes," answered Dr. Burgress, "but Miss Bakker could have had a child. I'm almost sure this victim is not Mary Alice Bakker, but I would like to verify a couple more things. Mr. Stewart, can you tell me if Miss

Bakker had a mole on the right side of her chin, or a light birthmark on her right shoulder, or a gold molar?"

"I don't know, but if I could use your telephone and make a collect call to the United States, I can get you an answer quickly."

"Let's go to the office and we will put the call through."

In about fifteen minutes Jeff had Mr. Bakker on the telephone.

"Mr. Bakker, I am at the morgue and I am pretty sure that this person is not Mary Alice. We need to be certain, though. Did Mary Alice have any birthmarks?"

"No, she had no birthmarks."

"Did she have any moles on her face?"

"No."

"Any gold teeth?"

"No."

"Mr. Bakker, did Mary Alice have any type of deformed extremity?"

"Yes, her little toe on the left foot was crooked. We had a brace on it when she was a small child, but it did not straighten it out."

"Just a moment, Sir."

"Dr. Burgess, was there any deformity on the victim's feet or toes?"

"No, Monsieur, her feet and toes are normal."

"Mr. Bakker, this woman is not your daughter; Mary Alice must still be alive. May I call you when I get back to the hotel? It may be quite late at night your time."

"By all means Jeff, call me any time. I'm so relieved that it's not Mary Alice. Thank you for a job well done. Good-bye."

After hanging up the phone, he went back to speak with Detective Pierre de La Salla.

"Bonjour, Monsieur Stewart. Are you going to continue looking for Mademoiselle Bakker?"

"Yes. Call me Jeff. May I refer to you as Pierre?"

"Oui, Jeff."

"Pierre, I would like to find out who the young lady in the morgue is. Have you any method of finding her fingerprints in Morocco, or maybe Algeria or Tunisia? This would be helpful for me to backtrack her to the connection with Mary Alice Bakker."

"It could be difficult. The headquarters for all fingerprints is in Paris. With the war so near and Vichy government infiltrating most of the government agencies, it will take some time, or maybe not at all. But Jeff, we can check to see if her fingerprints are on file in Morocco. This should take only about a week."

"I would appreciate that very much. I will check back next week. In the interval you can reach me at the de Zouaves Hotel. If I change hotels I'll call you with the new address."

He arrived back at the hotel at three PM and had a message from Claudette to call her. First, he wanted to speak with Marsh Bakker in New Orleans the time difference made it eight AM.

He asked the operator to get Franklin 3-4464 in New Orleans.

Twenty minutes later he picked up the receiver on the first ring.

"Hello darling, why did you not call me?" Claudette asked.

"I have just arrived back at the hotel and had to make a very important business call. I am now waiting for a telephone call from America. Can I call you back when I finish?"

"I shall be leaving for the cabaret in about fifteen minutes. I'll see you there?"

"I should be finished by then. If I am not there, I will be as soon as I can. Wait for me."

Five minutes later he answered the telephone and Marsh Bakker was on the line.

"Mr. Bakker, let me fill you in up to now and the plans I have, and see if they meet with your approval."

"Call me Marsh. What have you found thus far?"

"Detective Pierre de La Salla of the Casablanca Police is checking the fingerprints of the young lady in the morgue, not only in Morocco, but

France, Tunisia and Algeria. If I can identify her, maybe I can trace her back and see whether she had any connection to Mary Alice. The day I was in Agadir I met an American in the French Foreign Legion and he told me of some of the criminals who prey on young European women by enticing them to come to Morocco, Algeria or Tunisia, where they are sold into slavery for the purpose of prostitution. If they are beautiful enough, they are sold to harems for the wealthy. One of the passengers on the ship I later learned, is a deserter from the Italian Army and did some recruiting of European women. He was on his way back from New Orleans. I found out later, under an assumed name. A person gave me this information in the hotel lounge that informed me that he had still another name, and was connected to some type of criminal activity. Marsh, I think I can find out what we need to know, but it won't be easy or quick. These people travel in the circle of expensive nightclubs here, although not as expensive as the same type of clubs in America. Also, my twenty-dollar Sears, Roebuck suit doesn't fit in with this crowd. I had planned to move to a less expensive hotel, but it seems as if people of this type of activity patronize this hotel. The cost is high 600 francs per day. That is eight dollars a day and the hotel compares to the St. Charles in New Orleans."

"In other words, Jeff, you need more expense money. Well, OK. I want Mary Alice found as quickly as possible. You take on the life of the people you have to associate with. Tomorrow go to a large bank that handles international transactions and call me with the information I will need to transfer money to you. Would two thousand dollars be enough for the time being?"

"Yes, thank you. I will keep you posted on the events."

Jeff hung up and went into the bathroom to wash up in preparation for his meeting with Claudette.

Chapter Nine

It was a beautiful morning, as usual, in Marrakech, French Morocco.

Catherine went outside to the garden, her favorite place. The water from the blue Moroccan tile pool glistened from the sun as it came over the snow-covered Toubkal Mountains, some forty miles away. The snow-topped mountains made a beautiful picture, reflecting in the pool. She walked over to a lounge chair under a banyan tree where a pot of coffee was waiting on a table. Settling in a chair, pouring a cup of coffee and savoring the flavor, she looked at her surroundings. Beside the mountains, closer to her home, she saw the high eighteen-inch thick stone wall, painted white with broken glass imbedded on top of it. There was a large patio of deep red Moroccan tile, surrounded by a lush green lawn with palm and coconut trees landscaping the back area. She looked behind her at the large pinkish-red Moorish style, 30,000 square foot home. She almost wished her Grandfather Bakker could see her life-style.

Her earliest memory of her mother was sometime during her first three years of life. She and her mother lived with her grandparents, Sara and Henry Andrews, in a small town in the panhandle of Florida. Some of her early memories were the bitter arguments between her mother and Grandfather Andrews. He called her a whore, for going off to New Orleans and getting pregnant, then giving the baby the last name of its father. He told her she was living a life of sin and would go to hell. All through this, Grandmother Andrews tried to keep her out of hearing range of the arguments.

One day when she was six years old, a big shiny automobile drove up in front of the house. A nicely dressed man got out and went onto the porch where her grandmother was sitting in a rocking chair. He asked for Mary Jane Andrews and her grandmother told him she was at work at the shirt factory downtown. About this time her grandfather came out of the house with a shotgun and asked, "Are you the daddy of Mary Jane's baby?"

Turning white from fright, the man stammered, "You mean Mary Jane had a baby?"

"Yes, you low life son of a bitch. You did this to her, didn't you? Git outta here and don't ever show yore face around here again."

The man, still pale with fright, asked if he could come back and talk to her.

"Hell, no. Now, git in that shiny car and go, or the hearse will pick you up."

She found out later that the man was her father, Marshall Bakker. He went to the shirt factory and told them he had an emergency message for Mary Jane Andrews. She came downstairs, and after a long discussion, agreed to go back to New Orleans with him.

When she got home that night, she told her mother the whole story. She and Marshall Bakker had met and started dating, but his family was wealthy and felt that Mary Jane was not good enough for him. One day while he was away on a business trip, his father, Anthony Marshall Bakker, came to see her and offered her some money to leave. She refused.

The family business was manufacturing machinery for ginning cotton. Marshall's father called him in New York, where he had gone on business, and told him to leave immediately for Cairo, Egypt. The Egyptian Government wanted to purchase some machinery for ginning their cotton.

Mary Jane did not have a telephone, so Marshall could not reach her. He asked his father to tell her where he was going and that he would write. In place of giving Mary Jane the message, he offered her money to leave town. Mary Jane thought this was Marshall's way of breaking up with her. She refused the money, but it was too painful for her to stay in New Orleans, so she went to Pensacola, Florida. Just two weeks later she learned she was pregnant.

She worked and saved money until the baby was due. She entered the hospital using the name Mrs. Jane Bakker, and when the little blond girl was born, she was named Mary Alice Bakker.

Her mother kissed them good-bye and said to please stay in touch. Her father told Mary Jane, "If you leave with this man, don't come back home a'crying to me."

They went to New Orleans and married. After the wedding, when Mr. Anthony Marshall Bakker met his beautiful granddaughter, he fell in love with her.

Spoiled by Grandfather Bakker and her father, Mary Alice loved the attention she was given. Her mother seemed cold, just like Grandfather Andrews. She knew her mother and Grandfather Andrews loved her, but were unable to show the affection that Grandmother Andrews, Father and Grandfather Bakker showed. Her mother and Grandmother Bakker were much alike, caught up in society circles. Her mother was gone most of the day, leaving her to play by herself, with a maid to care for her. She loved the nights when her father was home. He would come up to her room and play dolls and other games with her. He was a good storyteller, and after dinner he would make up stories and read to her while she cuddled in his lap. After she began to grow into a young woman, they would spend hours just talking and having a good time. A happy time in her childhood was when Grandmother Andrews came to live with them after Grandfather Andrews passed away. Now, she had a woman to love and talk to. All through high school she had Grandmother Andrews to go to for advice, about female problems, her feelings about boys. She couldn't talk to her mother about these things. She would say, "Now, Mary Alice, when you get older we will talk. You are too young to know about these things."

Her father tried to give her some advice, but seemed uneasy talking about things she thought she should know. One night she overheard her father talking with Grandmother Andrews.

"Mom." He always called Grandmother Andrews "Mom." "Mary Alice is asking me questions that I am not sure how to answer. I know that Mary Jane does not tell her things she should know about at her age."

"Yes, Marsh, I've wanted to talk with her, but I didn't want to be the interfering mother. Mary Jane should be telling her about life."

"Mom, would you see that she knows the facts of life from a woman's point of view?"

After that conversation between Grandmother Andrews and her father, the three of them were inseparable, going to school activities, shopping, picnics and other outings.

She remembered when things began to change. Grandmother Andrews had a heart attack and passed away when she was in her last year of high school. By that time, her mother had become an alcoholic and had been in and out of treatment centers, but as soon as she was discharged she would start drinking again. Her mother was drunk on her graduation day and missed that important day in her life. A month later her father had to have her mother committed to a hospital for the insane due to alcoholism. During her first year at Loyola University her mother passed away, and the next month her beloved Grandfather Bakker passed away.

Away at school, with no parental supervision, she couldn't cope with the changes in her life and began to run with a fast crowd. Her father begged her to slow down and come home; but she would not.

In the last quarter of her fourth year at Loyola, with her grades failing, she didn't care what happened to her. The subjects she enjoyed and excelled in were Art and Drama. She had a fair voice and was a good dancer. She decided to quit school and go to New York to try for a show business career. But she felt depressed and started going to a psychiatrist for depression, one session a week. A couple of months later she landed a small part as a dancer in a large well-known nightclub. The new job went well and her spirits soared, so much so that she dropped the psychiatrist. A year later she lost her job for partying and drinking too much.

Trying to get her back on the straight and narrow, her father brought her back to New Orleans and put her in a mental hospital, the same one where her mother had been treated. By the second month, she was well enough to be trusted and was allowed some unsupervised time. The first night she went for a walk on the hospital grounds and met one of the male nurses.

"Hi, Ralph, what do you do for entertainment around here?"

"Not much here at the hospital. I go to a small bar about four blocks from here for a few beers before going home."

"Do you live alone?" She asked, as she moved up close to him.

He had been watching this beautiful girl and wanted to talk to her, but never had the opportunity before. Now was the time.

"Yes. If you would like to get away for a while, we can go to my place and have some drinks."

She edged closer until she was touching him and whispered, "Yes, Ralph, I have been thinking of you a lot for the past few days. But how can we get out of here without being seen?"

"I have a key to the back gate where the tool house is. Nobody is back there at night."

He took her by the hand and led her to the back gate. He could hardly contain himself thinking that this girl wanted to go to his place with him. They went through the gate and walked about two blocks to catch the streetcar. Still holding her hand, his heart was beating rapidly and his breathing was fast, in anticipation of what would happen when they got to his place. *What the hell is holding up the streetcar?* When the streetcar finally stopped, they rode about ten blocks before getting off at

Magnolia Street. While walking the three blocks to Ralph's apartment, Mary Alice snuggled up close to him.

When they entered the dingy apartment, Mary Alice kicked off her high-heeled shoes, while Ralph got two bottles of beer from the kitchen. Her feet hurt from all the walking. Suddenly, Ralph grabbed her, pinned her against the wall and started kissing her roughly. She could feel his erection, as he pressed himself against her, his right hand squeezing her left breast. Terrified, Mary Alice pushed him back, reached for her shoe and hit him in the side of his head with it. It stunned him long enough for her to grab one of the beer bottles, which was sitting on the table beside her. She hit him on the back of his head and he went out like a light. Reaching into his left front pocket, she retrieved three one-dollar bills and bolted out the door.

Catching the streetcar, she leaned back, tried to relax and think out her next move. The first person that came to mind was Mike Martel, a former boyfriend of her roommate at Loyola. He was from a wealthy family, somewhat wild, but they'd had some good times together until he and her roommate, Kate, broke up. She got off on Canal Street, went into the St. Charles Hotel and called Mike.

Mike met her at the St. Charles a short time later. They went into the restaurant and had dinner. Over dinner she told Mike of her problems and asked that he promise not to tell anyone where she was.

"Mike, could I borrow a hundred dollars until I can get my finances in order?"

"Sure, Mary Alice. Are you checking into the St. Charles?"

"Yes, but under an assumed name. Let's see, I knew a Catherine in the hospital and another person, a man whose last name was Ledbetter. I think they would go good together. Mike, meet Catherine Ledbetter. However, for tonight I'll check in as Alice Baxter."

"Glad to know you Alice or Catherine. Go check into the hotel and give me your room number. I'll call you tomorrow afternoon. If you feel better we can do the Vieux Carre."

"OK, Mike. I'll look for your call, but please don't tell anyone the name I am using or where I am staying."

Mary Alice checked into the St. Charles Hotel, room 901, informed Mike of her room number and went up to her room.

She was getting ready for a bath when she realized she had no clean clothing. She went down the street to Maison Blanc Department store and purchased some underclothes, an inexpensive dress and shoes. She would go by her house tomorrow after her father went to the office and pick up a few of her own things, but not many, as she didn't want anyone to miss anything.

Back at the hotel she took a long hot bath and got into bed. Turning out the lights, she began to make plans.

Grandfather Bakker had left her a trust fund, some property and a cotton plantation, which was leased out to a large corporation with the income going to the trust fund. Some stocks paid dividends that also went to the trust fund. Her grandfather had traveled extensively through England, France, Egypt and Morocco for business and pleasure. The area of pleasure was Marrakech, French Morocco, where, unbeknown to his family, he purchased a villa. The family thought that he was just renting it. When he was not using it, he leased it out to wealthy Americans and Europeans, with the profit going into Mary Alice's trust fund.

The next morning Mary Alice called attorney Clifford B. Barnett, who had set up the trust fund for her grandfather. They made an appointment for that afternoon. Arriving punctually, she was ushered into Mr. Barnett's office.

Mr. Barnett informed her of the status of her trust fund. "As you just turned twenty-five, the majority of the trust fund can be turned over to you. However, there is a clause that stipulates that the plantation must remain in trust until you are forty years of age, with the profits going to your account. However, if you want to live on the plantation and operate it, you have that option, after giving the lessee one year's notice."

Mary Alice told Mr. Barnett that she had no desire to operate the plantation. She also advised him that she wanted him to make the name Catherine Ledbetter a legal alias to use. The money from the bank account that came from Mary Alice Bakker's trust fund was to be redeposited into a new account set up in the name of Catherine Ledbetter. The property in Marrakech, Morocco was also to be transferred to that name. She wanted the alias established as soon as possible, because she wanted to get a passport. The state of Louisiana had just passed a law requiring drivers to be licensed and she wanted that in the name of Catherine Ledbetter, as well.

"One thing, Mr. Barnett, this information goes no further than this office, except the legal information that has to do with this transaction."

"I can assure you Miss Bakker, we will keep everything confidential. We will start using your alias now, Miss Ledbetter. There is very much legal work to do with the transferring of property and funds. It may take two weeks or more and you will be required to go before a judge for the name change. Where may I reach you?"

"Mr. Barnett, I do not want my name changed, just an alias. I will have to get an address as soon as you get the alias and set up a bank account. I am staying at the St. Charles Hotel, but will check out. Please have your secretary call the St. Charles and make a reservation for Catherine Ledbetter from Pensacola, Florida, to arrive about four o'clock. Can you extend me two hundred dollars until the transaction is completed? By the way, I will use your firm for a reference."

Mary Alice went back to the St. Charles and had a message to call Mike. She called and told him she would be registered at the St. Charles after four, under the name of Catherine Ledbetter. She checked out and went straight to Maison Blanc Department Store where she purchased some luggage, several changes of clothing and cosmetics. After having a late lunch, she used the restaurant's restroom to change clothes, and using the cosmetics she had purchased, she tried to alter her appearance. When she returned at the St. Charles at four-fifteen, no one seemed to recognize her. She checked in and was given room 815.

Mike called her and said he would pick her up at six and they would go to dinner in the Vieux Carre, (French Quarter).

The next ten days were a whirlwind of activity. She and Mike hit all of the nightspots in the Vieux Carre, drinking, dining and dancing the night away, sleeping most of the day. Time slipped by quickly.

One day the telephone woke her up about noon. It was her attorney, Clifford Barnett, who said he wanted to see her right away on an urgent matter. She made an appointment for two o'clock. Mary Alice rushed to take a bath and dress, almost running to get a streetcar so she could get to Mr. Barnett's office by two o'clock. The secretary ushered her in as soon as she arrived. She was seated in large overstuffed leather chair.

Mr. Barnett, a man about her father's age, weighing about two hundred thirty pounds on a five foot eleven inch frame, came rushing into the office. He was huffing, puffing and breathing heavily. His shaggy white hair stuck to the pinkish-white skin, which was wet with perspiration. He sat down, flopping into the big high back judges-style chair, looking at Mary Alice, while he took some legal papers out of his briefcase.

"Miss Bakker, I have some bad news. I'm really having a hard time telling you this. But, the fact is that your father, as trustee, has been draining the profits from your trust fund. Without going into the details of how it was done, I'll say this. If you are so inclined, you could have him arrested and if convicted, he would be in jail for a long time, up to twenty years."

Mary Alice was stunned. *How could he do this and still profess to love me?*

"Mr. Barnett, how much money is left in the account, if any?"

Opening some papers that appeared to be bank statements, Mr. Barnett answered, "I am afraid there isn't much cash, a few thousand dollars. The plantation is clear, but you cannot sell it until you reach the age of forty. You don't have enough money to operate it. However, we can open a new bank account and have the lease payments go into that account. Of course, you will also have to pay all the bills, such as taxes and upkeep on the plantation. There is a 30,000 square foot villa in Marrakech that is fully paid for, and there is one million, four hundred sixty thousand, and three hundred seven francs and 20 centimes in the account at Du Marrakech Banque. In American money that is, let's see, at seventy-five francs to the dollar, it comes to nineteen thousand, five hundred thirty-seven dollars and forty three cents, a lot of money in Morocco. Do you want to prosecute your father and see if you can recover the main part of the trust? I am not your father's attorney, so I do not know his financial status. Maybe you can get some of the money back, but probably not."

Mary Alice was numb. *I loved my father. Surely if he loved me the way he said he did, he would not have done this to me. Maybe he only loved me for the money. Grandmother Andrews and Grandfather Bakker were the only people who truly loved me.*

"Miss Bakker?" Mr. Barnett said.

She sat upright and she answered, "No, Mr. Barnett. Do not prosecute my father, but I want the money transferred to me now, today, and the deed and money in Marrakech transferred to my name. How long will the Moroccan business take to complete?"

"By wire about two weeks, but to finish the transaction, you will have to go to Marrakech and complete it in person."

"Start the procedure now, pronto. I will tell you now, I will watch my property and possessions from here on out like a hawk, and the first bastard that tries to steal one penny from me will be put in jail or done away with. My father can burn in hell and that goes for anyone else who crosses me. You are to tell no one, and I mean no one, where I am located or my new name. Is that clearly understood?"

"Yes, Miss Bakker, uh Miss Ledbetter. No one will know about these transactions. I promise you that."

Chapter Ten

During the two weeks waiting for the attorney to handle the financial transactions, Mary Alice's attitude on life changed. In place of being the fun loving, happy-go-lucky person she had once been, she vowed to take care of herself and to hell with other people. *It's give and take in this world and I'll do the taking. I will take the equivalent of my inheritance by hook or crook. Father will not get away with stealing the money, all he had to do was ask and I would have given it to him.*

On Saturday night she was waiting for Mike, seated at the bar at Armand's Restaurant and Bar on Royal Street, when the bartender told her she had a call. It was Mike.

"Hi, Honey. I am tied up and can't make it for a couple hours. Do you want to wait or go back to the hotel? I'll call you when I wrap this deal up."

"No, Mike," she answered. "I won't wait. I'll just have something to eat and go back to the hotel. Call me when you finish."

When she returned to the bar, the bartender slid a fresh cocktail in front of her and nodded to the gentlemen at the end of the bar. Looking down the bar, she observed a nice looking well-dressed man in his late twenties. He tilted his glass at her and she returned the gesture by holding her glass up and forming the words, "thank you" with her lips.

After a few minutes the well-dressed man came over and said, "Hello. My name is Gino. May I ask what is your name?"

"I am Ma...Catherine."

"What kind of name is MaCatherine and how do you spell it? My English is not so good."

"I am sorry Gino, the name is Catherine. It must be my southern accent. Where are you from?"

"From Morocco. I am here on business for a short time. Would you like to get a table?"

What a coincidence, he's from Morocco and I'm going there. I will not tell him of my impending trip, but try to get some information about the place.

"Yes, that would be fine. I am expecting a friend to join me later."

"Will this be a female or male friend?"

"Male, but not a boyfriend, nevertheless a good friend."

"Catherine, what kind of work do you do?"

"Well, at the moment I'm unemployed." *What the hell, he doesn't know me.* "I am in the entertainment field, a dancer, looking for an opening in show business, either dancing or acting."

"Really. Let's have another cocktail. I may have something that would be of interest to you."

After a couple more cocktails and small talk Gino said, "How would you like to make some big money in the entertainment field?"

"What do I have to do for this big money?"

"Well, it depends on how much you want to earn and what you would do to earn big money."

"Look, Gino, I have been around the block a couple of times. Lay it on the line, is it prostitution you're talking about?"

"Yes, but not a street walker or in a house of prostitution. This is high class. You will be with only one man, attending functions, restaurants, shows and other events. My clients will pay a lot of money for a beautiful fair-skinned blonde, and all expenses."

"What if I didn't like the man and wanted to leave, would it be a problem?"

"No problem, they would not want a girl that was unhappy. You could leave anytime. It would be less costly for them than a divorce."

"Well, Gino, I will have to think about it. It is still prostitution."

"Yes, Catherine, but think about this. What is it when a married woman stays with a man she doesn't love because he has money? It is married prostitution, but she is a prostitute just the same."

As she rose to leave she said, "I will have to think about it."

"OK, give me your telephone number and I'll call you tomorrow?"

"I do not give my number or address out to strangers. I'll be back here tomorrow night, same time, if I am interested. Good night. Thanks for the drinks."

Catherine walked up Royal Street. *What does Gino want? How much does he make on each girl he recruits? I wonder how much money can be made doing this?*

Early the next morning Mike called and apologized for failing to contact her the previous night.

"Let me make it up to you, have lunch with me?"

"Ok, Mike. I'll meet you at Jojo's on Rampart Street at twelve."

Catherine needed a male partner. She liked Mike and the qualities he had in meeting all types of people, especially the wealthy. Mike came from a well-known, wealthy family. His grandfather, Michael A. Martel, was a highly respected doctor, the founder of Martel General Hospital. Mike's father, Michael A. Martel, Jr. was also a highly respected doctor. Michael (Mike) A. Martel III attended Loyala University and was being groomed for a career in medicine. After four years Mike confessed he had majored in women, wine and golf, in that order. Mike had no interest in becoming a doctor; he was only trying to please his grandfather and father.

His grandfather passed away leaving Mike a small inheritance to be used as an income. After finishing four years of college, he tried a number of different things but found that selling and marketing suited him best.

Catherine knew a little of Mike's background. His grandfather was born in France and came to America to study medicine. Upon completing medical school he married his college sweetheart from New Orleans, whose parents were of French ancestry. Mike was fluent in French and with his smooth talk, good looks and a quest for adventure, he would be the likely candidate for a partner.

After being seated at Jojo's, Catherine told Mike about meeting Gino.

"You are thinking of becoming a prostitute in some foreign country?"

"No, Mike. Of course not, but the idea of getting young, beautiful women and grooming them in the proper dress and manners and charging for their services as escorts sounds as if it would be profitable. If the young women would have sex for money, we would charge accordingly. Would you consider going to Morocco with me as a business partner and see what we can do? We can meet with Gino tonight and gather more information."

"Sounds interesting. I'll meet you at Armand's, say about seven-thirty?"

"Sure, Mike. I'll go rest up; I want to gather some information. You give it some thought, too. If we work this out correctly, we can make a few bucks. See you at seven-thirty."

Catherine rested for a while, made a couple of phone calls, then went into the bathroom to take a bath. As she undressed, she looked at herself in the full-length mirror on the back of the bathroom door. What she saw pleased her, a five foot three inch frame weighing one hundred ten pounds, a fair complexion with a slight touch of pink, a well-developed bust, slim waist and shapely legs. Her full lips, when applied with the bright red lipstick she wore, gave her mouth a hint of sexuality. She chose a black cocktail dress with the thin straps, the hemline about two inches below her knees, and black high heeled shoes, both of which she had removed from her closet in her father's house, while he was at work. *This outfit is a little daring, but when I want something it always works to help me get it.*

Catherine was dressed and ready to go at six-thirty. *What am I going to do for forty-five minutes until it's time to leave? Oh hell, I'll just go now and have a cocktail, at Armand's. Maybe there will be someone there to talk to.*

She asked the maitre d' for a table in a quiet corner. He seated her at a round table where she took the seat nearest the corner, so she had a view of everyone entering the restaurant.

The waiter had just put her cocktail in front of her when she saw Gino enter. He walked over to the bar and took a stool at the far end, next to a big heavyset man, who looked to be in his fifties. When they shook hands, it appeared as if Gino passed something to Mr. Big.

Gino and Mr. Big had quite an animated discussion. She thought from the gestures they were making with their hands, that Mr. Big must also be Italian. Mr. Big began shaking his finger under Gino's nose, as his voice grew louder. He was evidently not pleased with Gino's reply, because his face turned an angry red, almost purple. He said something in a low whisper, then putting his thumb, forefinger and middle finger together and up to his lips, and threw a kiss at Gino, tossed a bill on the bar and stormed out of the restaurant. Gino motioned for another drink and went to the men's room. *Damn, what was this? A couple of queers having a lovers quarrel?* She quickly moved over to the bar and took a seat about four stools from where Gino was sitting, ordered a cocktail and went into the ladies room, taking her time to freshen her make up.

When she came out of the ladies room, she noticed Gino had not returned to his seat. It was several more minutes before he came back. When he saw Catherine, he picked up his drink and moved over next to her.

"Hi, Babe. How are things going tonight?"

"Hi, Gino. I'm fine. I am in a much better mood tonight than last night. You look as if you lost your last friend. Is something wrong?"

"A little business problem, nothing I can't take care of. You notice the man I was sitting next to?"

"No, I just came in, ordered a drink and went to the ladies room."

"A business associate and I just had a disagreement. Nothing I can't handle, just a little surprising. Did you think about the discussion we had last night?"

"You speaking of the prostitution caper?"

"Look, Babe, I'd rather say a mistress or hostess. Remember I am speaking of high class, wealthy clients."

"Gino, my friend will be along in a few minutes and we may come to some type of an agreement, but it will have to wait until he gets here. Let's have another cocktail."

About halfway through the cocktail Mike came in and Catherine introduced them to each other.

Ordering Mike a drink, Catherine said, "Gino, tell us the complete proposition, full details."

"OK. If you want to make big money, live well and have a good time, I have a client who is looking for a beautiful blonde, who is educated and knows how to associate with the wealthy society. You will have your own apartment and will be the mistress of a wealthy Arab oil baron. You will be one of three, a brunette, red head and a blonde. You must not go out with other men and must be available at all times to escort the client. For this you will be paid handsomely, fifteen hundred francs a month, an apartment, food and a clothing allowance."

"How much is fifteen hundred francs in American money, and how does the cost of living in Morocco compare to America?"

"The exchange rate is 75 francs for an American dollar, so the salary is two hundred dollars a month, a big salary in today's market. Remember, you would not pay rent, cost of food or clothing. To put things in perspective, the cost of a loaf of bread here in New Orleans is ten cents and in Morocco a loaf of bread, which is larger, costs about twelve francs. So twelve francs equals six and one quarter cents, therefore the cost of a larger loaf of bread is about six and one quarter cents. So you see what little you have to spend goes much further and the amount you save at the exchange rate can be great."

Mike said, "Thanks for the lesson on the cost of living and the exchange rate, but we have a different proposition for you. First, what are your fees for recruiting the women? Is it a one time deal or a monthly fee for the duration of the woman's stay?"

Gino said, "I am not interested in sharing my fee or disclosing it. If Catherine wants to make money, she can do with it as she pleases, cut you in or not, but you can not date her or live with her."

Catherine said, "Look Gino, I am not sleeping with Mike. We are good friends and will be business partners if we can work something out. Also, I do not sleep with men I don't care about for any amount of money. I will not put up with your bullshit or any wealthy Arab Sheik's bullshit. Now, if you want to make money tell me how much you make on a deal to procure a young woman. You may think I'm a pushover, but, Mr. Gino, let me tell you something. I have done a little checking on you and still have someone investigating your background. You are a little cog in a big wheel. You are in over your head and the Mafia will not accept any of your crap. I know you are deeply in debt to them. What would it take to get you clear?"

"OK, OK, I'll tell you. I get a hundred dollars a month, plus expenses," said Gino, "plus a two hundred dollar bonus if the woman stays four months and five percent or ten dollars per month of their salary until they leave."

"How much are you in the hole, and what would happen if you paid them off and changed jobs?"

"I owe them six hundred dollars. They want it now, or two hundred dollars a month plus twenty-five percent interest. If I pay them off I can leave them, but I would have to leave town."

"We have some plans. Are you familiar with Marrakech?"

"A little. I know of two clients there, but I can find other contacts in Marrakech. What do you have in mind?"

Mike spoke up, "We need contacts in Marrakech and someone here. We can tell you where to meet and procure young females. We will pay you one hundred twenty-five dollars a month, a bonus of two hundred a month if they stay six months, and five percent of their basic salary of fifteen hundreds francs a month."

"But I can't live in New Orleans, they would rub me out."

"What about Baton Rouge, have they anyone in that area?"

"No, they feel that New Orleans is where the young women come to look for adventure."

"Baton Rouge is a government city, and some colleges are located there. Many young women live there and might be looking for something more exciting than college or government work. What do you do to make contact with women?"

"I work as a bartender or manager of a bar or lounge. I have a friend who works at a lounge in Baton Rouge. She left New Orleans a couple months ago and took a job there. She might be able to help me find work."

"Fine, take a trip to Baton Rouge and see if you can get connected. Give me the names you have in Marrakech and call me as soon as you have made a connection."

Chapter Eleven

For the next three weeks Catherine and Mike made plans, calling Marrakech, making appointments for their future arrival.

She had moved from the St. Charles into a furnished one-bedroom apartment over Armand's on Royal Street and made arrangements to receive telephone calls at their number.

She had not yet heard anything from Clifford B. Barnett. She would give him one more day and if she still had no word from him, she would call him. *Everything is falling into place except for the damn attorney.*

That evening when she met Mike at Armand's, the waitress gave her a message to call Mr. Barnett.

The next day Mr. Barnett informed her that she had a court date for the following Thursday, to change her name to the alias and to sign some papers for transferring the money from the trust fund into that name.

She and Mike went to Baton Rouge to meet with Gino. He had found a job at the Hideaway Lounge, as night manager, and had made a few necessary contacts.

Upon returning to New Orleans, she completed the court and financial transactions, and got her passport in the name of Catherine Ledbetter. She was ready for a new adventure. When she arrived in New York, she made arrangements for Mike and herself to fly to London, then to Portugal, and on to Casablanca, with Marrakech as their final destination.

A week after arriving in Marrakech she had established her bank account, and had the Villa transferred over to her. Luckily, the villa was vacant at the time, so she was able to move in right away. A two-bedroom guest cottage on the premises, served as Mike's accommodations. The villa was a beautiful, large home, with a high thick wall around it with broken glass on top, to prevent intruders from entering the grounds.

A few days later the telephone was installed and she made contact with Gino's contact, the manager of the lounge at la Kasbah Restaurant. The manager, Roberto Gastroberto was also a deserter from the Italian Army and was an easy mark to make extra money. She made a dinner reservation for seven-thirty that evening at la Kasbah, which was across from the Medina on Boulevard el-Yarmouk. La Kasbah had a French and Moroccan cuisine. It was time to investigate the party scenes of Marrakech. Not knowing the city, Catherine suggested to Mike that they leave by six and do a little sightseeing.

When the taxi arrived, she and Mike asked the driver to take them to la Kasbah. On the way, Mike engaged the driver in conservation about Marrakech and the nightlife.

"Are you eligible as a tour guide, and what would you charge?" asked Catherine.

"Mademoiselle, I have been a taxi driver in Marrakech for eighteen years and I know the ins and outs of the new Marrakech and the Medina."

"Good, we will make use of you if you are fair about your fees and recommendations of places to go. However, you must be discreet."

"On that, Mademoiselle, you have my word of honor. What time is your reservation?"

"Seven-thirty and we would like to see, I think it would be called, the native quarters," answered Catherine.

"La Kasbah is across the boulevard from the Medina, the walled Arabic Medina, what you call the native quarters. Medina is the old city; it has been here in Marrakech since 1126. The Berbers settled it and the high thick walls, which surround the Medina, were constructed about that time as a defensive wall. In the early 1900's, French colonists settled the plains outside of the wall. The Kasbah inside the Medina is the living area with whitewashed, flat-roofed houses. Nothing has changed since the Islamic Middle Ages. Today, French is spoken by almost everyone and recently the Vichy French and Free French have begun populating the city. Also, the Germans and English are setting up outposts. The trouble in Europe is bringing all types of people into the city.

"About 1904, Morocco was divided between France and Spain, with France receiving the largest area, the middle and southern part. That is why we are known as French Morocco. Spain shares the northwestern part on the Mediterranean Sea at the Strait of Gibraltar and it is known as Spanish Morocco. We are at la Kasbah. I will park my taxi and we can walk across the boulevard to the Medina, but stay close to me. The pickpockets prey on tourists, if they are without a local guide."

They entered the Medina through a high arched gateway. The taxi driver told them that a gate was there until about 1930. It closed at sunset and did not reopen until daylight.

"By the way," Mike said, "what is your name? My name is Mike and my friend is Catherine."

"Arab's names are quite different from the French, English and other European countries. My full name is Abdullah bin Satman bin Haman Al-Fhalifa. Our family name is Al-Fhalifa, but you may call me Abdullah Satman or just Abdullah."

Catherine asked Abdullah, "What in the world do all those names mean?"

"Abdullah is my first name, bin means son. I am the son of Satman who is the son of Haman, my grandfather."

The odor in the Medina was full of exotic fragrances, mixtures of spices, oranges and other scents they could not identify. There was also the foul odor from wastewater running down the streets, as they had no sewerage. Mixed with this water was urine from humans, dogs, and donkeys. Waste dung lay in the street from the donkeys pulling carts, trying to squeeze through the crowds. Catherine and Mike were almost hypnotized by the sights, smell and sounds as they came into an area that Abullah called the Djerma el Fina, which roughly translates as "Court of Marvels." It was a souk, a market, with snake charmers, musicians, acrobats and storytellers. They could have spent several hours in this area but it was almost time for their reservation, so they returned to la Kasbah Restaurant, instructing Abdullah to pick them up at ten o'clock.

From the sidewalk they entered through a heavy wooden door, some twelve feet tall in an archway that was edged in colorful tile. After passing through this door, they found themselves in a lovely shady courtyard, filled with flowering bushes and plants. *I'll see about designing my entranceway to the villa this way,* thought Catherine. *Also, I do not have a name for the villa yet. I'll have to think of one.*

From the courtyard they entered the pink Moorish stucco building with another beautifully arched doorway that led into a room of deep red and black covered walls, and brightly colored tile floors. A heavy black desk stood just inside, where the tuxedo dressed matire d' greeted them.

They were seated in the large, elegant room, decorated with live plants, intermingled with small palm trees. Beautiful paintings hung on the black and red velvet covered walls. The tablecloths were pale blue linen and on each table was a crystal bud vase, containing a perfectly formed rose. The dining area surrounded the large parquetry dance floor. There were several private rooms to each side. As they were being seated, a belly dancer was taking her bows. On the stage were chairs and music stands for an orchestra. On the right side of the stage, an Arabian band was packing up their instruments, preparing to leave.

When the waiter took their order for cocktails, Mike asked where the restrooms and bar were located. The waiter indicated an area on the left side of the room. Mike excused himself and walked in that direction. Passing through the lounge, he noticed a tall bartender who fit the description of Roberto Gastroberto. When he came out of the restroom, he stopped at the end of the bar and asked the bartender, "Are you Roberto?"

"Oui, Monsieur, how may I help you?"

"My name is Michael Martel. My partner, Catherine Ledbetter, spoke to you by telephone. We would like to meet with you later tonight. What time are you finished with your duties?"

"I finish at twelve, Monsieur."

"OK, I will speak with you later. Miss Ledbetter and I are in the main dining room. If we feel that we can't stay until twelve, I will be back."

He returned to the table where Catherine and the cocktails were waiting for him. They clicked glasses. Catherine said, "Here is to a long and profitable relationship."

They had a couple of cocktails while they discussed some business details, then asked for the menu. When Catherine looked at it, she said, "Mike, I don't understand most of this. You speak excellent French, tell me what looks good?"

"Why don't we start with an appetizer? Here is something that looks good. A labenah, that is a thick creamy cheese, spiced with baharat, an Arabic mixed spice. It is used as a dip with Arabic bread called khubz. Would you like a salad, also?"

"Yes, Mike. Let's go for an Arabic meal."

"Garcon, we each will have rocca salad, and for the main course, uh Catherine, would you prefer, lamb, beef, chicken or fish?"

"Lamb or beef would be fine."

"Garcon, this kabsa on the menu, can they be had with lamb or beef or both?"

"Either beef or lamb or some of each."

"OK. Give each of us the kabsa and a side dish of full, and bring us a bottle of French wine, please."

After the waiter left Catherine asked, "Mike what is the meal we are having?"

"The kabsa will be a mixture of lamb and beef. It is the classic Arabian dish mixed with rice and taklia, which is a spice consisting of ground coriander and garlic. The side dish of full is a slow-cooked mash of brown beans and red lentils, dressed with lemon, olive oil and cumin."

The French and the Arabs eat slowly, savoring their meal. Likewise, Mike and Catherine took their time, discussing their pending business, the dinner, and generally getting to know each other better. When it was time for dessert, Catherine said, "Mike I am full, just a small piece of a cake or cookie would be fine."

"Here is a ma'amul, a date cookie."

The orchestra had started playing at nine. Mike looked at his watch and said, "It is almost ten o'clock. I should go out to tell Abdullah to wait for us. Roberto doesn't get off until twelve and I need to talk to him. Do you want to wait with me or return to the villa?"

"No, Mike, I'll stay. We can dance, it will help pass the time."

When Mike went to inform Abdullah to either wait or return in a couple of hours, Catherine was thinking about what an excellent dancer he was and how safe and comfortable she felt in his arms. *Hell, stop this! I can't mix business and pleasure. I've got to control my feelings and not let them get out of hand.*

The time went by quickly. Shortly after midnight, Roberto sent a message that he would meet them outside. When they got there, Abudullah was waiting as well as Roberto.

Roberto said, "I know a place in the Medina, where we can have a discussion in private."

Asked Mike, "What about women in the Medina bars or nightclubs or whatever you call these types of places?"

"Oh, this is a place that tourists frequent, also local Frenchmen with their wives, girlfriends or une femme soutenue, a une fille de joie. I can't think of the English words."

Looking at Catherine, Mike explained that he was trying to say, mistress and a lady of the night."

"Just a minute, what is the name of the place?"

"It is la Marrakech á Vol d'oisear."

Mike walked over to Abdullah and asked, "Abdullah we want to go with the gentlemen to the Medina, a place named la Marrakech á Vol oisear. Would this be a safe place to take a lady?"

"It is not the nicest place, so be careful. Would you want me to go with you?"

"Yes, please, and warn us if anything out of the ordinary takes place."

"Catherine, the name of the place is, roughly the Birds Eye View of Marrakech, and the place is what we would call in New Orleans, a joint. Do you still want to go?"

"By all means. I have to get familiar with all aspects of Marrakech."

The group of four of the most diverse people anyone could imagine started their journey to la Marrakech á Vol oisear.

Chapter Twelve

Jeff went down to Le Cabaret du Zouaves and upon entering found that the Cabaret was filled nearly to capacity, the noise level almost unbearable. Seeing Claudette sitting near the band, he worked his way through the throng of people. A large number of foreign soldiers were there and he recognized several of the uniforms, French, German, Russian, and Polish. There were some others he did not know. Sliding into the chair next to Claudette, he leaned over and kissed her on the cheek.

"I want to apologize for being late, but I had problems with the business back home. It has been taken care of, but I may have to go to Meknes for a few days. I'm not sure yet. Why are there so many people here tonight, and why all of the soldiers from different countries?"

"Jeff, you are all business. Aren't you happy to see me?"

"Oui, Mademoiselle, moi avoir le béguin pour. How is my French?"

"Not too good. I don't believe you have a crush on me. You are full of merde. Do you understand my French?"

"Not really. Did I say something wrong? I was only telling you I have a crush on you."

"Oh, Jeff, I understand, and I was telling you that you are full of shit. Let's speak English. I know more English than you know French and I don't understand Cajun French.

"Now to answer your questions about the soldiers. Germany has invaded Poland and is occupying part of that country. Russia and

England may enter into the war. France and Morocco are neutral, however, an underground movement in France opposes the French neutrality. They are called the Vichy and they are in Morocco. The troops in Morocco do not like each other, but they are in a neutral country. They, I think the English word is tolerate, each other until one side gets the upper hand. Enough of that, let's have fun. You haven't ordered a drink yet. Garcon, bring me another cocktail and my merde un gars a whiskey un apéro."

"What the hell did you order for me?"

"A good translation is, bring my shitty man a whiskey cocktail, but the tone was of amour. Let's dance while we wait."

"Mon chéri, I like my whiskey with a little water and my women avoir le chaud. I hope I got the right French of how I like my women."

"Yes, and I have the hots for you, too."

When they left the dance floor, Jeff spotted Gino at the bar with a couple of Italian Army officers engaged in a discussion. Hoping that Gino wouldn't see him, he changed seats at the table so his back would be toward Gino. Claudette looked at him and asked, "Are you trying to avoid your friend Bruno, or Gino?"

"Yes, there's something I don't like about him. I don't know what it is, but each time I see him, I have a feeling he is trying to get something out of me."

"From what I know, he is a low class. Oh, I can't think of the name, uh petit criminal."

"You mean small or insignificant, yes I will go along with that. Let's go up to my room and have some drinks. I want to faire l'amour à la papa avec mon chéri."

"That is the best suggestion you have made yet. I like to make love in a slow way, my dear."

Jeff went over to the house phone, called room service and ordered a bottle of whiskey, a bottle of champagne in a bucket of ice and two glasses.

"Mon cheri, let's finish our drinks and we will have champagne upstairs."

On their way to the lobby they saw an elderly woman entering the cabaret. She had a tray with a strap around her neck and on the tray was an assortment of corsages. This brought back pleasant memories to Jeff. He asked the lady, "How much for the corsage?" To his surprise she answered in his own words, "Whatever you think your chéri is worth."

He had seen the man before him give her twenty-five francs, about thirty-three cents. Jeff, remembering the old days, pulled out a fifty franc note and gave it to her, about sixty-six cents.

"Merci, Monsieur, merci."

Jeff felt a warm tingle go through his body. Was it the flower lady kindness or Claudette's perfume?

A few minutes after they arrived in the room, a knock came on the door. Expecting it to be room service, Jeff opened the door, and received a shock. There in the doorway stood Gino.

Quickly stepping outside in the hallway, Jeff said, "Gino, I'm busy. Call me tomorrow."

"Jeff, this is important, I need to talk with you now. I know who you are looking for and I know where you can find her."

"What do you know about me and whether I am looking for anyone or not?"

"I don't have the time to tell you the whole story, but I know about the girl from New Orleans, and I need help, and money, if...."

Bang! Bang! Bang! Three shots rang out. Jeff knew he was hit in the arm. He dropped to the floor and rolled around the corner. He lay still until he heard the door to the stairway slam. Then, peeping around the corner, he saw Gino lying motionless, with no one in sight. Slowly he got to his feet, as the door opened and Claudette came running out to him.

"Oh, Jeff, you are hurt. You are bleeding badly. Come in the room while I call the police and a doctor."

"Let me check Gino." Walking over to Gino, Jeff knew instantly that he was dead. He heard the lift door open and once again dropped to the floor. It was the police and the hotel detective.

Jeff went into the room and sat down while Claudette removed his coat, tie and shirt. Taking a couple of towels from the bathroom, she filled a large china basin with water and began to clean Jeff's arm. The bullet grazed his left arm just above the elbow.

An officer began questioning him, with Claudette interpreting for Jeff and the police.

"Monsieur, who is that person laying dead on the floor in the hallway?"

"I met him on the New Orleans Trader, a freighter, where he, myself and several more were paying passengers. I met him as Tom Brown. Mr. Brown and I rode the same carriage to de Zouaves Hotel. I had a reservation. Mr. Brown asked if they had a room and he was assigned to one a couple of doors down, in number 406. He came by my room after checking in and invited me down for a drink. While he waited for me to freshen up, he told me his real name was Giovanni Malfa or Gino. Later, Mademoiselle Meteron told me his real name is Bruno LaTorre. I had not seen him again until tonight when I went down to meet Mademoiselle. He was speaking with two soldiers at the bar. We left and came up here and before the wine was delivered a knock came on the door. It was Gino or Bruno or whatever the hell his name is. I walked outside and pulled the door almost closed, when three gunshots were fired. The first one hit my arm and I dropped to the floor, the same time as Gino. I rolled around the corner there in the hall, but Gino didn't move. I think the first shot went though Gino then hit my arm. That shot must have been the one that killed him."

"Monsieur, give me your passport. You are not to leave the country or even the city. If you move from this hotel you must notify us of your new address."

As Jeff was getting his passport, two detectives arrived. One of them was detective Pierre de La Salla.

"Aw, my friend, Jeff. How did you get into this? Are you getting close to the person you are looking for?"

"No, Pierre, I don't know the reason for this. I met the fellow on the ship coming over. He was using another name." Jeff relayed the story he had told the policeman.

Pierre said, "I believe I have seen this man before." Pierre walked over to a chair, next to a table with the telephone, and spoke with the hotel operator. While he waited for the call to come in, he went through Gino's pockets, turning them inside out and laying each item on the floor beside the dead body. Pierre found a set of keys, a hotel key to room 406, two loose keys, one could be a suitcase key, the other small key could be to a post office box, but no number or name was on it. He also found some American money, a quarter, and a dime, sixty francs, thirty centimes, a comb, a handkerchief, a small pocketknife and a wallet. When he opened the wallet, Pierre pulled out a number of bills, a total of seven thousand, three hundred francs. There was a photograph of an elderly couple with the names Sadie and Salvatore LaTorre and an address written on the back, and another photograph of a pretty young women about twenty-five or so years of age, with the name Carman LaTorre.

The phone rang. Jeff answered and said "Pierre, it's for you."

After Pierre finished, he walked over to the group and said, "Captain, that was headquarters. This man is Bruno LaTorre and he is wanted here in Morocco for a number of crimes, smuggling hashish, prostitution, and robbery, just to name a few."

"Jeff, are you all right, do you need to see a doctor?"

"No, Pierre, but do you have to keep my passport?"

Pierre walked over to the captain and explained whom Jeff was, and that he had helped them in the case of a young dead woman who was mistakenly identified.

The captain walked over to Jeff, apologized, and returned his passport.

After the fourth floor of the hotel was cleared of policemen, medical personnel, reporters and onlookers, Jeff closed the door and called room service for more ice to be delivered pronto.

"Claudette, do you feel like ordering a meal for us here? I would like to rest."

"Yes, Jeff, a quiet meal and a few drinks, without all the loud noise from the crowd and the bands, would be nice, only the two of us. What would you like to eat?"

"I would love to have a steak with potatoes."

"Steak, what is that?"

"It is your la bidoche, about one half inch thick and cooked medium well. I'll leave it in your sweet hands to order whatever you think best. I'll go wash up and fix a drink as soon as the ice and whiskey is delivered."

After the whiskey and ice came, Jeff put ice in the bucket with the champagne, poured about three fingers of whiskey with a very small amount of water in a glass, and fixed Claudette a champagne cocktail.

Holding his glass up, Jeff said, "Here's to a beautiful sexy nana."

The meal arrived, and Jeff and Claudette had a very relaxing meal before moving over to the sofa.

Jeff didn't know if it was the drinks, the perfume that Claudette had on, or the kissing and fondling, maybe all of these things, but this was the best he'd felt since Nicole's death. He began undressing Claudette, and then himself. He led her over to the bed, his head spinning from the sheer beauty of this French woman.

Chapter Thirteen

A loud, crazy ringing sound woke Jeff up. *What the hell was that strange noise?* He realized it was the awful sound of the telephone in Casablanca.

Reaching over and picking it up he answered, "Hello."

"Hello, Jeff. This is Pierre de LaSalla. I have identified the girl we had mistaken for Mary Alice Bakker. Do you want to follow this lead?"

"Yes, Pierre. When can I meet with you?"

"Let's see, it is now eight-thirty. Can you be at my office by eleven? I have to leave, shortly after twelve."

"Sure. I'll be there, maybe before eleven. Thanks. Good-bye."

He looked over at the lovely Claudette, who was still asleep or pretending to be. *Damn, can these French girls can make love! I have only made love a few times, but this was out of this world. Oh, well, I have time for one more roll in the sack.*

Jeff began to kiss her beautiful, round firm breast, while rubbing her belly down to the inside of her thighs. Claudette came alive quickly, and began responding in ways he had never experienced. As he kissed her below her navel, she reached down and gently guided his head to her vagina. *This is enjoyable, but how do I satisfy her.* She gently pulled his head upward and he knew when he had reached the spot.

After the passionate lovemaking, Jeff was exhausted. He rolled over on his back with Claudette in his arms. In a few minutes it was Claudette's turn. She began kissing his nipples and caressing his testicles and the inside of his thighs while kissing his stomach, lower and lower until she reached his penis. For the next few minutes he was in another world.

Laying in each other arms, he was more relaxed than he had ever been. Then his mind flashed and Pierre's face popped up. The clock read nine-thirty. *Damn, I've got to move fast.*

Jeff went into the bathroom, turned the water on to fill the tub, while he brushed his teeth. He was shaved, bathed and dressed in twenty minutes. Explaining to Claudette the rush while he was dressing, he asked, "Do you want to wait for me? I may be a couple of hours, but this is an important appointment I have to keep."

"Jeff, I have to report to work. I'll call in and tell them I will be there at twelve. This will give me time to go home and freshen up and change my clothes. I'll give you a call this afternoon."

After a passionate kiss good-bye, Jeff rushed downstairs to the front of the hotel and found a cab waiting at the curb. Giving the driver the address of the police headquarters, he laid back and closed his eyes to get a little rest.

I wonder what Pierre has found out about the girl. I may have to leave Casablanca to investigate her and maybe get a lead to Mary Alice Bakker. I sure hate to leave Claudette, but it will give me an incentive to finish this business quickly so I can get back to her.

He arrived at Pierre's office at ten-thirty, to find him going over the information about the girl. Pierre said, "The girl's name is Annette Coppola and she arrived in Casablanca two weeks before her death. Her death was caused by a gunshot behind the left ear. The blood was cleaned from her wound and body with alcohol and redressed to deter identification. This did not work, as the fingerprint bureau in Rabat had her prints on file. She was arrested once in Meknes in a prostitution ring, after that in Erfoud, a town on the edge of the Sahara Desert. She was uh, I don't know how to say it in English, la maquerlle and a uh, une oute at un bordel."

"I get part of it, a whorehouse?"

"Yes, she was the head of it and also worked as a prostitute."

"A madam who also worked as a whore?"

"Yes, that is it. She was arrested for housing an unlicensed foreign whore and on suspicion of murder. They could not prove anything, but she gave the police a tip about Bruno LaTorre, the man shot at your hotel door. They could not find Bruno and have been looking for him the past year or more. That is all I can tell you about this girl, except she had a boy friend at the French Foreign Legion Garrison at Erfoud. He did not have anything to do with the murder, as he was on duty at the border territory. Six months ago he was still at the garrison. His name is Conrad Goree."

"Pierre, I thank you for all of your kindness and information. I will go to Erfoud as soon as I can make arrangements. If I get back to Casablanca, I'll get in touch."

"Good-bye, my friend. I hope we will meet again."

Stopping for lunch at a restaurant on Le Boulevard de Paris, he had a nice quiet meal while thinking out his next move.

I'll call Claudette, and ask her to make my travel arrangements to Erfoud. This map shows that I can get there two different ways, by Rabat and Meknes or by Marrakech. They look about the same distance. Claudette will know which route is best.

It was after one o'clock when he called Claudette.

"Hi Claudette, how are you feeling?"

"Oh, Jeff, I feel much better now. Where are you?"

"I am at a restaurant on Le Boulevard de Paris. I just finished lunch and I have some sad news."

"What is the sad news? You are not leaving, are you?"

"Yes, I'm afraid so. I have to make some travel arrangements. Can your office do that for me?"

"Yes, you are not too far from our office. It is on the same street as your hotel, in the La Banque d'Etat. The Bank d'Etat's address is 3413 Boulevard du Zouaves. I'll be waiting for you."

Some fifteen minutes later, Jeff walked up to the counter and asked for Claudette. When he was ushered into her office, Claudette closed the door and gave him a full mouth kiss.

"Oh, Jeff. Where are you going? How long will you be gone? You aren't in any trouble, are you?"

"No, Claudette. I'm not in trouble and I don't know how long I'll be gone. Let me clear something up about my business. It is true, I have a small sightseeing business in New Orleans, also a small flower business, but I am also a private investigator and this is the main purpose of my visit to Morocco. I am searching for the daughter of a wealthy American. Detective Pierre de LaSalla just told me who the girl was that was killed, the one they thought was Mary Alice Bakker. She was a prostitute in Erfoud and she put suspicion on Bruno LaTorre. Some clothing she had on when she died, was purchased by the girl I am looking for. I don't know how long I will be, but I need to go to Erfoud. Can you arrange a travel plan to Erfoud? Which would be faster, via Rabat and Meknes, or via Marrakech?"

"Jeff, why don't I work out both plans and show them to you tonight. You then can decide which route you prefer. Let's say at your room at five-thirty?"

"That is fine, I'll see you at five-thirty, my love."

Claudette arrived a few minutes after five, looking as fresh as a daisy.

"Come in, my love. Would you like a snack and some wine?"

"Yes, I am tired. I think I'll pull my shoes off and let my aching feet rest."

Jeff ordered some snacks and wine and took the folder that Claudette handed to him.

"Jeff, I recommend you take the Marrakech route, it is a little closer. A train goes as far as Marrakech and the bus service is better from Marrakech to Erfoud. It will take approximately three hours to

Marrakech and about eight hours to Erfoud by bus. The other way, to Meknes is approximately the same by rail mileage and time as to Marrakech, but from Meknes to Erfoud is about eleven hours by bus. The trip from Marrakech to Erfoud is only eight hours. In my opinion, by the way of Marrakech is faster and better."

"Do you know what time the train leaves for Marrakech tomorrow?"

"Yes, there are two trains a day to Marrakech, one departs at ten AM and arrives in Marrakech about one PM. The next one departs about four PM and arrives there about seven PM. The bus departs from Marrakech to Erfoud at three-thirty PM and arrives in Erfoud about at eleven forty-five PM."

"Would it be possible to have the tickets ready at your office by nine AM?"

"Yes, I will go there early and get them ready."

"Let's order some food and more wine and get to bed early. I'll pack tonight and we will get up early and have breakfast on the way to your office. Is this OK with you?"

"Jeff, I have an idea. Why don't you pack and check out tonight and come to my place and spend the night. It's closer to where I work than this is. We can have breakfast and still be at the office in time to get your tickets and you won't have to rush so."

"Good idea." Jeff called down to the front desk and told them to have his bill ready within the hour, as he would be checking out that evening.

Claudette's apartment was only seven blocks down from de Zouaves Hotel. It was a beautiful apartment with a scenic view overlooking Boulevard du Zouaves. After having dinner in the little restaurant on the first floor, they hurried back to the apartment, so eager to make love, that they were nearly undressed by the time they walked across the living room to the bedroom.

Jeff was awake before daylight. He eased out of bed, taking the clock with him over to the window. The light from outside shone on the dial; it was four-thirty.

Well, let's see how sleepy Claudette is. Easing back into bed and snuggling up close to Claudette, he started caressing her breast and she came alive. Boy, did she come alive. They made love for over an hour.

Having worked up an appetite, they went to the Café Yasmina for breakfast. The cafe was only three doors from Claudette's office, so by eight-thirty, Claudette began working on the tickets.

When the tickets were completed, Claudette took the rest of the morning off to escort him to the rail station.

Arriving at the station, Jeff observed that the waiting room was large and crowded. Outside was a long platform with a roof over it. You could barely get through the people, who came with children, goats, dogs and other animals.

The train was a narrow gauge train like the trains of France and Europe, except they were older. When it arrived, people began pushing and trying to board the train, even before it came to a halt.

Jeff took Claudette in his arms and held her tightly.

"Cheri, I'll be back. I have your address and telephone number and I will call you."

"Jeff, my love, please let me know where you are and hurry back."

The train started moving and Jeff had to run along side of it and wait until two people in front of him grabbed the handrail and boarded. He grabbed the handrail and pulled himself up on the step with his right hand; he carried the heavy suitcase in his left.

Now he saw why everyone was trying to get on before the train stopped. It was crowded with people, some sitting on the floor. Further up front a goat or two were lying in the aisle. The noise level was high, and it seemed as if each person was speaking a different language. The odor of sweaty people, who hadn't bathed for a while, goats and chickens, hung in the air. The windows were open, and the hot air blew in, bringing with it some of the tannery odors mixed with the smells of the Medina section that the train was passing.

What a long tough ride this is going to be. Damn, three hours of this.

The train, with its eerie whistle, slowly snaked around Casablanca's Medina section like it was lost. After about twenty minutes, they began to see a little open land. They passed a French Army post on top a high bluff, overlooking the rail tracks and highway. A little further they passed an airfield that looked as if it was an Air Corps of some army, French or maybe Moroccan. Now they were in the open countryside, passing citrus trees, olive trees and some vineyards.

Being in this strange land, he was beginning to get a feel for it and the people, one person in particular, Claudette.

The train stopped and a horde of people departed with goats and chickens. Jeff stepped off the train to let some people pass. The sign at the station read: Settat, 113km to Casablanca. That was approximately 70 miles, and it had taken two hours to go a little more than half way.

As he climbed back on the train, he found an empty seat next to an Arabian woman, who was covered in white clothing from head to foot, except for her eyes. She avoided eye contact and stared out of the window. He noticed that the men across the aisle were giving him hostile looks. He moved over as far as he could to the outside of the seat without falling off, but the men kept their eyes on him. Jeff reached down and picked his suitcase up and went to the back of the car. Two men followed him, and then a third joined them. The three surrounded him, speaking in Arabic in strong hostile-sounding tones. The trainman came by and spoke to them and a loud conversation took place. They quieted down some and Jeff asked the trainman, "Did I do something wrong to these men?"

"No," answered the trainman. "You were sitting next to a Muslim woman and their religion forbids men and women sitting together in public places."

"I am sorry. I didn't know that. Please give my apologies to the men, as well as to the lady."

The trainman spoke to the Arabian men and lots of hand gestures later, the trainman turned to Jeff and said, "They accept your apology and they want to shake your hand."

"Jeff walked over to the Arabs and just as he reached them, the train went around a sharp bend in the tracks, throwing him against the car door. It flew open, and one of the men grabbed Jeff to keep him from falling out between the cars.

With bowing and hand gestures, Jeff was thanking the men, when a young Arab man came over and spoke to him in English. "Let me interpret for you. I am Ahmed and I have studied in Boston."

Ahmed spoke to the three men and they smiled at Jeff, nodded their heads and each one shook his hand. Jeff told Ahmed that he did not know about their customs and to give the men his sincere apology and thank them for catching him when the train lurched.

For the next thirty or so minutes, the men through Ahmed, enjoyed each other's company and learned some of each other's customs.

Ahmed invited Jeff to sit with him. When they were seated, he looked out of the window facing east and saw some high mountains. Ahmed told him they were climbing up the Atlas Mountains but would not go very high.

He had a delightful time with the three men and Ahmed. Before he knew it, he looked out of the window and noticed the train was pulling into the yard at Marrakech.

Chapter Fourteen

Catherine and Mike were dining at La Maison Bleue, a restaurant in a beautiful old palace, where the owner personally received the guests. For the past eight months they'd had a standing date to dine out each week and discuss the business. Over cocktails, to the accompaniment of Gnaoua music, they discussed Gino's departure and a possible replacement.

"Mike, did you find out what happened to Gino? Did he just leave without saying anything? Surely, he would ask for the money owed him. It is unlike him to do something like this."

"I called Jake Crusant at the Hideaway Lounge in Baton Rouge because I had not heard from Gino for a couple of weeks. The last time I talked to him, he told me he had two college girls ready to sign on. Jake said he had not been to work for ten days so he went by his apartment. The manager there said he gave up the apartment and said he was going home. I expect him to come by anytime. I have never trusted Gino and if he is in trouble, I want to be prepared when he shows up."

"Mike, I'll let you handle Gino, but I would like your advice on one of the girls, Alison Niepce, one of the last girls Gino sent us. She is a hothead and I think she is on hashish. At times she speaks foul language and is unruly. I can't control her as I do the others. She is trouble, but I do feel sorry for her."

"Look, Catherine, you can't let your personal feelings get in the way. Look at what happened to that girl that continued to fall in love with every guy that came to her."

"Oh, you're speaking of Annette. Yes, but she did finally find true love. A captain from the French Foreign Legion came to see her a number of times and she asked permission to go out with him when she was off duty. He asked her to marry him and go with him to the outpost where he was stationed. I could tell that she was madly in love. I even gave her some of my clothes so she would be nicely dressed when she got married."

"Do you know for sure she married the captain?"

"No, but they were supposed to get married by the chaplain at the post where he was stationed."

"Then you don't know whether she married or not. I heard that he didn't marry her and now she is a working girl in Erfoud."

"Catherine, you just can't feel sorry for people. Remember what you told me your thoughts were the day you found out your father had been dipping into your trust fund? You said and I quote, 'To hell with other people. It's give and take in this world and I'll do the taking.'"

"You're right, Mike. I'll take care of Alison. She will shape up or I'll kick her ass out in the street."

"Good girl. Let's have another cocktail, before dinner. You need to unwind and let your hair down tonight. What would you think about going over to la Marrakech à Vol oisear after dinner?"

"Oh, Mike, we do have fun there and we haven't been there in a month or two. Let's go."

The sun coming over the mountains woke Catherine up. Looking at the clock, she jumped out of bed and turned the water on in the bathtub. *Damn, I feel rotten.* Too many cocktails and up dancing until two at la Marrakech à Vol oisear, gave her a slight hangover. As soon as she finished her bath she buzzed for her maid, Suzie. She needed some strong coffee.

An hour later she felt much better, so she called Madam Danielle, at the un Bordel de Bonheur.

"Danielle, I will be over in about an hour. I want you to see that Alison is not busy, but do not tell her I am coming."

Arriving at the un Bordel de Bonheur, she walked into the parlor where four of the girls were seated, just in time to hear Alison telling two of the girls that she could show them how to make more money and have a better time. Alison looked up and saw Catherine, turned two shades of red and hurried out of the room.

Catherine closed the door, turned to the girls and said, "I just heard what Alison was saying. Let me tell you that you are working at the finest bordel in all of Morocco, with the nicest living quarters, best food and pay. Alison is going to the same place that Annette was going when she left to marry the captain. I am not sure, but I have heard that the captain did not marry her and she is still a working girl. The town is Erfoud, a small town of about nine thousand people, at the foot of the Atlas Mountains. A French Foreign Legion garrison of about six or seven hundred legionaires is located five miles from Erfoud in the desert. The legionaires get paid once a month, about 250 francs. They all get paid and within a few days all will come into Erfoud to visit the bordel and pay about 25 francs for service, with the money being split fifty percent to the bordel and fifty percent to the girl. Let's get real and see how much you can make. The price here at the un Bordel de Bonheur is two hundred francs. Your percentage is one third, sixty-seven francs with food and room included and you keep all the tips. With Alison and Annette, you will have to service over six sweaty, smelly Legionaries on a hard cot in a small hot room to equal the same money you receive here. After four or five days, most of them will be broke and business will be slow until the next payday. I am going up to tell Alison she is finished here, and all of you that would like to go with her, let me know and I will have your pay ready. You have my blessing. If there is anyone who would like to go, just raise your hand." No hands went up.

Catherine turned and went into the office, where she opened a book and quickly calculated Alison's earnings. She pulled some cash out of a locked drawer and went upstairs to Alison's room, where she found her packing her belongings.

"Alison, I wish you well with your new venture. You have pay for Monday, Tuesday and Wednesday, the slowest days of the week due you. You have serviced twelve clients at sixty-seven francs each for a total of eight hundred and four francs. Here is nine hundred francs. Please vacate the un Bordel de Bonheur in thirty minutes. Good-bye and good luck."

Going to the cottage in the rear of the villa, where Mike lived, she knocked on the door. She felt drained of all of her energy and strength and when Mike opened the door she almost fell in the chair.

"For Christ sake Catherine, did last night do you in that bad? What is the problem, are you sick?"

"No, Mike, I'm just tired. Not from last night, it was one of the most pleasant nights I have had in a long time. It was the firing of Alison and the loneliness I have been experiencing. It seems as if I don't have any female friends."

"Look, Catherine, the un Bordel de Bonheur is doing quite well. Why don't you go to Paris for a week or so and do some shopping, see some shows, and just relax. Forget about the business, I'll take care of it."

"Maybe you are right Mike. I'll think it over."

Back at the villa, she entered the wine cellar, selected a rare French wine, picked up a wine glass from the bar and went outside to the garden. She selected a chair facing the snow-topped Toubkal Mountains. Catherine loved to sit out here in the garden and gaze up at the mountains. Her best plans were made in this quiet surrounding. Now her thoughts turned to Mike's advice about going to Paris. It would be a nice holiday if she had a close female friend to go with her. She had friends, but no one close. She thought about Maxine, the owner of the dress boutique where she purchased most of her clothes. They'd had lunch several times and went out for cocktails one evening. She was fun and might make a lively traveling companion. Pouring another glass of wine, she took the glass and went into the screen and glass patio where she had a telephone extension. Looking up the exchange to Maxine's Boutique, she told the operator the number, and while waiting for Maxine to answer, almost panicked and started to hang the telephone up. Then, Maxine's voice came on the line.

"Hello, Maxine speaking. May I help you?"

"Maxine, this is Catherine. I was sitting here thinking about cocktails and dinner tonight. Have you any plans for the evening?"

"No, Catherine, however, I have had a rough time and may not be good company. My boyfriend and I parted ways a few nights ago. I do need company but I wouldn't want to spoil our friendship with the mood I am in."

"Well, I have had a bad day and my mood is not good either. Maybe over cocktails and dinner we can unload our troubles on each other. Tell me what time you close and I will pick you up, or name a place where we can meet."

"My manager will close. I'll leave now, go by my place, bathe, dress and pick you up. What is your address?"

"It is the Villa Marrakech on Boulevard de Santi, number 13913. That would be just north of Avenue d'Anta, the entrance is on the left side. What time shall I expect you?"

"Well, let's see, it is now four. I'll pick you up at six. Your villa, is it near the Villa Bakker?"

"Yes, in fact, it was the Villa Bakker at one time, but I purchased it and renamed it. Are you familiar with it?"

"A little. I will tell you about it later. See you at six."

"OK, six it is. Good-bye."

Just past six, Louise announced that Maxine was in the great room. Sitting in a dark red upholstered chair was Maxine, in a smart black cocktail dress about knee length with thin shoulder straps, cut low enough to show a little cleavage. A small white rosebud pinned to the left strap at the top of her dress and sheer silk hose with three-inch high heels completed her attire.

"Hi, Maxine. I didn't know where we were going and I wasn't sure how to dress. You are looking very, I believe the phrase is, a la mode or elegant."

"I thought when I suggested that white cocktail dress it would give you that sophisticated look, and it definitely does. Shall we go show our outfits to the clients of La Maison Bleue?"

At La Maison Bleue, the restaurant was almost full. The maitre d' recognized Catherine from the previous evening and seated them in the cocktail lounge where an orchestra was playing to a full dance floor. At the bar were seated military men from several different countries. A waiter appeared with two champagne cocktails and nodded to a table near the orchestra where two military officers were seated. Maxine looked and nodded her head and mouthed, "thank you."

"Well, Catherine, it looks as if the Germans have landed. Would you like to have drinks with them?"

"Why not? They are both good-looking, maybe we can have some fun with them."

Almost instantly the waiter appeared with a note in German, which neither could read. Maxine asked the waiter if he could translate it for them.

The waiter said that the officers wanted to know if they would accept an invitation to dine and have cocktails with them.

"We do not speak German. If they speak some French or English we would enjoy having a cocktail with them, but we have a business dinner to attend."

When the waiter went to the officers' table, Maxine said, "We should not give them our correct names. I will be Adele, what name will you use?"

"I knew a Lenore back home. Yes, Lenore will do."

After the waiter spoke with the Germans, he moved them to a table for four and escorted Maxine and Catherine over to them.

The tall officer blond introduced himself as Lieutenant Bertram Faust, and the other officer said in French, "I am Lieutenant Arnold Kepler. We are pilots in the German Avion and stationed at an airfield about twenty miles south of Casablanca. We are here for two days on a holiday."

Maxine said, "Hello, my name is Adele and my friend is Lenore. We live here in Marrakech. Are you with General Rommel's Army moving across the Sahara Desert?"

"No, we are a newly formed wing of the Avion, we are Luftwaffe pilots. Enough of war talk, we cannot discuss anything about the movement of the troops."

Bertam Faust had dark hair and cold blue eyes. He looked at Catherine and asked, "You have an American accent, have you lived in Marrakech for any length of time?"

"About a year, but I have been thinking of moving to Paris."

"That would be good, we are on a training mission and will be stationed back in Germany. France will surrender before winter and we could see each other in Paris.

"Would you care to dance?"

"Yes." *What a couple of conceited jerks these two are. I have to get Maxine to the ladies lounge and plan a way to get out of this.*

After a couple of dances they returned to the table where Maxine and Arnold were sitting, talking.

"Adele would you care to go freshen up?"

"Yes, I would; I feel as if my face needs to be repaired."

In the ladies lounge, Catherine said, "Maxine, let's wash these conceited fools out of our hair. We'll tell them we must leave for our dinner engagement and will meet them later, say about eleven o'clock. We'll give them the address of un Bordel de Bonheur and tell them to ask for Danielle. I'll call Danielle and tell her that when they ask for Adele and Lenore, to escort them to a waiting room and send two girls in and tell them Adele and Lenore will be late and take care of them."

The girls returned to the table to find another cocktail waiting for them.

Back on the dance floor, Catherine snuggled closer to Betram, while they finished a dance. Leading him off to the edge of the dance floor, she said, "Betram I have something to ask you. We have a dinner date with people we do business with. We discussed ways to avoid the date, but it would damage our business relationship. We both would like to be with you two. We'll cut the dinner short and meet you at a private club afterwards, if you want to."

"I would like to be with you. How long would you be with them?"

"Two hours at the most, let's see it is now eight, our dinner is at eight-thirty. We should be finished at ten-thirty or eleven. Meet us at this private club, the de Bonheur. Here, I'll write the address down, any taxi will know where it is. At the door, ask for Mademoiselle Danielle and she will take you to the lounge area. We will be waiting for you." She smiled seductively.

"Let's go back to the table and see what Arnold has to say."

They all agreed to meet at eleven o'clock at de Bonheur, and Maxine and Catherine departed in Maxine's automobile. They decided to go to La Marrakech à Vol oisear. They were seated at a table near the stage and dance floor and ordered two cocktails.

While sipping their drinks, Catherine said, "You know, Maxine, I was thinking of going to Paris for a little recreation, but after speaking with those German officers I don't think it would be a safe or pleasant place for a vacation."

"I will agree with you. Paris is a lovely city. I receive a great deal of enjoyment visiting there and would like to go there, if it was like the Paris of old. I need to get away from business for a few days. I have always enjoyed the beaches and nightlife in Agadir."

"I have never been to Agadir but have heard that is a fun city."

"Catherine, you want to take a few days off and so do I. If you would like, I'll call the Medina Palace Hotel in Agadir and make reservations. Would you like to go for a week? They have apartments and bungalows at weekly rates."

"That sounds wonderful. I haven't been to a beach since I left America and I do miss it. See when you can set it up."

Chapter Fifteen

Departing the train at Marrakech, Jeff made his way outside of the station where horse-drawn carriages and taxis were lined up waiting for passengers. Looking at his watch, he noted it was two o'clock. *Well, my bus leaves at three-thirty. I'll take a carriage to the bus station and see some of Marrakech.*

He picked out a white carriage with two white Arabian horses. He asked in Cajun, how long it would take to get to the bus station.

In English, the coachman asked, "Do you speak English?"

"Yes. I asked how long would it take to get to the bus station?"

"Monsieur, it is not far, maybe thirty minutes."

"I have to take a bus that leaves at three-thirty. Can you show me a little of Marrakech and have me at the station a little before three?"

"Would you like to see the best or the bad side of the city?"

"I'll leave it to you; some of both would be good."

The carriage was closed with windows that you could lower and raise. The driver sat up above the front window so that the passengers could get a good view. After a couple of blocks, Jeff spoke through a tube to the driver and asked him to stop. The driver asked, "Monsieur, is there something wrong?"

"No, I just wanted to know if I could sit next to you and maybe you can tell me a little about Marrakech."

From the driver's seat, Jeff had an excellent view as the horses trotted down the Boulevard el-Yarmouk. As the horse's hooves from his carriage and dozens of others clip-clopped along the cobblestone street, they were mixed with the rattle of taxis dodging heavily laden donkeys carrying sacks of goods. He again had that sensation of being in another world. The driver pointed out that inside the massive clay-colored defensive wall was the Medina, the old city. Ali bin Kouch, the driver, told Jeff that he would pass the souk just inside of the wall, but would not have enough time to stop. The carriage passed the souk, a large market, where all types of crafts were on display and for sale. There were wool-dyers with their garishly colored dripping bundles of wool hanging from the walls, metal workers, potters, venders selling clothing, fruits, nuts and vegetables. The carriage came out of the Medina onto Avenue de la Ménara and continued down to Rue de la Seville to the bus station.

The time was two forty-five. Jeff paid Ali and thanked him for his informative tour. He asked if Ali had a business card, and said that he would be back in about a week and would get in touch with him.

Inside the bus station was a mass of people, from different countries and tribes, speaking all types of dialects. Jeff made his way to the line at one of the windows for information. He was told the bus would be about ten minutes late and he could wait at the bus area out under the canopy for departing buses, at station thirteen. *Will thirteen be my lucky number?*

Walking over to station thirteen where several benches were occupied, he found one vacant space on a bench that seated four. Two Arabs, and a soldier wearing a French Foreign Legion uniform, were sitting on the bench. Jeff sat between one of the Arabs and the soldier. Sliding his suitcase under the bench, he spoke to the group. The two Arabs looked at him and nodded, while the French soldier said in broken English, "Good afternoon. My name is Jamie Pohlar. I am a legionnaire and I am stationed near Erfoud."

"Pleased to meet you, Jamie. I'm Jeff Stewart, an American on a fact-finding mission to gather information for my travel agency. I met a legionnaire in Agadir a few weeks back, who was stationed at Goulimime, but said they were moving to a post about a hundred miles south of Meknes."

"That would be where I am stationed, about five miles from Erfoud out in the desert, near the Algerian border. A detachment of troops came into the Sijilmassa outpost a couple of weeks before I came over to Marrakech. I think they came from Goulimime."

"My friend's name is Tony Marro. He is an American, or was; he said he is now a French citizen."

"He must have been in the Legion several years to become a French citizen. I don't think I have met him, however, I have been in the Legion for three years and have been stationed at a number of garrisons in Algeria, Tunis and here in Morocco. I am from Versailles, France, a small town just outside of Paris, and have been at the Sijilmassa outpost for about a year."

The bus pulled into space thirteen and people began to line up. Jamie asked Jeff if he would hold a place in the line for him while he tended to some business. As Jamie walked to the back of the bus, a black carriage, pulled by two black horses, came into the bus station, stopping at space thirteen. The carriage had frosted glass windows on each side with a cross, an angel and Mother Mary etched on them. Two men exited the carriage and went over to Jamie. After a couple of minutes conversation, one of the men walked over to two other men and they all went over to the carriage and removed a coffin. One man was on the top of the bus with Jamie, while the other men lifted the coffin up to them. Jamie pulled the coffin to the corner of the railing, lashing the coffin to the rail in the back and front. Other merchandise was placed on top, luggage, bags of personal belongings, along with two sheep and a crate containing three chickens.

The attendant or footman escorted Jamie to the last door of the bus. Before entering, Jamie spoke to the footman who came over to Jeff and motioned him to the last door with Jamie. There were five people in the last seat, two Frenchmen, an Arab, Jamie and Jeff. Jamie and Jeff sat on the outside near the door.

Well number thirteen is lucky thus far; this is going be a long ride so I have to make the best of it. However, it is not so lucky for the person in the coffin; I wonder who it can be.

The footman went around to the driver's side to the charcoal burner, put in some charcoal and turned the crank a few times, then came around and closed all six doors and guided the driver out of the station. Due to the gasoline shortage, caused by the war, many vehicles were equipped with charcoal burning tanks that produced a low grade of fuel to replace gasoline. The footman grabbed a handrail, pulled himself up on a small platform with a top and a seat. This is where the footman rode when the bus was in motion. His duties consisted of opening and closing the doors, loading and unloading parcels from the roof, and putting pieces of wood under the rear wheels on very steep inclines.

Jeff's mind was more on the coffin than on the problems of the war in Europe and shortage of gasoline. He wanted to know, but would not ask Jamie about the coffin. Maybe if he started a conversation, he could guide him to that topic.

As the bus left the city, the elevation began to climb and the bus struggled. The view was different from Marrakech and north to Casablanca. The low hills were almost bare of trees or bushes, but contained rocks of all shapes and sizes. At the first rest stop Jeff and Jamie walked around getting their legs limbered up. Below, an Arab was plowing a field that looked like a rocky desert, with a camel and a donkey hitched side-by-side pulling a plow. The plow was the same kind of plow that was used thousands of years ago. The only metal on the plow was a rough looking hand made plow shear, the balance was made of hand-hewed timber. Jamie explained that the camel was too dumb to follow a furrow, so the donkey was used to follow the furrow and lead the camel.

"Back when I was a kid and my dad farmed, I thought we had it rough, but seeing this Arab farmer and the way he works, we were well off," commented Jeff.

"I was thinking the same thing. We lived on a farm, a vineyard. Our father worked in the vineyard. My brother Simeon and I would speak about going to Paris and working when we reached the age to leave home. We both loved adventure and wanted to see the world. Simeon was a year younger than I, and we would make believe we were soldiers of fortune and have great adventures around the winery and vineyards. One-day a neighbor's son, an older person in his thirties, whom we had never met, came home on leave. He told us stories of his adventures in the French Foreign Legion. I was eighteen, then. Simeon and I would be spellbound for hours while he recounted his stories. We made a pact that when Simeon reached eighteen, we would sign up for the French Foreign Legion. The day after Simeon's eighteenth birthday, we enlisted over our parents' objections. My mother made me promise to look after Simeon; he was the baby. Today I am taking Simeon back to Sijimassa to be buried in Legion Cemetery. I have gone over in my head a thousand ways how to write Mama and Papa about Simeon's death. How can I justify not taking care of him?"

"Can you send his remains back to France?"

"The Legion would ship his remains back, but because of the conflict in Europe, France is on the verge of collapse to Germany, it is impossible at this time."

The bus was loading again, getting ready to move. Jamie seemed to be in a stupor, looking out over the fields as the twilight was fading into darkness. Jeff walked up to him and as Jamie turned, his eyes were filled with tears, his body began to tremble and shake. Here was a big strapping, six foot two inch, one hundred ninety pound, twenty-two year-old crying like a baby and trying to hide it. Jamie continued to say over and over, "How can I tell my mama and papa that I did not take care of Simeon?"

Jeff took Jamie's arm and led him to the bus. He boarded first so Jamie could be next to the door. By the time the bus slowly gathered power and got back on the highway, it was fully dark and the moon had not yet risen. Jamie sat silently in his grief.

"Jamie, I know the feeling of losing someone you love dearly. Why not just sit back and remember Simeon and what he would want you to do. When you are ready to talk about it, I will listen."

Jamie laid his head on the backrest. Jeff sat quietly waiting for Jamie to respond. He could feel Jamie's pain, remembering Nicole's death as though it was yesterday.

Facing the prospect of escorting Nicole and Pepe's bodies back to Fullerton, Jeff had the funeral home prepare the bodies for shipping. He went to the funeral home and selected the coffins and the shipping containers, and made arrangements for the undertaker to ship the bodies on the L & N passenger train leaving at six AM. He purchased a ticket on the same train. The train left on time and it was nine-thirty when the train arrived at Lake Charles for the transfer of the coffins and himself to a train that would depart for Leesville at ten-thirty. Jeff watched the removal of the two coffins from the train and their placement on a freight cart, which was pulled under the overhang to the far end of the station. Time passed slowly and at ten-fifteen the coffins were loaded on the northbound train to Leesville.

When he left the train at Leesville, he saw a somber couple waiting. Walking over to them, he asked if they were Mr. and Mrs. Grevy. Yes, was the answer.

An open model B Ford touring car, which had been cut off behind the front seat, with a flatbed made of lumber, turning it into a truck, waited. The two coffins were loaded onto the truck. Jeff and the Grevys rode in another car. They drove in silence, the five-mile journey out into the Kisatchie National Forest to the Fullerton Church and Cemetery.

The church was decorated with many colors of wild flowers, some roses and ferns. The coffins were placed in the front of the church. The coffins would be left closed due to the length of time since the deaths. The congregation opened with the singing of Bringing in the Sheaves, followed by Rock of Ages. The preacher delivered a fine sermon for Pepe and Nicole and closed the service with Sweet Hour of Prayer. After the service, Jeff went with Mr. and Mrs. Grevy to their home, where friends and neighbors gathered to express their condolences, bringing food and love.

Jeff spent the night with the Grevy's. Before going to bed, they sat in the living room with a fire in the fireplace and a kerosene lamp giving out a dim light. Mr. and Mrs. Grevy talked of Pepe's and Nicole's childhoods and the hopes they had for them. Jeff told of meeting Nicole and how they fell in love and the plans they had just started making for their life together. They all broke down and cried together. The next morning, they drove him to the train station to catch the ten o'clock train to St. Charles and then back to New Orleans.

The bus to Erfoud was rumbling along the winding road. The moon was out, and to the east you could see the sand dunes making shadows on the treeless desert. While looking at the shadows making strange patterns, it started to rain. When it rains in the desert the rain is very heavy and the winds blow extremely hard. Fortunately the rain lasted only a short time. Listening to the rain pelting against the top of the bus and windows and the motor straining, Jamie asked in a low voice, "Are you awake Jeff?"

"Yes, Jamie. Would you like to talk?"

"Yes, I would like to tell you about the last time I saw Simeon. Three days ago, he and two friends got three-day passes. He wanted me to go with them to Marrakech. I had duty the day they were supposed to leave and asked that he wait a day, but they insisted on leaving then. I told Simeon to meet me at the bus station the next afternoon. The next morning I went into Erfoud and while waiting for the bus, I met this girl from Rissani, a few miles south of Erfoud. We started talking and I went with her to Rissani and spent two days there. When I returned to the barracks at the Sijilmassa Garrison, the captain called me in and informed me that some Arabs had killed Simeon. One other soldier died this morning, and the remaining one is in the hospital in Marrakech. Supposedly, the three of them were in the Kasbah, trying to find a bar. They went through a gateway; the heavy door was open. The Arabs said they asked for women and a fight started. As they started to run out of the gate, a couple of Arabs closed the gate and about six or seven more Arabs caught them and beat and knifed them to death. How can I tell my mama that I did not go with Simeon to protect him? It is my entire fault for not going with him, and going with that girl, instead. My mama will disown me. If she knew Simeon was on top of this bus in a coffin with rain coming down on it, it would kill her."

Jeff asked the driver to stop the bus and see if anyone had any robes or skins to cover the coffin. The bus stopped and the driver found some camel skins one of the passengers had. It covered a little over two thirds of the coffin. Jeff pulled his coat off and laid it over the coffin, lashing the camel skins and coat to it. During the remaining journey, the rain stopped as Jamie told about their boyhoods between sobs. This was not a big strong brave French Foreign Legionnaire, but a little boy mourning the loss of his baby brother.

Chapter Sixteen

The bus pulled into the town of Tinejhir at nine forty-five for the last rest stop before reaching Erfoud. If the bus continued on its present timetable it would reach Erfoud about eleven forty-five.

There wasn't anything open except a large tent, which served Arabic gahwa (coffee), haleeb (goats milk), shai (tea), fatayer (bread pocket filled with lamb), khubz marcook (a thin dome shaped Arabic bread) and lahma bi ajeen (a type of Arabic pizza).

"Jeff, have you been eating Arabic food?"

"No, very little. What do you suggest?"

"Do not drink the mai, that is the water. It is bad tasting in this region and will sometimes make you sick until you get used to it. Drink just enough to quench your thirst. Try to get some quinine and take a little each day until you can get acclimatized to the water."

Jeff looked at the options and ordered the gahwa and the lahma bi ajeen; Jamie ordered the gahwa and the fatayer.

While waiting for the order Jeff asked, "Where is the toilet?"

"Let me see, just go around to the back of the tent, and find a place that has no one around and do your business behind a building, a sand dune, a bush, or any place that is private. If you have to go when someone is around, go ahead; no one will pay any attention to you."

Jeff went around the big tent. The only light was from the bright full moon. He walked far enough, until he felt safe and relieved himself. However, he had to use his handkerchief.

He returned just as Jamie was getting the food. There were no tables and looking around, most of the passengers were squatting while eating and drinking.

Before he had completely finished, the driver was ringing a bell to signal everyone to board the bus. He completed the lahama bi ajeen on the bus as it moved on the last leg of the journey to Erfoud. The full moon cast shadows on the mountains to the west as the road became flatter, and to the east sand dunes casting shadows made the area look very mysterious.

"Are you awake, Jeff?"

"Yes, Jamie. I was looking at the landscape and thinking how much different it is than in the southern United States."

"I feel as though we have become friends. Will you do me a great favor?"

"Sure, if I can. What would you like for me to do?"

"Would you go with me to the Sijilmassa Garrison for the funeral and burial of Simeon. You have given me great strength and I will need this tomorrow. I will talk to my Commanding Officer. Maybe he will give you permission to stay at the garrison's visitors quarters."

"Yes, I will be with you and everything is going to work out fine."

The rest of the bus journey was uneventful; Jeff and Jamie discussed their past lives. Jamie was more at ease that any time since Jeff had met him.

At eleven-thirty the bus pulled into Erfoud. After the passengers had unloaded, they all left the station, leaving Jeff and Jamie alone, except for the driver and footman. Jeff talked to the two men and they helped remove the coffin from the top of the bus. Jeff and Jamie had no place but the street to sleep. There were no nearby hotels and the bus station was closing. They put the coffin on the side of the bus station, opened Jeff's suitcase and removed two heavy cotton shirts, which they put on to protect themselves from the nighttime chill of the desert. They huddled beside the casket, trying to keep warm. The moonlight casting shadows from the sand dunes fell across the casket giving Jeff an eerie feeling.

Sometime during the night, Jamie's incoherent talking in French awakened Jeff. He was probably dreaming. The only words that Jeff could understand were "mama pardonner." Jamie was whimpering, and Jeff knew he was asking his mama's forgiveness. He knew Jamie was being tortured by the dream but didn't know if he should wake him. He reached over and touched his arm. It was wet with cold sweat, but Jamie did not wake up so he let him sleep. Jeff finally drifted back off to sleep, but was awakened by an eerie sound that made his hair stand up on his neck. Looking over at the coffin, a shadow of the nearby Mosque lay across it; the sound was coming from the tower of the Mosque. It was the six o'clock inflected intonation, the call of the mason going out from the Mosque, along with the sound of a one-stringed instrument.

Jamie awoke and they discussed the procedure for the day's events. First, they had to get Simeon to the garrison. Jamie explained that he needed to find a camel to transport the coffin. While Jeff stayed with the coffin, Jamie left to find transportation. About thirty minutes later he came back with an Arab leading four camels. One camel had a harness over his back for transporting goods. The three of them lashed the coffin to the camel's harness making sure that the coffin was in a completely horizontal position. Jamie said it would take about three hours to cross the five-mile desert to the garrison. They picked up some gahwa and khubz marcook, (bread). The camel driver had two pigskins of water, and the caravan started its trip across the desert at seven-thirty, estimated time of arrival at the garrison near ten-thirty.

The trip across the five-mile strip of desert was uneventful, very hot and very slow. At one point, Jeff had to stop and relieve himself, the water was upsetting his stomach. They arrived at eleven and proceeded to the chapel and unloaded Simeon. Jamie spoke with the chaplain, who would arrange for the service to be at sunset, about seven-thirty.

Jeff accompanied Jamie to his headquarters and reported to his captain, getting the full details of Simeon's death. He also received permission for Jeff to stay two nights in the guest quarters.

At the guest quarters, a room about six feet by eight feet with one cot, a small chest of drawers and a chair was assigned to him. Jamie left for his barracks but said he would return as soon as he bathed and changed into a clean uniform.

The toilet for the guest quarters was down the hall and a tub for bathing was next door. Most of Jeff's clothing was dirty, but he washed, shaved and put on the best clothes he had.

About an hour later, a clean Jamie came in with two of his friends and some food. The little room was crowded, and Jamie and another legionnaire had to be the interpreters, however, they all got along well. Jeff had made some more friends. *Now, if I could only find Tony Marro.*

Jamie told the group, "Stay here and entertain Jeff while I make a visit to headquarters. I won't be long."

Thirty minutes later Jamie returned and announced, "We have a visitor, let me introduce Sergeant Tony Marro from the 5th Cheval Brigade."

When Tony saw Jeff, in the true French custom, Tony kissed him on the cheeks. Jeff was not used to being kissed by men and tried not to let his embarrassment show.

"Gentlemen, let's go to our barracks and leave these two friends to get reacquainted. Jeff, I'll be back about seven. Sergeant, you are welcome to attend if you wish, if not I understand."

At seven-thirty the funeral began with the songs and ceremony in French. Jeff understood only some of the words.

The casket was carried to the military cemetery at the rear of the garrison and interment was in a mausoleum, which was in the rear defensive wall of the garrison. The wall was seven feet thick, ten feet high and four hundred feet wide. A small military band played the French National Anthem, the Marseillaise, and everyone saluted the flag and the casket. Jamie held up well until the casket was raised to its final resting place, on the fourth tier and fifty-one spaces from the left end of the mausoleum. Near collapse, he repeated over and over, "Mama, Papa, please forgive me."

Chapter Seventeen

That night, after the funeral, Tony invited Jeff to the garrison's saloon for a few drinks. Jeff reminded himself that if he ordered cognac, not to chug it down but to sip it slowly. However, the favorite drink here was beer.

In conversation, Tony asked how his investigation of the missing heiress was progressing.

"That is one reason I am in this part of the country. The information I received was that a women murdered in Casablanca, came from Erfoud, and wore some clothing belonging to the person I am looking for. The murdered woman's name was Annette Coppola and she had a boyfriend or husband, a legionnaire named Conrad Goree, a captain stationed here."

"There is a Captain Goree here. He's the commander of the 515 Camel Brigade. He has, or had a girlfriend who had some type of a business in Erfoud. I think Captain Goree is on patrol at the Algerian border. I can find out when he's due to return to the garrison if you would care to know."

The next morning Tony came by for Jeff to go to the mess hall for breakfast and then to find Jamie and see how he was faring.

Jamie was much better than the day before. His brigade was going on patrol at the Algerian border, to replace the troops of Captain Goree's brigade.

Tony received a one-day pass and was able to get Jeff and himself a ride on the truck going into Erfoud for supplies. Arriving in Erfoud, Tony advised him that the best hotel for an American would be the Tafilalet Hotel.

Hotel Tafilalet was not even close to being the grade of hotel as the Zouaves Hotel, but it was clean and the price was right, seventy-five francs a day. His room was on the second floor, only three doors from the washroom and toilets.

After checking in, Tony offered to accompany him to the police station.

In front of the hotel were several carriages waiting for passengers. Jeff and Tony climbed into the first one and asked the driver to take them to the police station where Jeff asked for the police commander.

Tony waited outside, when Jeff entered the office of Commander Andre Fosee. He introduced himself and gave the commander a letter from Policier Pierre de La Salla in Casablanca, stating the circumstances surrounding Annette Coppola.

"Yes, Monsieur Stewart, we have a file on Annette Coppola. Let me retrieve it and I will bring you up to date on her."

Commander Fosee read the file on Annette Coppola. "She was arrested on several occasions here for working as an unlicensed prostitute. Her license had been revoked in Marrakech for soliciting outside of the licensed bordel where she worked."

"Commander, could you tell me the name of the bordel in Marrakech?"

"Hmm, she was employed by the un Bordel de Bonheur. She was arrested for soliciting a legionnaire officer in a hotel."

"Sir, do you have the name of that officer?"

"Yes, it was Captain Goree. Annette's statement was that she was off duty when she met the captain in a lounge in la Réfugier Hotel, and after some drinks, dancing and dining, they went to his room. She claimed that she accompanied him for her own pleasure and did not accept any money from him. The captain was in Marrakech for three days, and she dated him each of these days. She said she fell in love with

Captain Goree and confessed to working as a prostitute. He asked her to come with him to Erfoud so they could be together. She told him she would only go with him if they were married. The captain went to the policier, filing a complaint that she solicited him at the hotel several times. They arrested her and after an investigation, voided her license. When she left un Bordel de Bonheur, she told the bordel that she was going to Erfoud to marry the captain. Upon arriving here she was unable to contact the captain, so she went to the local bordel and they hired her. She used her Marrakech license and applied for a license for Erfoud. When the license was turned down, we arrested her for working as a prostitute without a valid license. From our reports, the captain never contacted her, so she left Erfoud, one of the girls said, with a customer going to Casablanca. That is the end of our report on her."

Jeff and Tony went to the bus station to get the schedule to Marrakech for the next day. Two buses left, one at seven-thirty AM and one at two PM. Jeff purchased a ticket for the seven-thirty bus.

Tony and Jeff went to Tony's favorite lounge for an afternoon of entertainment, food, drinks and watching the belly dancers. Tony departed on the supply truck at six-thirty PM.

At seven-thirty the next morning, Jeff boarded the bus for the long ride to Marrakech, with an estimated arrival of approximately four o'clock.

It was a long, dusty, uneventful ride. Jeff dozed most of the way.

The bus pulled into the station in Marrakech at four-fifteen. Commander Fosee had given Jeff the name of a hotel, where he had stayed. At la Réfugier Hotel, he registered in a deluxe room for four hundred fifty francs a day (six dollars), the same class as the Hotel de Zouaves. Room number 215 was a large corner room.

Now, to get acquainted with Marrakech. He went down to the restaurant and lounge.

It had been a long ten hours since he left Erfoud. He only left the bus at the rest stops and walked to stretch his legs. He hadn't eaten, as the food along the way did not look appetizing. His last meal was breakfast in Erfoud about six-thirty that morning. He was hungry and wanted a steak. *What did they call it? Oh, yes, la bidoche.*

In the dining room he ordered some good wine and a meal, a steak with fresh vegetables. When he was ready to leave he felt much better and looked into the lounge. A band was playing and some soldiers were at the bar. He went to the bar and took an empty seat between a German soldier and a Vichy soldier. Both soldiers were sullen and quiet, and after two glasses of wine Jeff retired to his room for the night.

Jeff was awake early and went down for breakfast. When he returned to his room, he picked up the phone and called Claudette.

"Hi, Claudette. How have you been? I've missed you. It was a rough trip to Erfoud, but I am now in Marrakech at la Réfugier Hotel, room 215."

"Hello, Jeff. I am glad you are back and safe. Did you get the information you needed?"

"Yes, I found out something that will keep me in Marrakech for a while. Today is Friday, can you come down and spend Saturday and Sunday with me?"

"Oh, I was going to tell you something over the telephone, but I should tell you in person. I can't leave until tomorrow morning. Meet me at the train depot at one o'clock. I don't know if I can stay over, but I do need to talk to you."

"Sure, I'll meet you. Are you in some sort of trouble?"

"No. I'll tell you when I arrive tomorrow. I must go and get my work finished before I leave. I will see you tomorrow."

After hanging the phone up, Jeff sat in the chair and thought, *Well, that was a strange conversation. What is it that she didn't want to tell me over the phone and would come down here to tell me in person. I have only been gone a week; surely she hasn't had time to discover if she's pregnant. I hope not. She is a lovely and beautiful person and I care for her, but not enough to get married. If she were pregnant my duty would be to marry* her. Maybe it is something else, maybe just to get married. I am not ready, so I have to find a way to get out of it.

He had to get to work and follow up the lead of Annette Coppola. Getting a carriage, he directed the driver to take him to the police department. At the station, he went to the information desk and asked for Detective Louie Bennard. The clerk pointed to a gentleman who was talking to a lady and said, "I will inform Monsieur Bennard when he finishes with the lady."

Jeff looked over at Monsieur Bennard and instantly liked what he saw. He was a man in his thirties, about six foot one, weighing about one hundred ninety pounds, with black hair, a black bushy moustache, neatly dressed in a dark grey pin striped suit.

Louie finished speaking with the lady and walked over to Jeff and spoke in French, introducing himself.

Jeff put his hand out and said, "Bonjour Monsieur Bennard. My name is Jeff Stewart from New Orleans, Louisiana in America. I do not speak French very well, only a dialect of French called Cajun. I am a private investigator, and here is a letter of introduction from Pierre de LaSalla."

Louie took Jeff's hand, giving it a firm handshake, and replied, "My English is fair. How is my old friend, Pierre?"

"He is fine, and has been a great deal of help to me in trying to locate a missing young lady."

Louie read the letter.

"My friend speaks well of you. It looks as if you and he have become good friends. Let's go to my office so we can get better acquainted."

Louie's office was cluttered and looked like the type of place with more work than one person could handle. As they made small talk, Jeff gave a brief description of his background, and in return Louie filled Jeff in on his. Louie was thirty-one, three years older than Jeff, married at twenty-three, had no children. His wife of eight years, who was his first and only love had been killed one year before at the age of twenty-nine. Some criminals, who learned his home address, had come to his home to kill him, but shot his wife instead.

"I don't know whether I was lucky or unlucky to survive the shootout. As of this date, I have not found the killers. They took the love of my life, and I have been a little more reckless since. Not enough to get myself killed, not until I find the perpetrators and see that they are punished. For the few months after they killed her, all I wanted to do was to find them and brutalize and torture them before killing them. Now, I am going to a doctor, an older man, who specializes in family practice. He lets me talk as long as I want and probes me into talking about my wife. One day he said, 'Louie, your problem is hate, not love. You will always love your wife and that is good. Hate is another thing. It does not hurt the person you hate; they don't care if you hate them. It will eat you up internally until you are obsessed with hate and revenge and it crowds out everything else. Think positively. Remember your wife and concentrate on catching the murderers, however long it takes, and see that they are punished by the authorities.' That has changed my attitude and I am determined to find them and see that they get their just punishment."

It was ironic that criminals killed both Louie's and his first loves. Jeff told Louie of Nicole, and this became a bond for their friendship.

Louie looked through the files for an Annette Coppola and said, "Annette Coppola was arrested on a complaint by an officer in the French Foreign Legion, a Captain Conrad Goree. She was arrested for solicitation, her license was for a bordel and the captain made the statement that she enticed him to his room and then demanded money. Annette's defense was that she was off duty, met the captain for drinks and dinner, and he invited her to his room. She stated that she went for her own pleasure and really liked the captain. In fact, she fell in love with him and she was going with him to Erfoud and had never asked him for money. The captain was more believable, and the desk clerk at the hotel gave evidence that she entered the hotel with him. I went to the un Bordel de Bonheur and spoke with the madam, named Danielle, who said Annette was off duty, however, she had been warned before about solicitation while off duty. The un Bordel de Bonheur, at one time, had problems with complaints from customers about stealing money from their wallets, quoting a price on drinks and services and then overcharging them. They were on the verge of losing their license when the bordel was sold to an American Corporation from your city of New Orleans, the Vieux Carre Corporation. An American, Michael Martel is the President, but someone, I think in New Orleans, owns seventy-five per cent of the stock calls the shots."

"Louie, what does this Danielle look like? Is she an American?"

"No, she is not an American. She is originally from Paris, France. She has dark hair and is about forty-five years old. Tell me something of the person you are looking for and the circumstances surrounding the case."

Jeff gave him the information from the beginning to the present on Mary Alice Bakker.

"Jeff, it has been a long, pleasant and fruitful afternoon. What do you say to having a drink and dinner?"

"Louie, it would be a pleasure. I'll treat to dinner and drinks at the place of your choice."

"Jeff, I think we have a good friendship forming, so let's each pay for our treat, or if you pay for one, I'll pay for another. I'll pay for the first, for I know some places to start and you pick up the check on the next and so on. Would this be agreeable with you?"

"Sure, lead the way."

Louie's automobile was in the police garage and as they approached the car, Jeff noticed that the automobile did not have the charcoal burner in the trunk or a trailer with the charcoal burner. Louie explained that the charcoal burner did not produce as high an octane as gasoline; therefore the lack of power hindered them in high-speed chases.

Louie pulled into a parking lot next to a restaurant with a small sign outside that read in French, Chez Policier Club.

"This is a private club for all employees of the city of Marrakech and the country of Morocco, and their guests. It was formed by members of the police department but has expanded to include all employees of the city and country as honorary members. The name literally means at our house. The admittance to the club is very closely checked and as a guest you must show identification to enter.

We can have a good meal and drinks, however, meeting the opposite sex is not easy, due to the privacy policy. As couples or singles, we come here for food and drinks because the prices are much less than the public restaurants and lounges. Later, we can go to other lounges where the prices are higher but we have had our drinks and don't need to buy as many. Do you understand what I am trying to explain?"

"Yes, there are places in America that are much like this."

After being admitted, they were ushered to a table and they ordered drinks. The club's noise level was low and it was easy to carry on a conversation.

"Jeff, my wife, Necole, and I came here often. We would have a nice dinner, some drinks and go to Chelah for cocktails and dancing. Sometimes we would, I don't know the English word, but gaspiller, sometimes more than we could afford, we would go to Safir an expensive nightclub."

"In America, we would say squander or waste more than you needed to. Louie, you said your wife's name was Nicole. How was it spelled, N-i-c-o-l-e or N-e-c-o-l-e?"

"Necole's name was spelled N-e-c-o-l-e."

"What a coincidence, my fiancée's name was also Nicole, but spelled N-i-c-o-l-e. She was Cajun, which is of French ancestry. They settled in Louisiana over three hundred years ago and were called Acadians or Cajuns for short. They speak a dialect of French, which is what I know a little of.

"I had the same difficulty in adjusting after Nicole's death. I, too, wanted to catch, torture and brutalize the murderers. I worked with the

State of Louisiana Drug and Alcohol Division as an undercover agent. After the murders of Nicole, her brother, Pepe, and his girlfriend, Alma, I felt as you did. The night it happened, Art McGraw, another agent, gave me this advice, 'what happened tonight, you will never forget, and you will remember Nicole always, but time heals and life must go on. To be a good detective you must put even the most personal matters aside. If you don't, it could cost you your own life. I know what you are thinking, life isn't worth living, but it is.' I did have the satisfaction of apprehending the murderer, and it eased the pain some."

They completed their meal and were having coffee when Louie said, "Jeff tomorrow is Saturday. Let's relax and forget about the case until Monday. Casablanca and Marrakech are having a soccer match tomorrow afternoon. I can get some tickets, if you'd like to go."

"Any other time I would be happy to go, but I have to meet someone at the one o'clock train from Casablanca."

"A new love life?"

"No." Jeff explained the situation with Claudette.

"Here is my home telephone number; if you need someone to talk to I'll be home. I may go to the soccer match but I'll be home by five. Why don't you give me a call anyway, say, about five-thirty?"

"Sure, I'll call you. In the morning, I need to call my client in New Orleans."

Louie dropped Jeff off at la Réfugier Hotel at eight o'clock. In the elevator, he all at once felt exhausted; it had been a long day. Inserting the key in the door to his room, he could hear the telephone ringing. *That must be Claudette. I guess she can't make it, after all.*

Chapter Eighteen

He picked up the ringing telephone, "Hello, this is Jeff Stewart."

"Jeff, this is Marshall Bakker. I know it is getting late there, but I have been trying to find you for several days. Have you made any progress?"

"Yes, Sir. I left Casablanca about a week ago and went to Erfoud to check on the dead girl that had Mary Alice's clothes. Sorry it took so long, but it was an eight-hour bus ride and I had to contact a legionnaire five miles out in the desert from Erfoud. He and the police in Erfoud gave me information that brought me to Marrakech. I have been with a detective here who gave me some information, and will help me all he can. I now think Mary Alice may be in Marrakech, but is using another name."

"I called your hotel in Casablanca after you had checked out, then I called the detective that you worked with, Pierre de La Salla, who told me you had gone to Erfoud to check out the girl. He gave me the number of Commander Fosee in Erfoud. Commander Fosee told me you had left for Marrakech and that he thought you might be staying at la Réfugier Hotel. You seem to be on the right track. Jeff, it is imperative that you locate Mary Alice. Some new developments have taken place here. Let me bring you up to date.

"Clifford B. Barnett, the attorney who handled my father's estate, was arrested for misappropriating the assets of some trust funds he managed. One of those was the trust fund that was set up for Mary Alice.

The plantation would be inherited at a specific age, so he could not do anything with it. But other money assets were in negotiable bonds, stocks and rental property. Mr. Barnett sold the rental property and put the money in his own special account. The negotiable bonds and stocks were also sold and the cash was deposited to a different account, but also in his name. After Mr. Barnett was arrested, the money was confiscated and returned to the accounts of the rightful owners. Mary Alice got back all of her money, except about nine thousand dollars. Mr. Barnett's office was sealed, and he was arrested. He made bond and was released, however, he disappeared, forfeiting the bond. He has not been found, but the night of Mr. Barnett's release, his office was torched. The fire started in his file room and was intense, destroying all of his records. Keep on the job and find her as soon as possible."

"Yes, Sir. Would you have some one locally check out a corporation, called the Vieux Carre Corporation? The President is Mike Martel. He owns twenty-five percent of the stock. Here, they do not have a record who the chairman is, only that another person owns seventy-five per cent. The corporation owns an escort service for traveling businessmen, as well as a bordel named un Bordel de Bonheur. Mike Martel was seen in New Orleans about eight months ago with a young, blond woman. The detective here thinks the bordel is tied in with drugs, or at least was at one time. They arrested several patrons who were high on hasish, and admitted to purchasing drugs at the une Masion de Passe. This means the faded house. The name un Bordel de Bonheur means a happy brothel or happy whorehouse. The police were in the process of closing the place down and voiding their license when Mr. Martel made them an offer in the name of Vieux Carre Corporation and promised the police he would run a clean and orderly business. Up to this point they have not had any problems, except Annette Coppola, the girl who was killed in Erfoud.

"Also, get the names of any females in Mr. Barnett's papers, if there is anything left that was not destroyed by the fire, and get a complete background check on Mike Martel, as to who his friends were in business and back through college. With the help of Mr. Louie Bennard, the detective here in Marrakech, I'm sure we'll find Mary Alice. Send me the reports I asked for by aeromail. I know it's expensive, but it would sure speed things up."

"Thank you, Jeff, as soon as the businesses open, I will have someone on your request. Good-bye and be careful."

Jeff went into the bathroom, took a hot bath, hit the sack and slept like a baby until seven AM. When he awoke, the first thing he thought of was of Claudette and what she had to tell him. *If she is pregnant, maybe it was someone before him. I just can't imagine her knowing that it was me that made her pregnant in eight days. Oh, well, I will have breakfast and go meet her and find out the mystery.*

It was a long morning, he walked around the hotel area, sightseeing and watching people in the hotel lobby. A number of beautiful women passed by and they seemed to be staying at the hotel. *Hell, I am in trouble now with women; I'll just go over to the train station.*

Outside of the hotel he got into a carriage and told the driver to take him the long way to the train station.

Chapter Nineteen

It was a long hour before the sound of the train reached him. It was still not in sight, but would arrive at the station in a few minutes.

How should I act, happy, unhappy, puzzled? Well, I can't change anything now so I'll just try to act naturally and try to think straight as she tells her story. Hell, will that train never get here?

The trained pulled in and stopped, people began to get off with their luggage, baskets and animals. *I see she didn't make it. She should have called. Maybe I should have called. Oh, well, I missed a soccer game with Louie.*

Just as he turned to leave he heard a familiar voice, "Hello, Jeff. Over here."

He turned and Claudette was just debarking the coach. *Gosh, she is beautiful. What the hell am I thinking?*

She had only her handbag and a small bag that women carried personal things in.

"Do you have any bags that were checked?"

"No, Jeff. I am going back on the six o'clock train; I can't stay the weekend. Is there anyplace that we can go and talk?"

"Well, we can go to my hotel, not the room, but the lobby or in the lounge. Would that be acceptable?"

Damn, why do I feel so awkward? She is the same girl I was with a week ago, but she is so aloof and cold. Well, what the hell, I'll just be a gentleman and treat her as someone I've just met.

"Sure, Jeff, that would be nice. I would not like to sit on these hard benches all afternoon. How have you been, is everything going well with your investigation?"

Jeff found a carriage and told the driver to take them to la Réfugier Hotel. Luckily, it was the same carriage that had brought him to the train station. He tried to make small talk but the right words would not come out of his mouth. *Why didn't she just tell me on the telephone? It would've been a lot easier. Damn, won't the carriage ever get to the hotel? What will I do for the four or five hours?*

"Jeff, you are quiet. Is everything all right, or are you having some trouble with your investigation?"

"No, everything is fine, except you. I feel as if I don't know you, that you are a perfect stranger, trying to make small talk. When we get to hotel, let's go into the lounge and have a drink. God knows I need one to settle down."

When the carriage pulled up to the hotel, Jeff got out, helped Claudette out, paid the driver and escorted her to the hotel lounge.

"Would you like to have a drink?"

"Yes, I will have my usual vodka martini. Will you have one for old times, Jeff?"

"No, I think I will have a whiskey with a little water on the side. Maybe a double, I think I am going to need it."

After the drinks arrived, Jeff picked up his glass, held it toward Claudette and said, "To a lovely lady, salute."

Claudette did the same and said, "To a gentleman, salute."

After the toast Claudette said, "Jeff, this is the most difficult thing I have ever had to do. That is why I wanted to make the trip down and talk to you in person. Jeff, I want you to know that I truly love you, but I have to tell you something I should have told you when we first met, especially after I began to fall in love with you. I was engaged to be married, but we had some problems and parted ways before I met you. A few weeks after this happened; I fell in love with you. I thought maybe this was a rebound, but later knew it was for real. My boyfriend contacted me and wanted us to get together; I would not.

After you left, he called me and we went out. I had been to the doctor the day before and he told me I was pregnant. I knew the baby was his because I had missed my last period. For the baby's welfare, I agreed to marry him. We will be married tomorrow afternoon. I told him I had a tour this afternoon and would be back on the nine o'clock train. He will pick me up. I am so sorry that this happened, Jeff. I truly love you and will never forget you; I only hope you can forgive me."

Jeff sat there stunned. He felt bad for Claudette, but was relieved, a mountain had been lifted from his shoulders.

"Claudette, I respect your honesty; very few people would be this honest. Although I am losing you, I do wish you the best. I will never forget you, and I know you will be a good wife and mother. I am a nervous wreck and I need another drink. Do you want another one or should you have orange juice?"

"Jeff, that is why I love you. You are so thoughtful. But I can have another one."

"Did you have anything to eat before you left Casablanca, or on the train?"

"Only some fruit."

"Let's order a meal and sip our drinks until the food arrives."

After the meal, they went to the lobby and were talking like old times.

"Jeff, can we go up to your room? I am tired and would like to lay down and rest before the long trip back to Casablanca."

"Sure, you can rest until five, that will give me time to get you to the train station."

In the room Claudette pulled her shoes, blouse and skirt off and lay down on the bed.

Jeff was sitting in the chair when Claudette said, "Jeff, I want you to make love to me one last time."

Jeff was startled. He tried to think of something to say.

"No, Claudette, I love you, but I can't do that. I don't think I can because of the circumstances. I am not a prude, nor am I a very religious man. I only know if I was going to be your husband, and you were pregnant with my child, I would hope someone would not take advantage of a situation such as this. It is now three-thirty. I'll go downstairs while you get some rest and I'll call for you at five to take you to the train station."

"Jeff, I am sorry, I can't help the way I feel. If you would have me, I would marry you now. I know that would be asking the impossible, to have you marry someone carrying another man's child. You are right, maybe if you go downstairs it would be easier on both of us."

Jeff went down to the lounge and asked for a double whiskey, and put very little water in the drink; he needed the kick.

At five o'clock he called upstairs and Claudette answered.

"Are you feeling better now?"

"Yes, and thank you so much. I got carried away. I am fine now; I will be right down."

While waiting for Claudette, he called Louie.

When Louie answered, Jeff said, "Louie, Jeff here. I am at a the hotel getting ready to carry Claudette to the train station."

"Well, what happened, are you going to be a father?"

"No, she is pregnant by her ex-fiancé. I'll tell you the complete story when I see you."

"Jeff, there is a saloon near the train station I need to check out. Wait for me at the station. I'll be there a little after six."

Claudette came down looking as fresh and beautiful as ever. *She doesn't look pregnant; maybe I should have stayed with her. Hell, just get her to the train station on time.*

The tension was gone from both of them, leaving them with somber thoughts of what might have been. The trip to the station was made in silence. After giving Jeff a quick kiss on the cheek, Claudette boarded the train, which left promptly at six.

Chapter Twenty

It was past six-thirty when Louie picked Jeff up and drove a few blocks to Guita's Saloon.

They were seated in a private booth, with three walls that went to the ceiling and curtains that could be drawn for privacy. Louie explained that this saloon was like others throughout Morocco, patterned after the old-fashioned saloons in France. All the wood in the saloon was of heavy walnut or walnut-stained elm. They ordered drinks and the waiter set down a large bowl containing something that looked like snails.

"Jeff, these are escargot. The old saloons of France placed them on the bar and tables, free, to attract customers. Have you eaten them before?"

"Yes, but I have not seen them served this way. How do you peel them?"

"You don't. Take the escargot and put your thumb and forefinger over the opening like this, then crack the shell and pull the escargot out. If you like, dip it into some sauce and eat away."

Three men entered the saloon and went into the booth across from them, closing the curtains.

Louie reached over and closed their curtains, leaving a small opening for viewing.

"Jeff, I have seen one of those men before, I think at the police station. We have found that a number of saloons like this have been meeting places for the bandes. I can't think of it in English, bande with gun, bang, bang?"

"Oh, I get it. You mean, criminals or gangs."

"Yes, that is it. I think that one of those men has something to do with loaning money at higher interest rates than allowed. I had a tip that someone would be here to make trouble. The owner will not pay protection and has asked for help from the police. Another undercover officer is here, but I don't know who it is yet. I just returned home when you called, after being contacted at the soccer game. They told me to be here by seven."

The three men left the booth and walked toward the rear of the building, near the kitchen and office. Louie motioned Jeff to stay while he followed the men. As Louie approached the office he heard loud noises that sounded like furniture being overturned and bodies falling. He tried the door but it was bolted from the inside. He slammed his shoulders against the door until it flew open. A body was on the floor and two men were beating another man. As Louie burst into the room, one man pulled a knife to stab the man being beaten. Louie pulled his pistol, but at that moment was hit on the back of the head and he went out like a light.

Louie awoke to a blazing beam of hazy light shining down on him. Struggling to sit up, he found that he was too weak. Someone put a wet bar towel on his face. The sour smell of the stale alcohol snapped him to consciousness. Looking up he saw several policemen, Jeff, a man being treated by a medic, a man in handcuffs, and two men on the floor, both were badly injured. One looked dead, the other one had bandages across his chest and neck, and lay moaning, apparently in a great deal of pain. Jeff bent down, helped Louie to his feet and over to a chair.

"What happened, Jeff? The last thing I can remember is that a man was on the floor and two others were beating someone up. I pulled my gun and the lights went out. How long was I out?"

"Only a few minutes. The man near you, who is cut up real bad, is dead. He was your undercover man. The other man on the floor is the owner, Herman Nilting. The medic is treating one of the perpetrators whom you shot. The one in handcuffs is the other perpetrator."

"But, Jeff, I don't remember firing my pistol. Are you sure I shot him?"

"Your pistol is the only one found here, the perpetrators all used knives. I have never seen any knives of this type."

Jeff picked up one, holding it with a napkin and showed to Louie.

"That is an Arabian knife that is used by some criminals, maybe Arabs, maybe other people who want us to think they are Arabs. Are you sure there is not another pistol besides mine?"

"Yes, but if you didn't fire the pistol, then one of those two men did."

A police captain was questioning the man with the gunshot wound. Louie interpreted the questions and answers for Jeff. "The man's name is Nevin Rolf. He stated that his partner, Réne Munroe, killed the undercover officer then shot him, after Réne came up from behind and hit me on the head. Asked why his partner wanted him dead, Rolf answered that he knew too much and that the head of the bande organization didn't want him to talk about the Bennard episode."

Louie got very excited and wanted to question Nevin Rolf, but the captain told Louie that Rolf could not be questioned any further at that time. "Wait until later, then you can have a crack at him."

The captain said, "Louie, this is an order. Go home or some place where you can relax tonight and tomorrow. I want you at the office on Monday bright, early and fresh, because there is a lot of work to be done to clear this case."

Jeff said, "He's right, Louie. You do need to relax. Let's got to the Chez Policier Club, have a drink and a good meal and do some talking, OK? It's my turn to pay."

"As soon as I go to the restroom, we will be on our way."

As Louie approached the restroom, he noticed a group of people standing around watching as the medics loaded the wounded into an ambulance. One man, short in stature, wearing a red fez, seemed a little too curious about the activity and was noticeably nervous.

In the restroom, Louie met a detective he knew from the station.

"Albert, a little short man with a red fez is standing around the group outside. Did you notice him?"

"Yes, Louie. I don't know him, but his face and stature looks familiar. I can't place where I have seem him."

"Are you on duty now?"

"Yes, I am. I will be going to the hospital, and as soon as the doctors permit, I will interrogate them."

"Albert, do me a favor. If you find out anything or think of anything about Red Fez, I will be at the Chez Policier Club tonight for dinner and at home tomorrow. I am on the case, but Captain Velous asked me to take it easy and not report until early Monday morning. However, the more I know, the easier it will be to get organized Monday."

"Sure, Louie. You need the rest. Have a good dinner and if I get anything new I'll call you."

On the way to the club, Louie told Jeff about Red Fez. He felt a little suspicious of Albert, nothing he could pin down, he just seemed too friendly.

The club had entertainment on Fridays and Saturdays. Tonight, a well-known band and troupe of belly dancers were the featured act. They arrived early for a Saturday night and were able to get seats near the front.

In a closely-knit organization, news spreads quickly, and friends and acquaintances came by and greeted Louie. After about a half hour, things settled down and Jeff said, "Louie, let's order dinner. I think you know something more than you have said. Would you care to talk about it while we eat?"

After their dinners were ordered, Louie said, "Well, yes and no. There is something I would like to talk about. You see, being a detective, I guess I am suspicious of everyone, but I have a strong feeling I can trust you. You are an outsider and from the reports I have of you, you have your own agenda. Also, we have a lot in common. There has been no one I would trust since I lost Necole. I have to learn to trust again. Maybe it would help me to tell you of my suspicions.

"I didn't know the undercover agent, only that we had someone undercover trying to penetrate, 'le Royaume de Sang.' Loosely, in English, it is 'the Kingdom of Blood.' They are, as you call it, a gang, who deals in loans with excessive interest, extortion, protection, drugs, prostitution and other criminal activities. We have not found out who is, le roi, or the king. We know some of the higher-ups but we do not have enough evidence to arrest them. When I begin to get close to the higher-ups, people start disappearing or are killed. I believe with all my heart that they are responsible for Necole's death."

"Maybe some leads will develop from this episode that will result in you solving the case. On Monday I must get to work on my case. Do you know of anyone that will not charge an excessive fee to go with me and interpret? It would be helpful if they knew the records department of your government. I want to find out if any businesses or property are registered to anyone with last name of Bakker."

"There are a number of people registered with the Policier that will interpret in all languages. I'll check the first thing Monday morning. Visit my office at noon and we will have lunch and I will have some names for you. Let's relax and watch the show. I understand the belly dancers are outstanding."

These dancers were much better than the ones Jeff had seen in Erfoud. The show was unlike anything he had seen in New Orleans. The Arabian girls were beautiful in their costumes with the veils adding mystery. The lights were low, with only candles on the tables. It gave Jeff the impression the show was in a cave in the days of Ali Baba and the Forty Thieves.

"Jeff, what are you doing tomorrow, or I should say later today, as the time is one-thirty?"

"The record department is closed, so I guess I'll look Marrakech over and rest up for Monday morning. Why, do you have something in mind?"

"No, not really. I wanted to check out something before Monday morning. I have two contacts in the Medina section. If you want to see deep inside of Moroccan life, this may be of interest. One contact is a storyteller at Djemaa el Fna. In English this translates to Court of Marvels. This is at the souk. As you say, this place is like Ali Baba and the Forty Thieves, where snake charmers, musicians, storytellers, acrobats and other characters perform, and hustlers, pickpockets and the criminal element try to part people from their money.

"The other contact is at the north edge of Djemnaa el Fna square, where there are hundreds of stalls and shops filled with potters, wood turners, copper bazaars, wool-dyers, metalworkers and other hand made goods. My contact there has a wool shop. He attracts customers from Morocco and all over the world."

"Yes, Louie. Sounds like it would be an interesting experience. Who knows, maybe I can pick up a lead about the American girl. I think I had better get some rest. Are you ready to leave?"

"Yes, I'll pick you up at the hotel at eleven o'clock. Waiter, bring me the check."

"It's my turn to pay. How much tip should I leave?"

"Yes, your turn, and normally about ten per cent."

Chapter Twenty-One

Jeff awoke at seven, took a leisurely bath and shaved. He dressed in a pair of white duck trousers, a light blue shirt with full sleeves, no tie, a pair of dark blue Parisian suspenders he had purchased in Casablanca, and black oxford shoes. When he went down to the dining room, the de maison asked if he would care to have breakfast on the roof garden.

"Yes, that would be nice. How do I get there?"

"I'll call and have a table reserved. When you get on the elevator, push the button 'plafond,' that means roof."

This is an unexpected pleasure. I didn't know there was a roof garden for dining.

When he reached the roof garden, he was seated at a table near the wall on the east side.

As he pulled his watch from his pocket, the fob came loose. *I will get it repaired or a new one at the souk later today. Gee, it is eight-thirty and the sun is up over the mountains. I guess the reason they refer to Marrakech as the Red City is because of all the pink and rose-colored buildings.*

While he was eating his meal, he thought about the time he had spent in Morocco so far. *I have been here about three weeks and each day has been a new experience. What a beautiful view, the snow topped Atlas Mountains in the distance, with the pinkish buildings in between. The local citizens eating here are wearing those colorful gown-like clothes. Let's see, I believe they are called de-jel-bas. Yes, dejelbas. They look hot, but*

Louie said that they are really cool as the clothing holds the moisture inside and keeps the heat outside. Oh, well, I'll go down and wait for Louie.

Jeff was seated in the lobby near the window, watching the traffic pass, when Louie pulled in front of the hotel in his Fiat sedan. Sliding into the seat and greeting Louie, he noticed that Louie was dressed casually in light blue trousers and white shirt with an open collar.

Louie drove down Boulevard el Yarmouk in very light traffic. It was only a little after eleven on Sunday morning. They turned off and passed through a huge archway into the massive clay-colored defensive wall of the Medina section, which is crowded, even on Sundays, with heavily laden donkeys trotting through the sunlit alleys of the Medina. Louie had parked his Fiat at a lot along with camels and donkeys and they continued on foot to the souk. Arriving in the marketplace, Jeff was again amazed at the difference between this country and New Orleans. They came into a large open courtyard with people watching the acrobats, snake charmers, whirling dancers and other entertainers. The water bearers carried their water in a wild boar skin. The skin was removed and left intact, the belly sewed up leaving a hole to pour in the water or other liquids. The snout was open to pour the liquid out. Some had the strong Moroccan tea; others had different flavored waters, which they sold to passersby. Shops and stalls lined the walls on each side of an alley, which was covered by a metal grating. The smaller shops and stalls are cluttered and the owners hang their most colorful and unusual merchandise in the doorways and on the outside walls. Coffee houses, cafes and bars occupy the larger shops. On this day, the souk was crowded with the different Arab and Berber tribes, all in mostly white dejelbas garments, some with white turbans and some with the familiar red fez. Almost all had on the heelless sandals. There were people of many nations all talking in different languages.

Louie guided Jeff along the alleyways until he came to a doorway that was covered with a lightweight colorful carpet. Pulling the carpet aside, they entered a large room that was dimly lighted. At a corner table near the bar was a very large gentlemen that weighed in the range of three hundred-fifty to four hundred pounds. The gentleman was dressed in neatly pressed light gray trousers, white shirt, no tie and the traditional red fez.

Louie went over to the man and said, "Bonjour, Jacque. How are you on this beautiful day?"

"Bonjour, friend Louie, it has been a long time. Has crime ceased in our fair city, you haven't visited us recently?"

"No, the crime has not ceased. I have been extremely busy. Jacque, I would like for you to meet my friend from New Orleans in America. This is Jeff. Jeff, this is Jacque, who is the proprietor of this fine establishment, 'Sheikhdom du Jacque,' or Jacque's Kingdom."

"Welcome to the Sheikhdom. Have a seat and have a drink on the house. What will you gentlemen have?"

Louie said, "I'll have a vodka with a twist of lime. What will you have Jeff?"

"If you have whiskey, I will take that with a little water on the side."

Calling a waiter, Jacque said to Jeff, "I have a very fine whiskey from America. Would you like to have Jacque Daniels?"

"Sure, how did you get Jack Daniels over here?"

"I have connections with some people in New York."

After the drinks were delivered to the table, Louie said, "Jacque, we need some help," and he related the incident that happened the night before.

"Do you know of a Réne Munroe or Nevin Rolf?"

"Yes, and I dislike them both. They were in to see me to 'protect' my establishment."

"From who or what?" Jeff asked.

"They informed me that for 7,500 francs a month, no one would set fire or have fights or wreck all of the furniture. If a fire happened to break out, me being fat, may not be able to leave quickly enough and could get badly burned, or maybe die. I asked if I had to pay all of the money at one time and he said I could pay one half on the first and one half on the fifteenth. I asked them to wait while I go for the money and ordered them a drink. I went into the back and summoned my manager, Abdul Fahman. I asked Abdul to get two more fellows and go out to the table where I would be with the two men. When I nodded my head, they were to seize the two men and when I finished speaking with them, to take them in the back room and beat the hell out of them, bruise them, leave marks on their faces and bodies, then just show them their knives and throw the scums out in the gutter. I came back in and told the men that I had to send one of my managers to the banco to get the money; he should be back shortly. In a few minutes, Abdul and his two helpers came in. I nodded my head, and they seized the men and pinned their arms. I just sat there with my big fat ass in the chair. I motioned Abdul to bring them close to me. One of them, I think Réne, asked if I knew who his boss was. I said I did but in this part of the Kasbah I was the boss, and I was going to give him and his friend a small sample of what his boss could expect if they came back to this area. I told them that this was my area, and the next time he or anyone entered the Kasbah with merde like this they would be dead. Then I put my foot onto a chair and Abdul hit Réne in the belly and when he bent over, he made Réne kiss the bottom of my shoe. I nodded my head, and Abdul and the others took them into the back room and really gave them a beating. When they finished, they carried them to the alley and dropped them in the gutter. While they were still in the gutter, I had the janitor remove the pail from the toilet and pour the pisser on them. That was three months ago and I have not had a problem since."

"Jacque, if everyone who was approached by people like this, reacted the same way, my job would be much easier. You have been a great help to me. Let me buy you a drink. My friend, Jeff, is a private investigator and he is seeking a young lady. Jeff, give Jacque some details of the young lady."

Jeff related to Jacque the story of Mary Alice Bakker up to this point in his investigation.

"Jeff, a few years ago, an American by the name of Bakker owned a villa and used to have lavish parties. He would hire some of my girls to serve as escorts for his guests. I never met him, but my manager did. The manager is in Agadir for a few days on business. Come back about Wednesday, maybe he will remember more of the details."

"Thank you, Jacque. I like your place. You will see me often. If you don't mind, I'll sort of work out of here."

"Fine with me. Tell you what; see that table behind me near the wall? I'll reserve that for you. I need to go in the back and rest, the old fat man is tired. I will see you again soon."

Jeff and Louie moved over to the table Jacque spoke of. As Jacque was leaving, he stopped at the bar and spoke to the manager and pointed at their table.

"Well, Jeff, I see you have made a friend and he will be a good friend if you play fair with him. Let's finish our drinks and walk around the souk and see what is going on."

Walking along the alley, which was dimly lighted by the sun shining through the grated cover, the smells of mutton and fish cooking, leather tanning, and the sour smell of wool being dyed, filled the air.

What a difference six weeks has made in my life, since I left New Orleans.

Back in the open area, they stopped and watched the storyteller at work. Jeff could not understand the story, but people laughed and applauded. *Damn, he must be good.* When he finished his story, they walked over and Louie introduced him to the storyteller, Karim.

"Karim, have you seen anyone that has been trying to sell protection to any of the merchants, or wanted to sell or buy hashish? I am especially interested to know if Réne Munroe or Nevin Rolf have been active in this part of the Medina."

"No, Louie. I have not seen either of them around here, but over at Jemaa el-Fna, in the La Gazelle bar, I did see Nevin Rolf and two German officers having drinks and an animated conversation. I could not hear what they were saying but by the hand gestures, it was heated. I have seen them a number of times at the same bar."

"Thank you, Karim. Keep telling those good stories."

"Jeff, let's go by the La Gazelle Bar and have a drink, then we will call it a day, so we can get a good night's sleep."

"Fine with me. Today has been a great experience and I have enjoyed it."

The La Gazelle was designed on the order of Guita's Saloon, except the bar was much larger and there were more tables in the open. A small band was set up at the edge of the dance floor. They asked for a seat in the open room and were escorted to a table right in the center.

At this time of the afternoon, there were only six people at the tables, and twelve at the bar. They could not see into the booths. At the bar were two German officers and two others were seated at a table.

The waiter came over and Louie said, "My name is Louie and this is Jeff. My friend Karim, the storyteller, recommended this establishment as a friendly place with lots of foreign visitors. Jeff is from America and is looking for his sister who ran away from home over a family dispute. She is an American, a petite blond, very pretty. My friend Karim said that he had seen a girl of this description with a German officer last week. Have you noticed a young lady of this description with or without a German officer?"

"No, I haven't. I would have noticed if she were here with a German officer and I don't remember seeing a girl like that here, alone or with anyone else."

"What is your name?"

"Doran."

"Doran, why would you remember someone with a German officer?"

"I dislike Germans. The officers act superior to everyone else. I wish they would lose the war they started with France and get the hell out of Morocco. I'll get your drinks now, Sir."

"Louie, a German must have mistreated Doran; he is so bitter toward them."

"Probably a German picked up his girlfriend. I will go along with his dislike of the Germans and see if we can pick up anything else."

Doran returned with the drinks.

"Thank you, Doran. You know, I too dislike the Germans. I agree that they think they are much superior to us Frenchman. My ex-girlfriend went out with one, and she said he had lots of money to spend, more than she thought he made as a German officer. She learned that he was in the bande and made extra money intimidating business owners. She wanted me to earn extra money and when I refused she broke up with me. Would you know how I could get in touch with one of them?"

"Some of the German officers that come in here are not German officers."

"What do mean, German officers are not German officers?"

Doran leaned in close to Louie and said in a low voice, "There are some bande who have acquired German officer's uniforms and pretend to be German Nazi SS Officers. They approach German soldiers with French or Moroccan girls and shake them down, by accepting money to let them go. They go into businesses, and intimidate the business owners so they'll pay protection money to keep the German soldiers from fighting and destroying the place.

"See that German officer that just sat down at the end of the bar? Well, he is in here often, sometimes with a girl or another officer. I have to get busy or I will lose my job."

"Jeff, let's order another one and slowly sip it and see what will happen."

About ten minutes later, a nice looking brunette came in and the German officer and the brunette went into a booth. Louie motioned for Doran, and when he came over Louie said, "Escort us to the booth across from where the German officer and the brunette are seated."

After some fifteen minutes of not being able to hear what the couple was saying, Louie said, "Jeff, this might be dangerous, and if you don't want to get involved just say no. I want to go over to the booth and get tough with them and if necessary force them out the rear door, if there is one."

"Louie, I am with you. First, I will go back to the toilet to check for a rear door while you keep an eye on them. I'll be back in just a minute."

Going to the back, Jeff quickly saw a door, but it had a lock that looked secure. He eased around the corner near the kitchen. There, another door that was used to carry out the garbage was unlocked. Going back to the booth he described where the door was.

"Follow me to the booth and we will play it by hunches."

Louie went across the hall to the other booth with Jeff following. With one hand Louie drew his gun and the other hand quickly pulled the curtain back and surprised the couple as he slid in the booth beside the German officer, jabbing the gun into his ribs. Jeff slid in besides the brunette.

"You speak French?"

"Yes."

"You speak German?"

"Very Little."

"This is a surprise, a German officer in the German Army who speaks very little German. Where is your partner and don't tell me you don't have one, for I know you do? I just want to know where he is."

"I will meet with him later."

"Where?"

"I don't know yet."

"What is your name and what is the name of the brunette?"

"My name is Andre and this is my girlfriend, Marie. We are here on a date."

"Look ami, no more la merde. I know you are not a German soldier, but a dix franc henchman. What is your connection to Le Royaume le Sang? You have one opportunity to tell me. Now, what is the connection?"

"I have no connection."

"Jeff, take the girl and lead the way to the rear door."

Jeff clasped the brunette's arm, squeezed tight, pulling her after him.

Louie slid out of the booth and motioned Andre with his gun to come out. After he eased out of the booth, Louie pushed Andre in front of him as he pushed the gun barrel in the center of his back and pushed him after Jeff and the brunette to the rear door. After going out the door, Louie closed it and told Andre to bring the garbage cans over and place them behind the door. As soon as he finished, Louie hit Andre on the side of his head with the gun, almost knocking him to the pavement.

"My ami, that is a small sample of what you are in for. The same will happen to your girlfriend. Now, answer me. Who is your patron in the le Royaume le Sang?"

"I don't know."

Louie half turned toward the brunette and with a long sweeping swing of his arm, struck her head with the back of his hand, knocking her to the pavement. She began to whimper. Jeff reached down and pulled her to her feet and backed her against the building.

"Now, Andre, it will be your turn again and then hers. Now, who is your patron?

Jeff thought, *the word patron is employer or boss.*

"I receive my orders from Réne Munroe. I honestly have no knowledge where he gets his orders. I have not met anyone higher than Réne Munroe, I have only heard the first name of Réne's patron."

"What is that name? Are you sure you have not met him?"

"It is Albert and I have never met him or seen him, to know who he is."

"Give me your address and the brunette's address and it better be correct or I will seek you out no matter how long it takes and the results, when I find you, will not be pleasant."

Andre gave Louie an address and Louie ordered the two to begin walking down the alley toward the street. They disappeared from sight.

Louie and Jeff walked back in La Gazelle and sat in the booth. Louie summoned Doran for the bill, leaving him a generous tip and thanking him for his information and help.

Chapter Twenty-Two

Jeff awoke early on Monday morning to another beautiful day. The sky was a brilliant blue and the morning temperature was in the low 80's. He had ample time for a leisurely breakfast before going to Louie's office at noon. *It's too nice a day to stay in the hotel until noon. I'll go to the roof garden for breakfast and walk around the area for some exercise.*

Jeff spent about two hours walking and window-shopping. He purchased a shirt, tie and socks at one Marrakech's larger department stores, La Favette de Parisian.

When he left La Favette de Parisian, he was completely turned around and had lost his sense of direction. He pulled his watch out to check the time and noticed the watch fob was missing, so he went back into the store to find the watch repair department. While discussing the purchase of the fob, a young man standing nearby, who spoke very bad broken English, asked if he could be of help.

"Yes, after the repairman attaches the fob, I need to go to the la Réfugier Hotel. Could you direct me?"

"Yes, me have a voiture, you know, with de cheval, clop clop, uh horse."

"A horse and a carriage. How much to carry me to the hotel?"

"Oh, Monsieur, low price. Twenty francs."

The repairman had fastened the new fob and Jeff followed the young man to the carriage stand where a number of carriages and taxis were lined up. Jeff had gone out another entrance and that is where he got turned around. The young man directed Jeff to a white carriage, trimmed in gold, with the top down. Jeff noted that the gold-trimmed white seats were leather, probably camel leather.

The carriage made a U-turn on the busy boulevard. The heavy traffic slowed or stopped until they were in the outside lane heading in the opposite direction.

The driver turned around and said, "My name is Jules. I know Marrakech all over. I be guide for you? I take you to good places, restaurants, club, and girls and drink places. I price very cheap."

"Well, Jules, you may have a customer if you are fair, but if I think you are taking an advantage of me, I have a friend in the policier. How long will it take you to get me to the policier at 1415 Rue Ksour?"

"From hotel to policier, twenty or thirty minutes."

Looking at his watch, Jeff noted the time was eleven. "Let me take the clothing that I purchased to my room at the hotel and we will go to the policier station. I am having lunch at twelve with my friend who works there."

On the way to the policier station, Jules asked if he wanted to see some nightlife. "I have places with lots of girls to meet and have you a grand time."

Maybe I can get a lead. "Jules, do you know a bordel that has American girls? I have been gone from America a long time and would like to associate with an America girl so I can converse and understand her. Later you can take me to where the French and Arabian girls are."

"Yes, I do that. What time do you want me pick you up? I wait at the policier for you?"

"No, don't wait. Pick me up from the hotel at seven PM and I will see what you have."

"Will do. No carriage, I have automobile for tonight."

At the information desk, Jeff asked for Louie and was directed to his office on the second floor.

"Good morning, Jeff, I have made arrangements for an interpreter to meet us at a café for lunch. Shall we go?"

"Yes, I'm anxious to get to the enregister bureau and see if I can find anyone by the name of Bakker."

"Don't discount the remarks made by Jacque. He may operate a saloon, but he is straightforward with his friends. I think I am a friend and he seems to like you. To assign you a table shows that he does. You may search the license bureau for a bordel and escort service that might be registered in that name or any name that would be used as an alias."

They were seated at the café when an attractive, well-groomed woman approached the table and spoke to Louie.

"Jeff, I am pleased for you to meet Paulette. Paulette, this is Jeff."

"Hi, Paulette. I am glad to meet you."

Jeff looked into the bluest eyes he had ever seen. The eyes were surrounded by a pretty face with an extra smooth, light complexion, and set into the waviest natural blond hair he had ever seen. As he scanned her face, he saw it was small and perfectly shaped, with a sensuous mouth. Looking down further, he saw a petite body with curves in the right places. She wore a dress showing just enough cleavage.

"Hello to you Jeff. It is a pleasure to be working with you." *My, I hope I can keep my mind on business. Louie shouldn't have done this to me.*

After lunch was finished, Paulette said, "Jeff, are you ready to go to the enregister bureau?"

"Yes, Paulette. Louie, I'll call you later."

Outside, they went to a parking lot where Paulette had a small Fiat. Pulling his lanky legs inside, he was humped over to keep his head from rubbing the top.

Paulette gunned the engine, and the car took off down the boulevard, expertly weaving in and out of traffic.

Arriving at a large building that looked as if it were a courthouse, Paulette parked and they went to the second floor.

"Paulette, I want to look for the records of property owners, starting ten years ago. I am interested in a person by the name of Anthony Marshall Bakker purchasing any property. Also, if he owned any business or was ever arrested."

"Yes, Jeff. We will have to visit several departments. This will take all afternoon and maybe we will have to spend some time tomorrow."

"OK, is there anything I can do?"

"Yes, as I ask for the record books, carry them to the table over there, and when I finish, bring them back to the clerk."

The clerk placed the first book on the counter. Jeff saw why he needed to carry it to the table for her. The book was about thirty inches wide and twenty inches tall by five inches thick. All entries were handwritten.

Paulette worked rapidly, scanning the pages and making notes for two hours. She announced that she had some information but would need to go upstairs to the business bureau, where another hour was spent. It was now four-thirty and the bureau closed at five.

"Jeff, we do not have time to check the policier records today. If I picked you up at nine in the morning would that too early?"

"No, Paulette. You may pick me anytime, earlier if you prefer, if the bureau opens that early."

"The bureau opens at eight o'clock. Would eight be good for you?"

"Eight o'clock will work for me."

"Fine. I'll drop you off at your hotel. Where are you living?"

"At la Réfugier."

"That is a good hotel and the lounge is nice."

"Would you like to stop by for a drink to relax some?"

"OK, for one drink. I have a date tonight and will not have time for more than one."

In the lounge, Paulette ordered a glass of wine, while Jeff ordered his usual whiskey and water.

"Salute, Paulette. Thank you for the work you did today. You are quite fast."

"Salute, to you Jeff. I wish to help you complete your mission."

After some small talk, Paulette finished her wine and got up to leave. Jeff walked her to her automobile, went upstairs to bathe and change clothes. When he finished, it was six-thirty; he walked outside for some fresh air before Jules arrived.

Slowly walking and window shopping, he was approached by a women in a tight, short dress with the neckline low enough to reveal about half of her breasts.

"Bonjour, Monsieur, du vous vouloir sauter une femme?"

"Sorry, I don't understand. I speak very little Francais."

"Oui, you are English?"

"American."

Jules drove up just then and walked over to the woman. They engaged in a short conversation, and then she turned and walked down the street.

"Jeff, that was une pouffiasse. I think you call her bad girl uh, yes, a slut. No good to pick up on the streets. I take you to nice place when you are ready."

Jules had on a nice suit with a tie. How much do you charge for the evening as a guide?"

"Oui, I take good care that you see the best shows and places until one AM for 500 francs."

Let's see, five hundred francs at seventy-five francs for a dollar, is about six and a half dollars.

"OK, Jules. Do you know a restaurant and lounge where American girls go?"

"There is a restaurant lounge where some American girls go, also an element of characters hang out; you may not like some of them."

"Are they gangsters or rowdy? I think you may say chahuteur."

"No gangsters or chahuteur, but some of them are odd, men and women, I not know the English words."

"OK, Jules, let's go. We may not stay long, but I would like to check it out."

Arriving at the Qurik Restaurant and Lounge, they were seated in a booth along the wall with a good view of the stage. Jules asked Jeff, "What you want to drink?"

"I normally drink whiskey with water, however, this is a new experience. What is your favorite drink?"

"I like the Cognac, as you English say, highball."

"Jules, I am an American, not English. I will take a Cognac highball with a little carbonated water and a twist of lemon."

I will sip it and not chug-a-lug it down like on my first one.

The drinks arrived and after a salute, Jeff began to sip his drink. Hmm, I could get to like this; it gives that warm feeling quickly.

The floorshow started and the first act was a man and woman slow dancing. As the music tempo picked up to a moderate beat, and the dancers responded. The music continued to get faster and the dancers kept up with the beat, while removing pieces of clothing, until they were totally nude. Still dancing, they began to fondle each other until they were aroused. You could tell by looking at the male. The audience began applauding and shouting, "baiser-baiser-baiser." Jeff asked Jules what baiser meant, and he said, "I don't know the American word, but it is to do this. Balling up his left hand into a fist and his open right hand he made a slapping sound and a motion that Jeff interpreted as having sex. Then the male threw the female on the floor and went for it as the curtain closed.

The show's next act was two girls dancing. As they danced, they began removing their clothing until they were completely naked, to the applause of the audience. They began to kiss and fondle each other. The louder the applause, the more vulgar their gyrations became. Just short of the sexual act, the curtains closed to the screams of the audience. "Encore, encore."

New Orleans was never like this.

Then two men came out who danced and also stripped, but stopped short of the sex act.

A comedian was next, but Jeff could only pick up a word or two. During this period, his eyes roamed around the room, looking at people having a good time. As his eyes reached the corner of the opposite wall, he saw a face that looked familiar. The show was over for now, and the lights came up, but the curtain closed on the booth across the opposite wall. By now, Jeff realized the club was a queer and lesbian hangout. He also noticed a transvestite. He asked Jules, "Are there any straight people here? I thought there would be some American girls, but I have not seen any."

"All types of people come here, but a great many tourists come in. Look over by the back wall. See those four girls? They are tourists."

A commotion erupted on the opposite wall. A number of people were fighting.

Damn, they are three women.

"Jules, let's get the hell out of here. I don't want to get messed up in a brawl."

They got the waiter's attention and asked for the check. The waiter took his time and by the time he returned with the check, the policier had arrived and quieted the crowd down. Jeff paid and they quickly made their way to the door. The policier had the three women in handcuffs and was leading them out.

My God, one of them is Paulette.

"I wonder what they were arrested for?" he asked Jules.

"They are females lovers. I think you call them 'odd.' Two of them are fighting over the other one."

It was only eleven, but Jeff had had a long day.

"Jules, take me to the hotel. I will call it a night."

"You want me get you in the morning?"

"I have your telephone number. If I go out tomorrow, I'll call you."

Undressed and laying in bed, watching the neon lights illuminate the wall of his room in red, blue and white, he tried to put things in order.

Tonight was a bust on getting any type of information. I don't know if I want to use Jules or not, I am not sure he understands what I want. Hell, I'm not sure of what I want except to find Mary Alice Bakker.

He had trouble getting to sleep, however, he awoke early and went up to breakfast. A misty rain was falling, the first to interrupt the scenic view at breakfast time. Up on the roof garden, they rolled open a canopy to cover some of the areas. Seated next to a wall and the railing, the view was still outstanding. While taking in the view, the waiter appeared.

"Mr. Stewart, you have an overseas call waiting for you in your room."

"Tell them to hold on, I will be there in a minute."

Not waiting for the elevator, he rushed down the stairs to his room where Marshall Bakker was on the line.

"Jeff, Marsh Bakker here. I wanted to get you before you left the hotel. The seven hour difference makes it difficult to call. It is two AM here now.

"I have checked the Vieux Carre Corporation. The president, Mike Martel, is from a prominent family here in New Orleans. Michael Martel was a fair student, and could have been very successful, except he loved to have a good time and craved excitement. His friends said, in college he majored in girls, beer and golf in that order. He was last seen with a blond, a Susan Whitehurst, in the Vieux Carre. The Whitehurst girl stated that she dated Mike a couple of times and has not seen him since. The chairman of the board of Vieux Carre is a Catherine Ledbetter and she owns seventy-five percent. Catherine's last known address was the St. Charles Hotel. Now, here's an odd coincidence, or maybe not. Clifford Barnett, the same attorney who embezzled Mary Alice's money and disappeared, represents her. Catherine Ledbetter does not have a police record, nor have we found a birth certificate with that name in the Louisiana Health Department.

"We found some charred papers in Mr. Barnett's files that had part of an address, Boulevard de Santi, Marra. It was on a piece of scorched paper and I can only assume that the Marra is for Marrakech.

"Oh, one other thing. Mike Martel purchased an airline ticket to New York under the name Mike Wertal, that is we think it was he. Have you any further information since I last spoke with you?"

"Yesterday I was at the enregister bureau, which is like our courthouse, and I have an address that I am going to check out this morning. Through a detective here in Marrakech that I have become friends with, an element of the underworld told us an American who had used his company for service was named Bakker. After I finish at the enregister bureau, I will try to contact the person and follow it up."

"Fine, Jeff, keep up the good work. I hope we can find Mary Alice soon."

Paulette was waiting when Jeff went downstairs.

"I asked the clerk to call your room, but he told me your were on an overseas telephone call. Are you ready to go?"

"Yes, how was your evening?"

"It was very nice, except I tripped on a step and my left cheek hit the doorway. It is nothing, a little bruise. How was your evening?"

"It was pleasant. I had dinner and a few drinks and went to bed."

"Would you mind if we stopped for breakfast? I overslept and did not want to be late for you."

"Swell, I was just sitting down to order breakfast when I received the overseas call and I haven't had anything to eat."

Paulette pulled into a lot and they went inside a small café and ordered breakfast. While waiting, Jeff asked, "What did you get from the enregister bureau yesterday?"

"I have the address of where an Anthony Marshall Bakker purchased a villa about ten years ago."

Damn, why didn't she tell me this last evening, I could have asked Mr. Bakker when he called this morning. I should have asked. I guess I had her on my mind and she turned out to be lesbian.

"What was the address of the property that he purchased?"

"It was 13913 Boulevard de Santi."

Could this be the same address that Marshall told me, Boulevard de Santi?

After breakfast, Paulette drove back to the enregister and looked to see if Anthony Marshall Bakker had anything listed in the policier blotter.

After an hour Paulette said, "The policer was called to a villa owned by an Anthony Marshall Bakker, six years ago April, 1933 for a group of people fighting. It states here two people were arrested, and again in July 1933, a person was arrested for crashing a private party. The one that was arrested stated that he was contacted to bring three prostitutes to a wild party and stayed to protect their interests. I have found no other record under Bakker. Are there any other names you would want me to search?"

"Yes, if you have time before the enregister closes for lunch, would you check to see who lives at 13913 Boulevard de Santi? Afterwards we can have lunch. I would like to go to the Medina to an establishment named, Sheikdom du Jacque."

At lunch, Paulette informed Jeff that Catherine Ledbetter owned the villa at 13913 Boulevard de Santi. The deed had been transferred from Anthony Marshall Bakker's estate some eight months earlier.

"I also checked for the corporate officers of the Vieux Carre Corporation and the only person known to live in Marrakech is the president, Mike Martel, whose address is 13913-B Boulevard de Santi. The letter denotes an apartment or a separate dwelling on the same property.

That is odd. Anthony Marshall Bakker was Mary Alice's grandfather and he's been dead for years. The villa's deed was transferred after the disappearance of Mary Alice. Who is Mike Martel and what happened to Mary Alice Bakker? Where is she?

"Shall we go to the Sheikdom du Jacque?" asked Paulette.

"Yes, maybe it will not be too busy at this time and Jacque will have time to give me some information."

"I have never been to this establishment, but have heard of it. You get around, to have been there and know the proprietor personally."

"I was introduced to him by Louie, who is a personal friend, and he invited me to drop by anytime."

After parking Paulette said, "I know approximately the location of the street. If you recognize any of the streets or shops let me know."

Ten minutes later Jeff recognized the street and as they turned the corner, the sign of Sheikdom du Jacque appeared.

After entering the Shiekdom, Jeff saw Jacque sitting on his throne, an oversized chair, and his bulk of nearly four hundred pounds, wearing his red fez and a goatee that he had begun growing since Jeff's last visit. He wore a white Egyptian cotton dejelbas and his presence dominated the room.

"Good morning, Jacque. How are you? I would like to introduce you to my friend Paulette. Paulette, this is Jacque."

"Well, my good friend, I see that you have found one our fair beauties, or is this the lady you were searching for?"

"No Jacque, Paulette is an interpreter that Louie recommended. Do you know of anyone who might have had any contact with any American girls?"

"When you and Louie were here, my manager who had some contact with the Bakker group was in Agadir. He is back now."

Jacque told the waiter to ask Dave to come out.

After the introductions, Dave, Paulette and Jeff went over to the table that Jacque had reserved for him.

Paulette interpreted the conservation between Dave and Jeff.

"A couple years or so past, our escort service was contacted to furnish six girls, three Americans and three Arabians who would mingle with the guests. They told us there would be six males, and they wanted a troupe of Arabian dancers for entertainment, also a bartender. We made the arrangements. I went with the troupe to see that they were taken care of and to collect the money. The person who gave me the deposit said Monsieur Bakker would pay the balance.

"I met Mr. Bakker, who had six guests, two Americans, one Englishman and three Egytians. We arrived at seven o'clock, about thirty minutes before the meal started. The guests were having cocktails and hors d'oeuvres when we arrived. After the introductions were made, they paired off, the three Egyptians with the American girls, the Arabian girls with the other three guests.

"The troupe of Arabian dancers was an independent group and was called on as needed. The six escort girls were on our payroll and out of un Bordel de Bonheur, which we owned at that time. The party progressed very well, everyone was having a fine time, when one of our girls, one of the Americans, came out of an upstairs room, ran down the stairs screaming, 'I'll do most anything but I will not let him do it to me in the butt. The pig pinned me down and forced me to lay him in this fashion. I am leaving.'

"She ran out of the door, into the street and disappeared. Approximately thirty minutes later the policier arrived and the owner, Mr. Bakker, informed them that the girls worked for me and I was arrested. When Jacque went to the policier department the next day and spoke with the authorities, the charges were dropped. We had problems with the un Bordel de Bonheur, because we could not find a good manager. The authorities had begun proceedings to close the place down, when an American made Jacque an offer. He accepted the offer so that he could concentrate on his businesses here in the Medina."

"Dave, did you or Jacque see the person who purchased the business?"

"No, it was handled entirely by the attorneys. However, while I was in Agadir, I met two beautiful women from Marrakech. One was originally from Paris and the other was an American. I received the impression that the Parisian girl knew something about the un Bordel de Bonheur."

"In what way did she give you this impression?"

"In a conversation with them, I mentioned that at one time I had managed an escort service that had a couple of American girls working there. The Parisian girl said that she had American clientele from un Bordel de Bonheur who were very good clients. I asked what affaire she was in and she answered that she was a tour guide. She never alluded to the subject again."

Paulette asked, "Did the American girl say what she did or the reason she was in Agadir?"

"No, I assumed that she had just arrived. She stated she was on vacation and was enjoying the beach, because it had been some time since she had been to a beach. She was very friendly."

"Did you get their names?"

"Yes, the American's name is Janice and the Parisian is Michelle."

Jeff thanked Dave and asked if he would like to have a drink. He said he had to get back to work and would send the waiter over.

Over the drinks, Jeff asked Paulette, "Do you think the girls in Agadir have any connection with un Bordel de Bonheur or the missing Mary Alice Bakker?"

"I doubt it very much and it will be tough to trace them. We can go to the un Bordel de Bonheur and I'll act as your interpreter. You do not understand one word of French, but are inquiring of a missing American girl who worked at the Bordel."

Some forty-five minutes later, Paulette parked the little Fiat at the curb of a pink Moorish style building. Jeff opened the door, turning his body to the right, swinging his legs out of the Fiat and lowering his head, he unfolded his tall, lanky body out of the Fiat.

Jeff turned to Paulette and said, "This is odd, a female and a male going into a house of prostitution. Do think it will look suspicious?"

"Maybe, but these houses get all types of requests so nothing is a surprise to them."

Knocking on the door, a buxom peroxide blond who appeared to have had a rough forty-five or so years, answered the door.

Paulette, "Are you the Madam?"

"Yes, how may I be of service?"

"My name is Paulette and I am the interpreter for Monsieur Stewart. He would like to inquire about someone. He will pay a fee for your information."

"My name is Danielle and I will give information as long as it does not put any of our employees or clients in jeopardy. Let's go to the parlor."

They passed through an entrance that had deep red felt wall covering, into a parlor that was also decorated in deep red, black and gold, with ornate sofas and chairs. The table lamps had multicolored glass panel shades and on the wall were gaslights that had been converted to electric lights, with small wattage bulbs. It was a rather large room, presently occupied by two couples. An old Victrola was playing some French music or at least music that Jeff did not recognize. As Paulette, Danielle and Jeff entered, one couple departed for the staircase. Danielle seated them in the far corner near the Victrola where they could not be overheard. Just as they were seated, Danielle went to the Victrola and gave the handle six or eight turns on the crank, before returning to Jeff and Paulette.

Paulette interpreted for Jeff. "Madam, do you have any American's employed here at this time?"

"Yes, I have one girl, a redhead about thirty years old from the city of Chicago."

"In the last year have you had any other girls from America working here?"

"Yes, two other girls worked for a short time. One, a blond girl, later took a job as a companion to a sheik near Erfoud."

Jeff's heart pounded a little faster as he asked the next question, "What was her name and do you know what part of America she was from?"

"Her name was Frances DuBois and was from Spokane, Washington."

"Madam, did you ever hear her speak of Mary Alice Bakker or New Orleans, Louisiana?"

"No, she spoke very little of her life."

After a number of other questions that did not reveal any useful information, Jeff paid Madam Danielle. As she escorted them to the door a thought flashed through Jeff's mind.

"Madam Danielle, did you know an Annette Coppola?" *I will bluff this one.* "She worked here at one time."

"Yes, the poor girl fell in love with a client, a captain in the French Foreign Legion, and went to him to marry. I heard later that she was murdered. I don't believe the captain did it."

"She had on some clothing, labeled made in America. Do you know where or how she got the clothing and why do you think the captain did not kill her?"

"Well, Monsieur Stewart, a person from Casablanca that Annette said was an old boyfriend came by and she asked for the night off. When they returned they had a loud argument out front. Her friend said in a loud, angry voice in Italian, 'You dirty slut, if you tell anyone, I will trace you down and kill you for that.' About two weeks later he came by and asked for her and one of the girls said she went to Erfoud."

"Did you hear a name that she called him, and what about the clothing?"

"She called him Neno or something like that. She may have received some clothing from the, 'à la mode Maxine.' Sometimes they have American clothing and they sell slightly used fashions at a bargain. The girls sometimes buy slightly used clothing or the DuBois girl may have given them to her."

After Paulette asked for and received the address of à la mode Maxine they departed.

The hour was getting late and Jeff asked Paulette if she would care to have dinner with him.

"Yes, that would be nice. There is a small Italian restaurant just around the corner. We can stop there if you like."

"Sounds good, let's do it."

After they were seated, Jeff asked if she would like a glass of wine.

"Yes, it has been a long day and I missed my sleep last night. After dinner I am going home and go to bed."

They made light conversation during the meal while consuming more wine.

"Jeff, I must tell you that you have been the most perfect gentleman. You have not tried to do as most men, give a female a few drinks and get her into bed. Thank you."

"Paulette, you are beautiful woman and I am happy to be seen with you but I would never try anything unless the person gave some indication she was interested. You have been a perfect lady and a pleasure to do business with."

"Jeff, maybe I am exhausted and the wine is getting to me. You have been honest with me, so I will be with you. I wish that things were different with me. I think we would make a nice couple. However, that can't be. You see I like women. You are the only man I thought I could change for, but I know I can't. Last night my lover and I had a big fight at a club and I was arrested. That bruise that I told you I received from a fall. Well, it was from a fist. I am feeling sorry for myself and thought how nice it would be to be like other women and have a nice man like you, but it will never be."

"Paulette, we can be friends. We do not have to be lovers. If it would help you, I'll go home with you and sit in a chair and you can talk until you fall asleep, then I will quietly leave."

"Thank you, Jeff. You are a good friend and having someone listen to me would be nice."

Jeff walked into the bathroom and looked at his watch, it was eleven forty-five. He covered Paulette with a blanket and quietly eased out of her apartment, making sure the door was locked and headed for la Réfugier.

Chapter Twenty-Three

Over their second cognac cocktail while planning their trip to Agadir, Maxine said, "I just remembered, I have two discount coupons for the Medina Palace. I got them last year, when my boyfriend and I were in Agadir. We stayed at the Satife, next door to the Medina Palace, but I admired the Medina so much that I went over one afternoon and looked around.

"The hotel design is similar to a Moorish palace, with a huge lobby and large rooms. The restaurant is roomy, with high ceilings and several palm trees in the center, and the lounge is out of this world. The bar is shaped in an S curve approximately seventy-five feet long.

"We went to a show there one night. The stage is about four feet high with a large dance floor directly in front of it. They have excellent floorshows with entertainers who have played at the some of the finest establishments in Paris. One of the more memorable acts was the dolphin show. A huge water tank rolled from under the stage covering the dance floor. The hotel is on the Atlantic Ocean with the beaches on one side and an inlet with jagged rocks on the other side. The Palace draws saltwater from the inlet into the hotel dolphin pool. Two girls played with the dolphin in the pool; it was really a great show. The stage show was taken right out of the Follies in Paris and I was told it was just as good as the Follies.

"Anyway, I met the manager and told him that I wished we were staying there instead of next door. He gave me a coupon that is good for a two-week visit, and I think I have two months left before it expires. Would you like to stay there?"

"Maxine, I'm with you. I say, let's go as soon as we can, but I'd rather have a room instead of a bungalow or an apartment."

"I agree. I will make reservations to start on Friday. We can leave on the Friday morning train at ten and be at the hotel about two.

"Let's have another cocktail and call it a night. I will call the Medina Palace first thing in the morning."

On Friday morning Maxine and Catherine met at the train station to depart on their vacation. Catherine said, "Maxine, I have only left Marrakech one time in the ten months I have lived here, and that was to go to Casablanca for two days. I caught the night train there and back, so I have not seen any scenery of Morocco outside of Marrakech and Casablanca."

As they boarded the train Maxine said, "You take the window seat. Let's try for the left side of the coach; the view will be better. We should be able to get good seats, as we are in the reserved first-class coach. No animals are allowed in the first-class coach section, and the majority of the passengers can not afford the fare."

The train left on time and wound through the city, just outside the walls of the Medina. They passed the ruins of the Palais d'el-Badia, a three hundred sixty-room palace of marble, onyx, mosaic, and stucco with carved ceilings covered in gold leaf. The remains of the wealthy slave and gold trader palace are the setting of the annual folklore festival, which Catherine attended the month before. The train changed direction from southwest to south and there was the beautiful view of the mountain she saw each morning from the courtyard of Villa Marrakech. As the train slowly picked up speed, the High Atlas Mountains with the snow on top loomed larger. From the sound of the engine and the air getting thinner, she knew they were climbing higher in the mountains.

"Maxine, I expected the terrain to be flat as we approached the ocean, but we are climbing higher."

"In a few miles we will be at the village of Asni, which is at the foot of the High Atlas Mountains. From there we will climb to an elevation of over four thousand feet, before we descend down to the valley on the other side. It is about a three-hour trip to make the seventy-five miles to Taroudannt on the other side of the mountain. From there to Agadir is only an hour. The train has to travel slowly due to the height of the mountains and the winding railroad track. However, you will see the most scenic views of the mountains and the valley below. It is worth the slow trip."

The trip from Asni over the mountains to Taroudannt lived up to Maxine's description. Thirty minutes from Taroudannt, the Atlantic with it blue and turquoise waters appeared with the clean white sandy beaches.

I have never seen such beautiful white beaches before. The beaches of the Gulf of Mexico at New Orleans have a grayish color to the sand compared to these beaches.

Maxine must have been reading Catherine's mind, as she spoke, "The beaches here are nice, but as we get nearer to Agadir the sand gets even whiter and finer."

The train approached Agadir, where the ships sail between the rocks on each side of the channel. Catherine went over to the other side of the coach to an empty seat and looked up on the high hill above the town, where the fortress-like wall surrounded the Kasbah.

"Maxine, we should go up there while we are here. Maybe there's something different than the Kasbah in Marrakech."

"Each Kasbah has some differences, but basically they are much alike. We went up to the Kasbah and found a delightful place where some French Legion soldiers and other foreign soldiers were visiting. The name of the place is Fosse Café; we will pay it a visit while we are here."

"My French is not very good, I thought Fosse was hole."

"Yes, that is correct. In English, it is Hole Cafe. It is downstairs, as you would say, in the basement. It is unique. You go down about twenty steps, where you can get drinks, eats, water pipes with tobacco or hashish in the tobacco. They have floorshows, with Arabian dancers and music. Not only can we get some sun while we're in Agadir, but there are other places to see. I want go to Inezgane, which is not far. There is a large market there that opens each Tuesday.

"The fact is we didn't do too much outside of the hotel. Sig, short for Sigmund, my boyfriend at the time, did not want to leave the hotel. Sig was a pilot in the newly formed Luftwaffe German Air Force. He had completed training in Germany and was assigned to the unit that bombed Austria. When the Luftwaffe had completed its mission, Sig's unit was shipped to Morocco to train and prepare for the war in North Africa. He and the other pilots he met here would sit around all day, drink and relive their exploits. This is the reason we broke up. Remember the two German officers at the La Masion Bleue that we ditched? That is why I wanted to use an alias, because the German officers and pilots are self-centered conceited bores."

The train was coming into the Agadir station. The building was made of thick stucco walls in the Moorish design. The sun and the heat from the water, baked the clay until it was similar in color to the buildings in Marrakech, slightly pink. The station had a cover over the loading platform with a wall on the outside. It was almost as if you were coming into the building.

When they went inside to claim their luggage, an Arab dressed in a dejelbas garment wearing a red fez, was holding up a sign that read la Medina Palace. Maxine walked over to the man with the sign, who informed her that he was the concierge from the hotel and was there to pick up the passengers. She gave him the tickets for their luggage and they went through the spacious main terminal, with its marble and mosaic floors in an array of different patterns, high carved wooden ceilings painted in muted colors. The walls were decorated with arabesques in plaster. Palm trees were planted at various locations around the main lobby.

They were ushered into a six-passenger Mercedes automobile, with the top down. A couple, a man and a woman in there fifties, with Italian accents, were the other guests. On the way to la Medina Palace, the Mercedes skirted the center of town, passing the fishing and trade port. Camels and donkey carts, loaded with merchandise, crowded the narrow streets. The Atlantic was visible, but not the beaches. The Mercedes came to the top of a hill and below in its entire splendor was the long, wide beautiful beach of white sand. The beach was not crowded, although there were some people swimming and sunning. A few had their colorful umbrellas up. Finally, the Mercedes pulled up in front of la Medina Palace, another building of the pink Moorish design with the exception of the entrance. The roof and the driveway were covered with dark green tile. Upon arriving in their large luxurious room, number 227, they observed a pitcher of fresh water and two bowls, one with fresh fruits, the other with nuts. Their holiday was off to a glorious beginning.

Catherine walked over to the door to the balcony. Opening it, she found that the room was facing west. Looking down the short slope, she saw the beach and the Atlantic Ocean.

"Maxine," Catherine said, "it's three o'clock and I am starved. Let's go down and have a bite, then change into our swim suits and hit the beach."

"Yes, we think alike. We will ask for an umbrella and towels, and rest up from the train before we explore the night life."

Laying on a towel, watching the Atlantic with it turquoise water and gentle waves rolling on the white sandy beach, Catherine thought, *why haven't I been here before. I am more relaxed than I have been for about a year. My troubles seem to have been long ago. New Orleans was never this peaceful. I wonder if my father misses even cares or me. Well, let him enjoy the money.*

"Catherine."

This brought her out of her daydream. "Yes, Maxine."

"It is five o'clock. Let's go to our room and bathe and dress for tonight. We can take our time. In fact, I would like to have a German beer. That is the only thing that Sig introduced me to that I really enjoyed."

On her way through the lobby, Maxine stopped and ordered four beers to be delivered to their room. Asking about reservations for the dining room and lounge, the concierge informed her that he would make them a reservation in the lounge dining area near the stage.

"Mademoiselle, would this be for two and do you want to make the reservation for the early show at eight or the second show at ten-thirty?"

"Yes, for two and the eight o'clock show," looking at Catherine who nodded her head in approval.

In their room, they relaxed while drinking their beer. Catherine said, "Maxine, we're on vacation and we haven't anything planned for tomorrow. Let's have dinner at nine in the main dinning room and go to the lounge for the ten-thirty show. What do you think of this idea?"

"That's fine with me. I'll call the concierge and have the reservation changed, and then we can have the other beer and take a little nap before we bathe and dress."

After a leisurely, delicious seafood dinner, they went into the lounge at ten and were seated near the front. At the table near them were two smartly dressed military officers in white uniforms with gray and gold trim.

The waiter came over and told them that the two officers wanted to buy them a drink.

"What army are they in?" asked Maxine.

"They are in the Italian Army. I believe they are colonels."

"What do you think Catherine, shall we use our aliases and see what happens?"

"OK. I guess Lenore is ready. Are you, Adele?"

"Yes, we will accept their offer."

"If they were German officers they would have asked to join us. I guess they will ask after a drink, or will it take three?"

A surprise, when the waiter returned with the drinks, he said that the officers asked if they could join them.

They agreed and the two officers came over. Still standing, one of them put his hand over his waist, bowed slightly and said in French, "Good evening, ladies. My name is Roberto Palermo and this is my friend Vincenzo Catola. May we be seated?"

"Sure, Roberto. My name is Adele and my friend is Lenore. I am French and Lenore is American. Do you speak French or English?"

After being seated across from each other, Roberto looked at Adele and said in broken English. "You American?"

"No, I am French, but I speak English as my friend Lenore does not speak much French."

"Are you on vacation or do you live in Agadir?"

"We live in Marrakech, and yes, we are on vacation. Where are you stationed, here in Agadir?"

"No, we are stationed in Addis Ababa, Ethiopia."

Vincenzo spoke for the first time in broken English, looking at Lenore. "We can not say where we are located or the purpose, only here in Agadir we are on leave."

The show started, and another round of drinks was ordered.

After the show was over, they discussed how much they enjoyed it, the follies, and the live dolphin performing in the tank with the two girls dressed as mermaids, especially when the dolphin removed the mermaid's bra.

After they finished their drinks, Vincenzo remarked, "Shall we purchase a bottle and go up to our room?"

"No, thank you. We are going to the beach tomorrow, you can join us there if you wish."

On Saturday, Catherine awoke and looked out at the sky in the west. She saw that the clouds were dark and it looked as if it was raining.

Walking softly to the bathroom to avoid waking Maxine, she attended to her morning necessities, and then went onto the balcony. It had rained earlier. The skies were still dark and a strong wind was blowing. The waves were too high and rough for swimming. She noticed some people walking on the beach, even in this weather and at this early hour of seven o'clock.

I don't know why I am feeling so depressed. Maybe a good walk in this weather will clear my head.

She walked along the beach, with the strong, cool wind blowing an occasional spray of salt water into her face.

Well, I can take a bath when I get back to the hotel. I need something to clear my thinking. Why is it that I only meet men here in Morocco who want to spend money on one or two drinks and go to bed? I would love to meet someone who is romantic and let things develop naturally. Mike, I know, is or was a womanizer, but I am developing feelings for him. Maybe it's because I am lonely and have not met a decent man. When I get back to Marrakech I'll see if we can do more socializing. I hope on his part, it would not be just for the money. Here I go again, thinking that all men want is sex and money. How do I separate the two and tell when the feeling is real or it's the money they are after? I'll call Mike tonight with the excuse of finding out how business is. If he does not give me any type of a hint or hope, I'll let my hair down tonight-in Agadir.

Realizing that she had walked further than she intended to, she turned to go back and faced the couple that rode from the train station to the hotel with them yesterday.

"Good morning. How are you?"

In broken English the man said, "Good morning. I am fine. You are English?"

"No, I am American. I was lost in thought and did not realize I spoke in English. My French is not too good. Are you French?"

"No, we are from Italy. We will turn around and walk back with you, with your permission."

"I would be delighted to have your company. My name is Catherine Ledbetter." Oops I should have said Lenore. "Call me Lenore, my friends do."

"Very good to meet you La Nore. My name is Giovanni Palermo and this is my wife Giulia. We are from Foggia, Italy."

Strange that they have the same name as the colonel we met last night.

"Our son is a colonel in the Italian Army and was stationed in Addis Ababa, Ethiopia but was sent on special duty to Marrakech. He was given a seven-day leave and we will meet him here in about an hour at the hotel. If we walk a little fast, it is because we are anxious to see him. It has been two years since he was sent to Ethiopia and we have not seen him from that time. He suggested that we meet him in Agadir and arranged our itinerary to arrive here yesterday."

Odd, last night the colonels spoke as if they had been here a couple of days. I won't mention I met their son last night."

Entering the hotel, a French policier approached the Palermos and asked that they accompany him to their son Roberto.

Catherine went to see if Maxine was in the dining room. She was not. As she approached her room, standing outside of the door were several policiers, as well as Giulia and Giovanni Palermo. Mrs. Palermo was sobbing uncontrollably, while Mr. Palermo was holding her head on his shoulder and stroking her, murmuring something softly in Italian. The door opened and a French policier asked her to wait outside.

Startled, Catherine asked, "What in the hell are you doing in this room and where is Maxine?"

"Someone will be with you in a minute, Mademoiselle."

"No, where is Maxine? I demand that you tell me."

"Mademoiselle, this is an official order. Wait outside!"

A policier removed two chairs from the room next door and put them in the hall for the Palermos to sit on.

The policier, which would not let her in, left her with another officer and went back into the room. A few minutes later he returned, gently put his hand on Catherine's elbow and escorted her into the room.

Six or eight people were in the room, and as her eyes scanned the room, she saw an Italian officer on the floor. The officer was face down; a vast pool of blood was running from underneath the body.

She looked wildly around the room but did not see Maxine.

"Where is Maxine?" she screamed at the men.

A man who was bent over on the other side of the bed, got up and came around to Catherine, saying softly, "Mademoiselle, calm down and I will try to help you."

Catherine looked up at the tall man in a light grey pinstriped suit. He had black hair, brown eyes and a bushy mustache, with the most pleasing smile she had ever seen. Instantly, she liked and trusted him.

"I just want to find my friend."

"Please be seated and I will tell you."

Catherine took a seat and the tall man seated himself in front of her and shielded almost half of the room.

"Mademoiselle Ledbetter, my name is Louie Bennard. I am from Marrakech. I am a detective, investigating a gang in Marrakech. My associates followed two men down here from Marrakech on Thursday, and I followed you and Miss Maxine Vensel from Marrakech yesterday."

"Why, and where is Maxine? Why don't you tell me?"

"We want to be sure the person we think is Maxine Vensel, really is that person. We need for you to identify her. Come with me."

He led Catherine around the foot of the bed, where she saw what looked like a body under a sheet between the wall and bed.

Louie slowly pulled the bloody bed sheet back, to reveal the face that was almost unrecognizable. The face had been shot several times and blood was everywhere. Catherine felt her stomach churn and she was getting queasy. She tried to suppress the vomit that was leaving her stomach on the way up. She took off for the bathroom and made it just in time. She heaved and heaved until she was weak and felt as if her stomach was heaving dry air and she was choking. Louie came in, wet a washcloth and began washing her face.

Afterwards, it seemed like hours before she was able to go back and sit down in the chair. She was weak but felt better, when Louie said, "I know it is difficult, but would you try to identify the person on the floor."

With Louie holding her, she went back over to the body. She tried to look quickly, but could not identify the person. She looked again and the dress on the person was the same as a dress Maxine had hung up in the closet. Again, peeking at the face she felt her stomach churn again, not from the gruesome sight, but from recognition. It was Maxine.

"Yes, Mr. Bernard, that is Maxine."

"I am sorry Miss Ledbetter, but I must ask you to view the Italian officer and see if you recognize that person."

As he slowly turned the body over, Catherine saw a mass of blood, flesh and bones. She could not recognize the person; it looked as if the entire face had been blown away. She felt her knees give way. Mr. Bernard put his arm around her as he said, "Do you recognize any features at all, hair, ears, neck or hands?"

"No, only the hair looks something like Roberto Palermo, but I am not sure."

"Gentlemen, remove the bodies to the morgue and clean them up."

"Miss Ledbetter, I have to impose upon you again. Later this afternoon we will pick you up and take you to the morgue to make certain we have the correct name and information about your friend. Also, we would like you to take another look at the man after he has been cleaned up, to see if you recognize him. I will have someone escort you to another room. If you feel better after you refresh yourself, perhaps we could go to lunch; you can talk, and I will listen?"

"That is nice of you, Mr. Bennard. It may take me awhile."

"Please call me Louie. It is now twelve. Would one o'clock be a good time to pick you up?"

"Yes, Louie, I'll be ready. That will give me time to lay down for a few minutes and relax."

In the room, Catherine lay across the bed and tried to put together the puzzle. *I didn't know Maxine very well. She was private about her life, but we did enjoy each other's company. I was never invited to her home or met any of her friends. Maybe she was a loner by design, not by choice. I was so hoping for a friend to pal around with.*

The telephone woke her up, "Hello."

"Catherine, Louie here. Are you ready for lunch?"

"Gee, Louie, I fell asleep. It will take me a few minutes to get dressed, can you wait?"

"Take your time, I'll be in the lobby."

He surely is a thoughtful person, polite, kind, also good looking.

Some fifteen minutes later she went down to the lobby, where Louie was patiently waiting and reading some reports.

"Feeling better?" And without waiting for an answer he asked, "Do you have a favorite place to go?"

"I feel better, but I would like to eat. We only arrived yesterday and this my first time in Agadir. Maxine told me there was a nice place to visit in the Medina section; the name is Fosse Cafe."

This girl is either naive or smart. The Medina is not a place for good dining. I'll give it a shot.

"Do you know how to get there?"

"No, I assumed that Maxine knew how to get there. Don't you know how to get around in your own city?"

"This is not my city. Don't you remember, I told you I am from Marrakech and my associates followed the two men on Thursday and I followed you and Miss Vensel yesterday."

"No, I don't remember. Finding Maxine murdered has really upset me."

"I have the use of a policier automobile and I will get directions from the concierge."

After getting the directions, they went out and got into an old beat up automobile and started for the Fosse Café.

Is this man really a policier? I have not seen a badge or identification and it is strange, him being from Marrakech and driving an old beat up automobile, claiming it is on loan from the Agadir policier. What am I getting myself into? I wish Mike were here.

"You are very quiet. Is there any problem you want to talk to me about?"

Just as the automobile turned into the street from the docks toward the center of town, she saw a policier station and said quick and loud, "Louie, pull into that station and stop."

Louie glanced at her, but did as she asked. "Now what do you want to do?"

"I would like to go inside."

She opened the door and walked briskly into the policier station and up to the desk.

"I speak poor Francais, can you help me?"

"Oui, I speak some English. How may I help you?"

Louie came up behind her, spoke to the officer, showing his identification and said, "I am Detective Louie Bennard from Marrakech, and I have a loan of one of your automobiles. Here is the permit. I think the young lady wants to be sure I am who I told her I was."

The desk officer looked over the paperwork and answered, "Yes, Mademoiselle, Mr. Bennard is a Detective from Marrakech and the automobile is on loan to him."

"Thank you, Officer." Turning to Louie, "I am sorry, but the car made me skeptical. After the murders, I am very nervous."

"I understand, Catherine. Shall we continue on our trip? Maybe a cocktail and lunch will make you feel better. I promise, no one will bother you."

I believe him. He sure has a way of calming my fears.

They came to the high stucco covered walls and large archway of the Medina. Near the wall was a parking lot almost filled with camels and donkeys tethered to large stones, and a few automobiles. Louie squeezed the old battered automobile between a donkey hitched to a cart full of hay and a camel. Louie went around the automobile and opened the door and placed himself between the camel and the automobile. Catherine exited, looking at the hissing camel. Going through the narrow streets, Louie took her hand and she held tight. His large hand made her feel good and safe. After a few more turns she saw the sign with an arrow pointing down. They were at the Fosse Café. Going down the dimly lighted, winding stairs made her think, *this is like Halloween. I'm glad I'm with Louie.*

They were seated at a table near the back of the Café.

"Catherine, what will you have?"

"I will leave the ordering to you, I enjoy beef." Mike said that was always safe to order. "I would like to have a small steak, or I think they refer it to as beef, and I think I'll have a drink. Will you have one?"

"I am on duty and cannot drink, but you should have one to settle you down. What is your preference?"

"A cognac with tonic water and a twist of lime."

After Louie ordered, he looked at Catherine and said, "Are you sure you didn't know the man that was slain at the hotel?"

"I don't think so. Maxine and I met two men last night. We had a couple drinks and watched the show with them and tentatively agreed to meet on the beach this morning. I woke up early. Maxine was still asleep, when I left for a walk. I walked for about thirty to forty minutes up the beach. As I turned around to come back, I met a couple that rode in the automobile that brought us from the train to the hotel. We introduced ourselves to each other. They said they were Giovanni and Giulia Palermo. We walked back together for maybe thirty-five minutes. Their last name was the same as one of the Italian officers we met last night. They stated their son, Roberto Palermo, a colonel in the Italian Army, was stationed in Addis

Ababa, Ethiopia and recently transferred to Marrakech. He obtained a leave and they agreed to meet him here for a vacation."

"That is odd. The officers arrived Thursday afternoon from Marrakech and the Palermos flew to Marrakech and came down by train on Friday. Both parties were in the hotel Friday night, but did not see each other. I am curious why the son did not seek out his parents or the parents did not seek out their son on Friday night. Surely, each knew the other should be at the hotel.

"Catherine, I hate to ask you, but I would like you to take a closer look. The morgue will examine the bodies and clean them up to look much like they did in life. There will be differences, such a swelling, discoloration and broken bones, but I think you may identify him as the man you saw last night."

"Oh, Louie, I do not relish viewing the bodies again, but if it will help to catch the killers of my friend, I'll do it."

"If you can give me all of the information you know about your friend, Maxine Vensel, that would go a long way in helping solve this tragedy."

"I realized after this happened that I really don't know too much about Maxine. She was an outgoing and friendly person, but she never talked about herself. She told me she was born in France and I had the impression that it was Paris. Anyway, she had lived in Paris. She had parted with her boyfriend recently, a German Luftwaffe pilot. The reason we stayed at la Medina Palace was that last year Maxine and her boyfriend stayed at the Satife Hotel, next door. She had two discount coupons for la Medina Palace, which is a much better hotel. We arrived in the afternoon yesterday and last night met two officers in the lounge. It was the first and only time I saw them."

Louie had an enjoyable lunch and really liked being with Catherine, but he was in Agadir on policier business and had to conclude the case and get back to Marrakech.

After leaving the Fosse Café, Louie guided the old automobile through the narrow streets to the morgue. Catherine was understandably nervous. Louie put his hand on her arm and felt her trembling.

"Don't be nervous Catherine. I know it is unpleasant but it has to be done. Just look and see if you can recognize the man you met last night. Afterwards I will drop you off at the hotel so you can rest."

After entering the building, Louie guided her down the hallway. Catherine could already smell the scent of death, and a sharp irritating odor drifted up her nose. She almost lost her breath. Noticing her color and breathing, Louie stopped by an office and spoke to a white-coated person who gave him a small vial. Louie asked her to sniff it. She recognized the smell of ammonia and concluded that is was smelling salt. Louie explained that the irritating odor was formaldehyde, a chemical used in the morgue and funeral homes as a disinfectant and preservative. At the morgue laboratory, she was ushered over to a chair and asked to wait. As she looked around the walls and floor of the tile room, the smell of the formaldehyde got even stronger. Several tables with sheet-covered bodies were visible.

Thank God the bodies are covered.

After a few minutes she was ushered into a room where a body was covered except for the head.

Louie asked, "Catherine, do you recognize this person?"

A cloth, the size of a handkerchief, was covering the left side of his face, and Louie explained that this part of the face was unrecognizable, but maybe she could recognize the other part.

The man on the table had four spots, two on the forehead and two on the right cheek, as if four large pimples had been removed, and he was devoid of any color. His right eye socket was just an empty hole.

"The face looks thinner than Roberto's, however, the hairline looks familiar. Yes, now that I've taken a closer look, I think this is the man who introduced himself to me as Roberto Palermo."

"I do not like asking you Catherine, but it's very important that you are certain, one way or the other. Would you take another look, to be sure?"

She forced her eyes to focus upon the man's face, then closed them and reflected how Roberto had looked last night. Opening her eyes and again looking at the face she answered, "The face and hairline look the same, although, his head is smaller than I remembered. But that is probably because of the way he died. Yes, Louie, positively and without a doubt, this man is the man I met as Roberto Palermo."

"Thank you, Catherine. That confirms that this man is not Roberto Palermo."

"What? I don't understand. I just identified him as Roberto Palermo."

"Yes, but Mr. and Mrs. Palermo viewed the body and stated it was not their son. Apparently this man was an imposter. We went to the hotel but the Palermos had checked out and said they were going back to Marrakech. No trains or planes are scheduled for departure until later. The policier have stationed officers at both places."

"We want to be certain of Maxine Vensel. Would you like to take a minute before you look?"

"No, I want to finish this gruesome task."

Guiding her over to another table, Louie slowly pulled the sheet down from the top of the head.

First, Catherine noticed the hair was not as blond as it had been; maybe blood changed the color. As the sheet slowly moved down, Catherine gasped, then gulping in fresh air, she cried out, "Oh, Maxine, who did this to you? This can't be happening." Turning to Louie, "That is Maxine, but I don't know who would do this to her."

Louie went over to her, put his arms around her and said, "Everything will be fine. You are sure this is Maxine?"

"Yes, I am positive beyond any doubt that this is Maxine Vensel."

"Let's go to your hotel where we can discuss the situation as it now stands. Perhaps if I tell you what I know and my theory, conceivably, it could bring back some incident that you could relate to."

How good it is to get out of that awful foul smelling place. I wonder why Louie thinks I know something that will help his case. I know nothing about these people except Maxine, and very little about her. I do like the attention Louie is giving me.

Arriving at la Medina Palace, Catherine asked if they have moved her possessions to the room she had rested in.

"Oui, Mademoiselle, you are in room number 331. That room also faces west. You still have the view of the beach and ocean."

Room 331 had one large bed rather than twin beds, giving more room for the added sofa. Opening the door to the balcony and a window on the front side, a cross breeze blew in, moving the curtains and cooling the room.

Louie seated himself on the sofa and Catherine said, "Would you care for a Coca Cola or some other drink?"

"Well, I am taking myself off duty, so I will have a dry martini. Anything we discuss will be off the record. If anything comes up in our conversation, I will not use it unless I have your permission. I really want to know you better, for personal reasons."

"Thank you, Louie. I prefer a martini, also, but I don't care to drink them alone and have not found anyone else who likes them. I'll order up a pitcher of dry martinis and see if they have any type of snacks."

After ordering, Catherine excused herself and went into the bathroom. She washed her face and looked in the mirror. *Damn, I'm ugly. How did the men I dated think I was beautiful; maybe it was the money that was beautiful? I guess the day's stress has given me a dull headache and now my stomach is cramping again. My hair is a dirty, stringy blond color, my skin is pale, I have pimples all over my face and my eyes are bloodshot. They look like rat's eyes peeking up from a mousetrap. I'll finish up and go out and down several martinis, which always helps my stomach.*

I can't put it off any longer. I should have known when I get horny and bitchy this would happen, and what a bitchy day this has been.

"Louie, would you hand me that small blue case by the bed?"

She opened the case and reached inside for her sanitary belt and napkin pad. After putting it on, she reached back inside the case for her Lydia E. Pinkham Female Tonic. *No, on second thought, I'll just substitute the martinis for the Lydia E. Pinkham. They work better, anyway.*

She brushed her thick blond hair until it cascaded around her petite face and down to her shoulders. Her eyes, the color of the deep blue Atlantic Ocean, looked wide open and cheerful. The light rouge and powder covered her pale skin and three pimples, and the medium red lipstick made her mouth look sensual and soft. Looking in the mirror she saw a neatly dressed woman, five feet five inches tall, weighing one hundred fifteen pounds, a curvy body on a pair of shapely legs.

OK, Mr. Louie Bennard, here I come.

As she entered the room, she heard a loud whistle, and Louie looked as if he was seeing her for the first time. On the coffee table the pitcher of martinis and glasses were waiting.

Louie came to his feet and said, "Catherine you are trés bien beauitful."

"Thank you Louie, let us toast our friendship."

"This may not be in good English but here it goes,
Here is your martini,
I spiced it with love,
I stirred it with care,
And here's to you mon chére."

"Oh, thank you, Louie. That was truly a beautiful toast. I have never heard another as beautiful. Louie, I can't give a toast as good as that, but I'll speak from my heart.
I have known some,
Loved none,
Hope you are the one,
Here is to you."

The two clicked glasses, looked into each other's eyes, put their glasses on the table and embraced, pressing close until their lips found each other's. It was a long and passionate kiss.

Catherine felt a sexual excitement that was turning into an almost uncontrollable biological urge.

Louie felt his head spinning and an impassioned yearning for this woman. He pressed her breasts to his chest while his hand found the way to her crotch. Feeling the pad, his hand moved to her soft firm buttock. This was the first sexual excitement and craving he'd had for anyone since Necole was killed. The thought of his wife snapped him out of the ardent impulse. Releasing his embrace on Catherine he said, "I am sorry. I got out of control. You are the first woman that I have kissed or been excited by since my wife died."

"Louie, I am sorry about your wife, I thought that you just did not like me."

"Oh, no. Instantly, I liked you and after being with you and the kiss, my emotions just went wild. I guess I feel guilty about my wife."

Catherine refilled the martini glasses and said, "I have never loved a man. I have been fond but never loved, so I don't know the feeling. Maybe if you will tell me about your wife and how she died, I would be able to understand. It might help you to talk about it."

Louie looked into this woman's beautiful blue eyes. He felt as though he could see her soul and he trusted her.

After finishing that martini and another, Louie had told Catherine his life story and about losing his wife, Nécole.

By now, both were a little high on martinis, although the telling of Louie's difficult tragedy had somewhat sobered them to a point of being on an emotional low. Time had slipped away and it was nearly eight o'clock.

"Catherine, let's take a short walk, maybe down to the beach for some fresh air and have something to eat. Maybe we can get our true feelings in order and talk about us?"

"I'll go freshen up. I will only be a few minutes. Would you like to use the bathroom first while I get my clothes together?"

"Yes, thank you."

On the street in front of the hotel, Louie reached for Catherine's hand, grasping it lightly but firmly. They started walking. Not a word was spoken, but Catherine knew by the tender feel of his hand that she had fallen in love. They walked around the hotel, down the wooded walkway to a narrow boardwalk leading to a short pier. Walking out on the pier with the moon reflecting on the blue Atlantic they stopped at the end. Louie turned to her and said, "Nécole, I am sure, would approve of you. Would you do me a, I don't know how to say it in English, a uh deed? Just help me to understand that it is proper to love you, that I am not forsaking Nécole."

"Louie, I have never loved another man, other than my father and grandfather. I now know what loving a man feels like. You will never forget Nécole, and I don't want you to, but your life must go on. You will love again. I'm hoping it will be me, but whoever it is, remember Nécole, but let go of the love for her. There's not a thing you can do to bring her back."

Louie put his arms around her and pulled her close. The moon was shining over his left shoulder onto her face and her blond hair.

"I do love you and with your help, maybe I will learn that I should not have a guilty feeling about it."

With their arms around each other they walked back to the hotel for dinner.

Over dinner Louie said, "Catherine before you answer, think about what I am saying to you. I want to be with you, hold and kiss you and spend the night holding you. I know that the time is not good for sex, even if you did not have your period. I am lonely and I have found you. I do not want to lose you, just cuddle and caress you."

Looking Louie in the eye for a moment, Catherine said, "Louie, I know that I love you and I want you. Please stay with me tonight. I'll trust you, but you must be the strong one. At this time of the month I've always wanted sex, although, I've never had it when I had my period, but with you I have no will power."

"I know that I love you, but to be more than sure it is not just for sex, let's wait until we get our emotions under control.

"When we get to the room, I have to call my hotel and see if I have any messages."

Back in the room, Louie called his hotel and made notes. Hanging up, he called another number and talked for about ten minutes, then he called Marrakech and spoke another ten minutes.

Catherine had changed clothes while he was on the phone. She wore a light blue silk nightgown almost the color of her eyes.

Louie thought, *God she is sexy, even in a long nightgown.*

"Honey, I am finished in Agadir on this case. I will have to go back to Marrakech to try to complete it. When do you plan to return to Marrakech?"

"We just arrived on Friday afternoon, but with Maxine gone, I don't care to stay by myself."

"Get your ticket and I'll take it to the train station and exchange the return ticket for one leaving tomorrow. I have to get my ticket validated for tomorrow, anyway. While I am there, I will check the schedule. I believe a train leaves at ten and gets to Marrakech around two. I also have to go to the policier station to clear up some matters. I'll be back later."

"Fine, I do not want to stay here without you. I'll pack while you're out so I can be ready in the morning."

When Louie returned, he undressed and got into bed, turning out the bed light. Louie turned and put his arm under Catherine's head, pulling her close. The sweet smell of her body and hair almost took his breath away. After about an hour of kissing and cuddling, Louie dropped off in a deep sleep. Catherine laid wide-awake thinking of how to break the news of her real name. *Louie may not take to this very well, especially the business I'm in. Maybe if I wait to find the right moment it would be easier. Her night was spent drifting in and out of sleep, but she still had not resolved how to tell him. Maybe an opportunity will present itself before we arrive in Marrakech.*

Up bright and early they bathed, dressed and went down to breakfast. Over breakfast they made plans.

"I have checked with the policier, and they will let me use their automobile this morning. They will pick it up from the train station later. It is now seven. If you check out now, then we'll have time to ride around and see some of Agadir before going to the station."

"I'll be ready in five minutes."

Louie guided the automobile through the narrow streets to the train station and looked up to the high wall surrounding the Medina.

"Let's take a tour up the mountain on the far side of the Medina for a view of the city."

"I would like to take one last look at the city. Under a different circumstances, I would love to stay here, especially with you."

Louie was deep in thought as he made the twists and turns around the Medina and parked in a spot high above it. They sat and gazed at the beautiful view below, the old world city of the Medina with the high stucco walls, surrounding a cluster of buildings that was hundreds of years old. Beyond the old city was the modern city with the Moorish styling and lush green foliage, and just below, the white sandy beaches and the blue Atlantic, calm with slight waves washing ashore.

Catherine's mind placed the Villa Marrakech in the setting below.

"A franc for your thoughts?"

"Oh, I was just thinking what it would be like to have Villa Marrakech sitting down there, and us being together. Louie, I am a dreamer and the things I dream very rarely come true."

"Your villa must be special to you. There has been a bit of secrecy about you, like you've been hurt by someone close to you. I will not probe at this time, but when you feel the need to talk, the invitation you gave me goes something like this. You will never forget the person, who hurt you, but your life must go on and you will trust again. I hope you will put that trust in me.

"It is getting late. We should go to the train station."

"Louie, I promise you that I am trying to get the courage to tell you of my problems, but I am afraid and with all of this business about Maxine, I can't get my mind clear enough to think. I will soon, though."

"Let's agree that we will not speak of our problems on the trip back to Marrakech. After we get home, we should not see each other for two days. That will give us time to think our problems over, and at the end of this period decide if our problems are worth telling each other and casting them aside. If we can do that, our love will overcome anything. On the trip back, let's just get to know each other better. I know at this point I love you, and I will try to solve my problem about Nécole."

Louie started the automobile and guided it back down the hill. Catherine moved over as close as she could, with the shift gear in the center of the automobile. Putting both legs around the shift gear her body was touching Louie from the shoulders down to the knees.

I know what my answer will be if I can wait two days. I have to get my mind in order so that I will not look like an awful person.

The train departed on time. Louie was seated in the aisle seat and Catherine was next to the window. Louie asked the porter to bring two pillows, then he put the seats back and the pillows under their heads, and with his arm around Catherine, they snuggled and reclined. They didn't have to speak, they were content just to hold and be with each other.

The trip passed uneventfully, and at one fifty-five the train arrived at the Marrakech station.

Louie found a taxi and dropped Catherine off at Villa Marrakech. They walked to the door, he took her in his arms and they kissed.

I don't think I can last two days without him, she thought.

I have to be strong; I really don't like the time frame of two days that I placed upon us. Maybe I'll call her after one day, he thought.

Louie walked slowly back to the taxi, laid his head back and ran the last few days through his mind as the taxi drove him home.

Chapter Twenty-Four

On Thursday night, Louie and Jeff went to the Chez Policier Club for a beer and a light dinner.

"Jeff, I have to go home early tonight and get a good night's rest. I have to be up early tomorrow to go out of the city on a case. I will be gone for a couple of days. Will you still be here when I get back?"

"It's almost certain that I will. I haven't found any good leads yet. I think tomorrow I will go to la Gazelle and speak with Doran, and then I'll go over to Sheikdom du Jacque and nose around. I won't ask where you are going. When you return, give me a call."

Jeff sat in his room reading some notes, when he came across a reference to un Bordel de Bonheur that the manager at the Sheikdom talked about. Also, Marshall Bakker said that the Vieux Carre Corporation, of which Mike Martel was part owner, owned it. He remembered that Annette Coppola once worked there.

I guess I'll have to go to the whorehouse and find Mr. Martel first. Maybe Paulette can meet me in the morning and go with me as a cover and interpreter.

Jeff asked the operator to ring numéro, deux, quatre, un, sept, huit.

"Hello, Paulette. Jeff Stewart here. How are you?"

"Hello, Jeff. This is an unexpected pleasure. I am fine and you?"

"Fine. How is your time for tomorrow? I need to go to the Medina and to un Bordel de Bonheur, again."

"Ha! You won't need me for the bordel. They know what you are there for."

"You don't understand. I am still trying to trace down the owner and I also want to go back to the Sheikdom du Jacque in the Medina and a bar named la Gazelle."

"Fine. I can make it at ten. Should I meet you at the hotel?"

"Yes, I'll be waiting for you."

At seven the next morning he took the elevator to the roof garden for breakfast, and after eating, he lingered, just admiring the beautiful mountain on the clear sunny day.

Promptly at ten, Paulette arrived. They decided to go to the Sheikdom du Jacque first, and then to la Gazelle and make the last stop un Bordel de Bonheur.

When they greeted Jacque at his private table, he looked at the two of them and said, "You two are out early. What brings you here, or are you winding the night down?"

"No, Jacque. We are looking for a Mike Martel. Do you happen to know him?"

"I haven't seen Mike for a few days. He and his friend Maxine were in for a couple hours. I think they were going out of the city. That is, Maxine said she was going south for a few days, and I assumed that Mike would be going, too."

Jeff thought he would take a stab in the dark. "Jacque, who is Mike's partner? I thought he had an American for a partner."

"Oh, his partner is a lawyer and he is an American, but he is in and out of Marrakech. I believe he resides in London," answered Jacque.

"I was under the impression that his partner was a woman."

"Well, Jeff, I am not sure. They are both very secretive. I think there is more to them than it appears."

"Do you know the name of the lawyer that you think might be Mike's partner?"

"No, but I heard that he was also an associate of Réne Munroe."

"Maxine is a blond. Does she resemble this photo?"

Jeff showed Jacque a photo of Mary Alice Bakker.

"The hair looks similar. Other than that they do not resemble one another. You may try la Gazelle. I understand they frequent that place often."

"Thanks, Jacque. We'll stop by there."

"Jeff, be careful. Some of le Royaume de Sang, you know, the Kingdom of Blood gang controls that part of the city and they are moving to acquire more territory. I told you how they tried to move in here, but I stopped it thus far."

"Yes, Jacque. We will keep our eyes and ears open."

In the automobile, Jeff asked Paulette, "Are you afraid to go with me? If so, drop me off. I won't mind."

"Oh, no. It is intriguing and I am not afraid with you. I think we make a good team."

Upon arriving at la Gazelle, they were seated in a booth and Jeff requested Doran for their waiter.

"Hello, Doran, remember me?"

"Yes, you and the other detective were in not long ago. What can I get for you?"

"What will you have, Agnes?"

"I'll have a cognac and tonic water."

"Doran, bring the lady her drink and make mine a whiskey with water on the side."

After Doran left, Paulette asked, "Jeff, why did you call me Agnes?"

"I did not want him to know our real names. While we are here, refer to me as Cliff."

When Doran returned with the drinks, Jeff removed a twenty-franc note and slid it toward the waiter, keeping his hand on the bill.

"Doran, I am looking for Mike and Maxine. Have they been in lately?"

"They were in Wednesday afternoon and stayed for about an hour."

Jeff pulled out another twenty-franc note and laid it on top of the first one, his hand on top of the bills.

"Doran, I will remove my hand if you can tell me anything of interest that they spoke about, such as travel plans, or something about their business."

Looking around carefully, Doran answered, "It is not safe to talk about some people; you know they would kill me in a flash."

Jeff pulled out another twenty-franc note and held it in his right hand, "How much of this do you want?"

Doran walked away and returned with two more drinks. "I overheard Maxine say she would be leaving Friday morning for Agadir."

"Did she say with whom?"

"It was a strange name like Kasarine."

"You have been helpful Doran. All of this is yours if you can tell me what Mike's response was."

"He said that he and Réne Munroe would be leaving Thursday and would meet her there."

"Anything else?"

"No, Sir."

"Thank you, Doran. This is yours," Jeff said as he pushed the three twenty franc notes over to him.

Doran put the tray on top of the francs, picked up the glasses, tray and bills.

In the Fiat, on the way to the un Bordel de Bonheur, Paulette said, "Jeff, what do think of the trip to Agadir? It is odd they are going different days."

"It is strange. I would contact Louie, but he is out of town on business. Hmm, I wonder if the trips all of these people are making have something in common. Let's see whether we can find Mike or Maxine before they leave. We can get Maxine's address form Danielle. Is there a Post Office nearby?"

A few blocks away, Paulette pulled into a parking lot at the Post Office.

"Paulette, go in and get an envelope, a couple sheets of paper and a stamp. When you return we will address the envelope to Mike Martel at the un Bordel de Bonheur."

At the bordel, Paulette asked for Danielle and when she arrived Jeff, with Paulette translating, said, "Madam, I have an official envelope for a Mr. Mike Martel. Is he here?"

"No, I'll deliver the message to him."

"I'm sorry, Madam, but this is an important official message and he must receive it and sign for it. If this is not delivered today, he will lose a great deal of money. I would not like to be in the position not letting him receive this important message."

"If it is that important I will give you his address, but he will not be home until five. His address is 13913-B Boulevard de Santi."

"Mr. Martel will thank you for this. Oh, yes, the lady here would like to purchase a nice dress. You told us once before of a nice dress shop. What was the name?"

"I don't remember. There are many shops."

"You remember, you stated Annette Coppola may have purchased some used clothing there?"

"Oh, you are speaking of à la Mode Maxine; I will go find the address."

A few minutes later she returned and handed Jeff a piece of paper with the address written on it.

In the small Fiat, Paulette said, "Jeff, à la Mode Maxine's location is between here and Boulevard de Santi. Would you like to stop by there first?"

"By all means. Let's drop in and you can do some window shopping and nose around."

"Jeff, help me with some of your American. What is window shopping and nose around is that some way of smelling the shop?"

"Ha! No, it is a type of American slang. Window-shopping is, looking but not necessarily purchasing and nose around is just looking or snooping. I think in French, or anyway Cajun, it is fouiner."

"American is more confusing than English."

Paulette found a parking space in front of the à la Mode Maxine. Inside, Paulette asked the sales person for Mademoiselle Vensel.

"Mademoiselle Vensel left on a one week vacation yesterday. She did not leave an address; she said she would call in every other day. I don't expect to hear from her until Monday."

Back at the Fiat Jeff said, "Well, Paulette, let's go by number 13913 Boulevard de Santi, and see if we can get lucky and find Mr. Mike Martel."

Arriving at 13913 Boulevard de Santi, Jeff looked for 13913-B. The complex had a stucco wall, about five feet high around it, with shrubbery in front almost as high as the wall. The wrought iron gate was locked and only a large villa with a red tile roof was visible. Paulette parked, and they walked down the sidewalk until the wall made a right angle and continued dividing the property from another property. Turning and walking back past the Fiat about a half a block, they saw a single gate and a driveway leading to a much smaller house than the villa. A small sign had the number 13913-B. The gate was locked.

Back at the main house, the gate was also locked, but on the side of the wall at the end was a mailbox and a button. Jeff pushed the button and held it for a few seconds. No one appeared. He rang three more times before a maid in uniform came to the gate.

Paulette spoke, "Mademoiselle, I have a special letter for Mademoiselle Ledbetter. The officer must see her sign the receipt."

"I can accept the letter for her."

"No, Mademoiselle. It is a very important letter that contains a matter of a sum of money and the officer must see her sign the receipt in person."

"I am sorry, but Mademoiselle is out of town and will not be back for a week."

"This is an extremely important letter about finances. Perhaps if you can give us her telephone number, we can ring her and read the information to her and if she would care to give us permission to leave it with you, we can do that."

"I have her number but was instructed not to call unless it was an extreme emergency. Come up to the house with me."

Walking toward the house on the curved driveway, Jeff thought, *Look at the beautifully landscaped yard. I know the cost of living and goods is less in Morocco, but this life style must cost a fortune.*

The foyer of marble and tile into the main room looked almost like some of the palaces he had visited. Entering into a smaller, cozier room, decorated in Arabian motif, with deep red, black and gold colors, they were seated in camel leather chairs. The housekeeper, Camille, handed Paulette the telephone and a number. The number was for la Medina Palace in Agadir.

"Mademoiselle Ledbetter's room please?"

"Mademoiselle Ledbetter went out. May I take a message?"

"No, we will call back. What room is she in?"

"Mademoiselle's room number is 227."

Paulette related to Jeff the conversation with the hotel. Jeff looked as his watch.

"Paulette, it is five o'clock and they may be out for the evening. Let's call it a day. Would you care to have a drink and dinner?"

"Yes, Jeff. I was wishing you would ask. Let's go by my place so I can freshen up and dress, then to your hotel so you can freshen up. Tonight is Friday, maybe we will be able to relax and rest tomorrow."

"Sounds good. Thank the maid and get the telephone number here."

Paulette's apartment was in a stylish neighborhood. The decor was tasteful and surprisingly feminine.

"Jeff, help yourself to a drink at the cupboard while I bathe."

Jeff fixed a whiskey and water and sat down on the overstuffed sofa.

It is hard to believe Paulette is a lesbian. Her clothing, make-up and mannerisms are all feminine. She is beautiful, gracious, has a pleasant personality and is just fun to be with. Oh, well, what the hell, we'll just hang out and have fun.

Quicker than most women, Paulette was dressed and ready to go in no time. As she emerged from the bedroom, Jeff let out a low whistle. She was gorgeous in a short black silk dress with thin straps, which showed the curves of her body and her long shapely legs.

"Would you prefer to go by the hotel and freshen up or use my bathroom?"

"I will need to change clothes, however, I'll never equal your fashion."

As they entered the hotel Jeff asked, "Paulette, what would you like to drink while you wait for me to get dressed?"

"I'll have a cognac to start. I would like this to be a special night. I don't know why, but I feel as though I am a normal person."

Jeff looked puzzled. "Gee, Paulette, I think you are normal even above average. I'll drink a cognac with you."

Jeff ordered four cognacs to be delivered to his room. "We'll have a couple while I'm getting prepared for our big night on the town."

Jeff went into the bathroom, bathed, shaved and put a towel around his waist to come out to get his clothing.

This time, Paulette let out a whistle.

"This is only a hotel room and not as large as your apartment. I apologize."

"Don't, you look great in just a towel. Do you mind if I ask a question?"

"No, not at all." Jeff reached for his drink, held the glass toward Paulette and said, "Salute, to a beautiful date. What would you like to ask?"

"Well, it is embarrassing to ask. If you would prefer not to talk about it, that would be fine, but I was looking at your left foot. What type of accident did you have?"

"It was no accident. I was born with a clubfoot. As you see, it has no toes. But, I did not know it wasn't normal until the kids at school teased me about it. Then I became sensitive, so I tried harder to be like other kids. I learned to run, jump and do everything they could, but I still had a little limp."

"I never noticed a limp. Your walking looks fine to me."

"After I made enough money, I had a special shoe made and when I wear it I don't limp as much."

"Jeff, I would love to do something tonight. If you can't, don't be embarrassed, but I haven't danced with a boy since I left high school. Can you dance?"

"Yes, not very well, but I do enjoying dancing. I'll finish dressing and we will go out and as they say in America, cut a rug. That means to dance."

A few minutes later, he returned, fully dressed and received another whistle.

Paulette said, "We do make a handsome couple. Let's enjoy the evening."

Getting into the Fiat, Jeff said, "This your city, so lead the way. I feel my mission is about accomplished, things are narrowing down to a couple of possibilities."

"Are you thinking Maxine is the person you are looking for?"

"That's one of the possibilities. The clothing that Annette Copola was wearing once belonged to Mary Alice Bakker and Maxine is in the clothing business. It would be easy to acquire new clothing and to sell or donate her former clothing. She also has a connection to the un Bordel de Bonheur. I don't know the extent of the connection just yet. Mike Martel also has a connection to the un Bordel de Bonheur, and Maxine and Mike have been observed together and seem to be close to each other. They both have gone out of the city; the puzzle is why Mike went on Thursday and Maxine on Friday. Also, the Ledbetter woman connects in some way with the two and she has also left the city. I wonder if they traveled to the same destination and if Louie's trip has any connection with the two?"

"What is your other possibility, the Ledbetter woman?"

"Yes, Mike lives on her property or the property that once belonged to the same estate. I have not found that she has any ties with the un Bordel de Bonheur.

"Let's put off the shop talk and discuss business some other time."

"I assume that shop talk is business talk. As you Americans say, check. We are almost at the La Jeunesse where the food is French and Moroccan with Oriental music and belly dancing. They have an excellent floor show and a band for dancing, I think you will love the atmosphere."

At La Jeunesse, they were seated in the center of the restaurant, with a good view of the stage where the band was playing, while three belly dancers performed.

"Paulette, I feel like celebrating. First, out with a beautiful and charming women who I have enjoyed working and relaxing with, and second, seeing the end of the tunnel of my mission. Would you care for a bottle of champagne? That is, if it's not too expensive. I am on a expense account but it is limited, somewhat."

"Jeff, you are the first man since high school I have enjoyed being with and I would like to celebrate also, for I think with you I have found my true self. I do not want you to be offended, but I would like to pick up the chéque for the champagne."

"There is no need for that, I just have to be careful with the expenses. What do you mean you found your true self?"

"I insist that the champagne is on me, and later I will tell you the meaning of finding my true self."

Paulette ordered champagne made from grapes whose cuttings were imported from France, grown and harvested in Morocco. It was an excellent wine to be aged only a short time.

The belly dancers completed their act and the band was preparing to set up for dance music. Jeff noticed a female on stage that looked familiar. He walked over toward the stage and realized that she was a well-known vocalist from America.

"Good evening. Aren't you Jo Bacon from America?"

"Why, yes. I can tell you are an American, too, and I would guess from Louisiana, by your accent."

"You are correct, New Orleans. I have seen you perform in New Orleans several times. I see you are ready to begin. A friend and I would be pleased if you would have a drink with us after your set."

"Thank you, when I take my break I'll come over to your table."

When the band started playing, Jeff asked Paulette to dance. He held her close and the perfume she was wearing, along with the champagne, was getting to him. She was noticeably pressing her body against his.

It is hard to believe she is a lesbian. I don't know how to proceed with her, the way she is acting.

They danced, talked, and drank more champagne and the time passed quickly. The band was taking a break and Jo came over. "I'll be back shortly and will have that drink with you. It is nice to talk to someone from home."

About ten minutes later Jo came over with a gentleman, who she introduced as her husband. After being seated Jeff asked, "How did you get to Morocco, is the band on tour?"

"No, we live here now. I was born in Saint Louis and became a blues singer. I traveled all over America and then to England and France. Returning to America, I realized that being colored did not matter in England or France, but in my own country I could not enjoy the fruits of my earnings the way I could in other countries, so I found a singing job in Paris. I'm better known in Europe than I was in America. I met my husband in Paris. We have been married for four years. The war in Europe was beginning to be dangerous for my husband. He is for Free France, so we had to leave. Enough about me, what about you?"

"Jo, I have lived in New Orleans for more than ten years. I am a private investigator, here in Morocco looking for an American girl. In New Orleans, I used to see you perform on Bourbon Street. In fact, I would give you a corsage once in a while, and when I went home I would play some of your songs on my harmonica. I also played for you one time."

"No, you're not the flower man, are you?"

"Yes, I was, and I still own the business. I have someone else managing it, now."

"What happened to the limp, or was that an act?"

"Yes and no. I only limp slightly while wearing my special shoe."

"Jeff, who is the person your are looking for?"

"A young lady whose real name is Mary Alice Bakker. I don't know what name she is using now."

"Do you have a photo of her? A few Americans live here and American tourists drop by occasionally. Maybe I have seen her."

Jeff pulled out the well-worn photo of Mary Alice and handed it to Jo.

"That face looks familiar. I believe she has been in here, but I can't say I met her. If you will tell me how I can get in touch with you, I'll let you know if she returns. I must get back to the dressing room to freshen up for the next show. It has been a pleasure to meet someone from the States and New Orleans."

Paulette and Jeff had more champagne, danced and talked until one AM.

While dancing Paulette snuggled up close to Jeff and said, "I am having a wonderful time and I hope what I am going to say will not spoil our friendship. Would you spend the night at my apartment with me?"

"Paulette, I would love to do that, but are you sure about having a man with you?"

"Yes, I am almost sure. Let's go, and we can talk about it when we get to my place."

When they arrived at the Fiat, Paulette went over to unlock the door on the right side and as she turned she collided with Jeff. As he put his arms around her to keep her from falling, they embraced and their lips found each other's. They kissed passionately for several minutes. A lustful craving for sexual contact surged through each of them.

Finally, Paulette pulled away. "Jeff, I know what I want. Let's go, and I will explain my feelings when we get home."

In the apartment, Paulette said, "Jeff, I will make some coffee while we talk. I do not want to be inebriated at a time like this."

When the coffee was ready, Paulette spoke, "Let me tell you of my background. I was born just outside of Paris to a middle class family. I have one sister and one brother; I am the middle child. When I was thirteen and just getting interested in boys, a neighbor about twenty years of age was home from college. I'd had a crush on him from the time I was nine or ten. We met one afternoon he asked if I would like to take a drive in the country. I was very flattered that an 'older man' would want to go out with me. He drove out in the country and he told me how beautiful I was. We parked by a lake in a wooded area and began to kiss. His hands were fondling me and it excited me. When he started to undress me, I got scared and I tried to stop him. His mood changed and he got really rough with me. He hit me in the body; I assumed later, so the bruises would not show. He told me he would kill me if I didn't undress, and I still refused. Then he pulled me out of the car and put me on the ground, putting his knee in the pit of my stomach, he slapped me and took my clothes off. When he saw I was menstruating, he became more outraged and mean, hitting me in a frenzy of blows. He had undressed and he ravished and assaulted me. I believe it continued for about two hours. After each time, he would tell me that if I told anyone he would take me off in the woods and do this again for days and then kill me. When he was finished, he let me go to the lake to wash and clean up, then he took me home.

"After that, each time I got near a male I would get tense and almost go into a nervous breakdown. I lost weight and my parents began to worry about me, so they made an appointment with a doctor. The doctor could not find any medical reason that would make me lose weight and be nervous, so he recommended my parents take me to a psychologist, a Dr. Marie Antrone. Dr. Antrone was a lady in her early forties. She was very gentle with me. I finally told my story of the incident at the lake and how I was afraid around any males, even my father and brother. The doctor told me this was normal, that I had to accept males as the animals they were. Most of the female population accepted this behavior for financial security, food, clothing, housing and the maternal instinct to bear children. The instinct was strong in the female because they are taught that the greatest reward was to bear children. She said that some women were like her, enjoyed the company of other females and had no interest in bearing children. Females were strong, but gentle and loving. She advised me to be friendly with males, but associate very little with them, however bond with females.

"As the visits became more frequent, she was telling me what a beautiful young girl I was, and that we should become closer. On one occasion, she invited me to the seashore for the weekend. My family's perception was that this would be beneficial to my full recovery, as my demeanor had greatly improved since I began seeing Dr. Antrone.

"After arriving at her cottage, we went swimming and later to dinner. As we were preparing to go to bed, Marie suggested that we share the same bed to discuss some of the aspects of my problem.

"Lying in bed, the discussion turned from my problems to telling me how lovely and caring I was. She put her arms around me and pulled me close to her and cuddled and fondled me. As she kissed my breast, her hand moved down between my legs. I felt, for the first time, a sexual desire since the rape incident. There was no grasping and squeezing of my breast; her hand was gentle, not the rough groping of my vagina as the man who forced himself on me. The man's penetration was forceful and rough, as he jabbed me in the vagina with his penis and seemed to suffocate me with his heavy body on top of mine. Marie gently caressed my vagina while kissing my breast, and stomach, until her head was between my legs. I did not know what an orgasm was until then; it was pure sexual excitement and I was lost in another world. Afterwards, the gentle treatment of Marie fondling me, made me feel that I was alive again. I was with Marie three years before she was killed in a train wreck. I was not involved with another woman steadily until I met

Jeanie. I had been with her for about three months, when we had a disagreement and a fight in a nightclub. Since I've been working with you, I find that my interest in women has diminished some."

They had finished their second cup of coffee. Paulette went into the bathroom and came out in a very sheer, white nightgown and said, "Jeff, get undressed and I'll discard the nightgown and let nature take its course."

In bed, Jeff took Paulette in his arms, kissing her full sensuous lips, moving down to her breasts and kissed each of them while slowly moving his hand down between her legs, and nature took it course.

Jeff woke up to the smell of coffee and looked around. He was in Paulette's bed, with the sun shining through the window on him. Paulette came out of the kitchen in her sheer nightgown. *God, she is one beautiful and sexy woman.*

"Good morning, Jeff. Go to the bathroom and I will have some coffee and toast waiting when you finish."

Over toast and coffee Jeff said, "There is not much we can do until Catherine and Maxine return from Agadir. Today is Saturday, would it be all right with you if we revisit the Villa Marrakech and show the photo of Mary Alice Bakker to the housekeeper? I should have done it yesterday."

"That is a good idea, and after we visit the Villa Merrakech we can relax for the rest of the weekend."

"Before we go, I think we should take a trial run at sex and see if it is as good as it was last night."

"Jeff, we think alike."

They removed their clothing and had torrid sex, then relaxed in each other's arms, revitalizing their bodies, until they had restored their strength and again made love.

At eleven-thirty, they headed for la Villa Marrakech. Arriving at 13913 Boulevard de Santi, it took some fifteen minutes or more for the housekeeper to appear at the gate.

As Paulette interpreted, Jeff said, "Madam, in my official duties, before I contact Miss Ledbetter, I must know I will be speaking to the correct person. It is very important that the correct person receives this money. Here is a photo of the person we know as Catherine Ledbetter. Is this the person who resides here and is now in Agadir at the telephone number you gave us? The housekeeper looked at the photo for a couple of minutes and replied, "This must be an old photograph, for she is younger and has a different hair style."

"Yes, Madam, the photo was taken about two years ago. Can you say this is the same person who lives here?"

"Yes, that is Mademoiselle Ledbetter, but she is more beautiful now. Have you spoken with her?"

"We will this afternoon, now that you have made the identification. Thank you, Madam."

Leaving the villa, Jeff said, "Paulette, I think we have found Mary Alice Bakker. I will have to call my client and give him an update. If you would take us to the la Réfugier Hotel, I can report the progress. Afterward, we can finish the weekend on our own. However, I have a better idea. Mary Alice will be gone for a week. I think my client would want me to go to Agadir, at once, and confirm that this really is her. After I speak with Mr. Bakker, and depending upon the time, we can leave either this afternoon or early in the morning for Agadir. If you would be free at least until Monday, I would like you to come with me."

"Yes, I will make a couple of calls and have my assistant cover for me."

Arriving at the hotel, Jeff gave the hotel telephone operator Marshall Bakker's telephone number to place a call for him. It would be seven AM in New Orleans.

At two-fifteen Jeff picked up the ringing telephone, "Hello, Marshall."

"Yes, how are you Jeff? Have you any good news?"

"I'll put it this way, about ninety percent good news. That is, I'm almost sure I have found Mary Alice."

"That is wonderful news! Is she safe and in good health? When can I see her?"

"Not so fast. Let me tell you where I am in the investigation. At the Villa Marrakech, which was willed to her, the housekeeper has identified the photo of Mary Alice as the present occupant and owner."

"Good job, Jeff! I'll make arrangements to fly over to Marrakech tomorrow."

"Hold on Marshall. I have not met Catherine Ledbetter. She left Friday to go to Agadir for about a week. With your permission, I will leave in the morning for Agadir to confirm the true identity of Catherine Ledbetter."

"Hell, Jeff, you don't need my permission. Just call me promptly, I will be at the office tomorrow and you will be able to reach me wherever I am located. Jeff, be sure to tell her about Clifford Barnett. I have her money in a special account. Barnett has vanished. The police believe that he has left the country. He could be there, so be on the alert and careful. I'll be waiting for your call."

Jeff looked at his watch; it was two-thirty. "Paulette, how long would it take us to drive to Agadir?"

"It is about one hundred twenty-five miles over the mountain. I would say at the best travel time it would be about seven or seven-thirty if we leave by three. This time of the year the sun doesn't set until about seven-thirty, so we may make better time."

Looking at his notes, Jeff gave Paulette a telephone number and said, "This is the number of la Medina Palace in Agadir. Call and make reservations for us to arrive between seven and eight o'clock."

After three and a half hours over the narrow mountain highway, they arrived at la Medina Palace and checked in. They freshened up and went to dinner.

As they were eating Paulette said to Jeff, "Listening to the conversation here in the dining room, we missed the excitement. Early this morning, they found a man and a women dead, in one of the rooms."

"What was the circumstance surrounding the deaths?"

"The table on my left said it was a lover's argument, the table on my right is saying it was gang killing. No one really knows."

"I have more concern about finding Catherine Ledbetter. When we finish, let's retire to our room and let nature take its course. We will find Miss Ledbetter in the morning."

"Jeff, all of a sudden I do not have any appetite. I think nature is better."

Waking up, Jeff looked at Paulette sleeping, then at his watch and saw that it was after eight o'clock. *Damn, how did I sleep so long? I was tired from the long drive and Paulette makes a good sleeping pill.* He touched Paulette's breast slightly, rubbing her nipple with his forefinger. Paulette opened one eye then the other and reached out and pulled him over to her, and for the next thirty minutes or so, nature took its course.

"You can use the bathroom first and dress. I will make a call to Miss Ledbetter's room.

"Operator, room 227."

"Miss Ledbetter checked out early this morning."

"Did she make reservations elsewhere?"

"Monsieur, I believe she on the way to Marrakech by train."

"Do you know when the train departs for Marrakech?"

"I believe it departs about ten o'clock."

"Did Mademoiselle accompany Mademoiselle Vensel to Marrakech?"

"Oh, no, Monsieur. Haven't you heard about the tragedy?"

"What tragedy?"

"Yesterday morning Mademoiselle Vensel and a yet to be identified Italian Army Officer were shot and killed by an unknown person."

"What about Mademoiselle Ledbetter, was she injured?"

"No, she left this morning with a detective from Marrakech."

"Was she under arrest or did she go willingly?"

"I believe she went willingly. The newspapers stated no arrests have been made."

"Thank you."

Damn, what rotten luck. I knew I should have gotten up and not had that last piece.

When Paulette came out of the bathroom she said, "Why the long face, anything wrong?"

"Yes," and he told her of the departure of Catherine and the slaying of Maxine and the Italian Officer.

"That is bad, however, we can make a holiday out of it. If we had not come to Agadir, we would be doing something in Marrakech. Relax, we can spend a couple of hours here and take our time driving back. We can leave here by noon and arrive back in Marrakech around four."

"You do make a good partner. I should go to policier to see whether they will give me any information."

At the station he asked for the person in charge of the Maxine Vensel case. A detective came out and introduced himself, and asked if he could assist them.

Jeff spoke. "We were looking for a Catherine Ledbetter and Maxine Vensel, and learned that Maxine Vensel was killed, and Catherine Ledbetter has returned to Marrakech with a detective. Was she under arrest?"

"By what authority are you requesting this information?"

Showing his ID he said, "I am an American private investigator, searching for a missing American woman. This is her photo. Is this the person that is named Catherine Ledbetter?"

"Yes, that is she. She was not arrested. However, a detective from Marrakech is escorting her back."

"Would the detective be Louie Bennard?"

"Yes, do you know him?"

"Yes, we have become close friends and he has given me assistance in trying to locate this person."

"Detective Bennard and Mademoiselle Ledbetter have become very close. Detective Bennard was in Agadir on another matter, investigating Maxine Vensel and an American by the name of Mike Martel. Maxine was murdered, but no one has observed Martel, either before or after the slaying."

"Thank you. We will be departing for Marrakech. I will contact Louie when we get there."

Arriving in Marrakech at four-thirty, Paulette drove to her apartment.

"Jeff, why don't you stay here tonight and you can make plans for tomorrow. I will help, if I can."

"You know as much about this case as I and maybe understand it better. Your input would mean a great deal to me. I will call the hotel to see if I have any messages."

Louie had left a message at three-thirty for Jeff to call him. He picked up the phone on the first ring.

"Hello, Louie here."

"Louie, this is Jeff. How are you?"

"Friend, I am, as you Americans would say, 'down'. To me that is discouraged, I have had three days of ups and downs. One thing that I am discouraged about should make you happy."

"I am sorry about your discouragement. Tell me about it, or better yet, why don't you come over to Paulette's apartment and we can discuss it here?"

"So you and Paulette are close. I thought she was a lesbian."

"No more. I'll put Paulette on and she can give you the address."

Within the hour, Louie came in and they greeted each other as if they had not seen one another for months.

Paulette made them all drinks and Louie brought them up to date on his adventure.

"Jeff, I believe the girl I have fallen in love with is your missing Mary Alice Bakker. I think she is struggling with identifying herself to me. We have agreed not see each other for two days. I thought that would give her time to think things out."

"Louie, I have come to the same conclusion, that Catherine Ledbetter is Mary Alice Bakker. I have ruled out Maxine. The main reason is that she is French, but she plays some part with Mike and Catherine. She is a friend to both, as Jacque, Doran and others have seen her with each of them. Paulette and I traveled to Agadir to see her and found out about the murders and you and Catherine. We had visited Villa Marrakech, and the housekeeper identified the photo of Mary Alice as being Catherine. I planned to see Catherine tomorrow. I need to wrap this case up, for Mr. Bakker is waiting to come here, but I will wait until the day after tomorrow."

"No, you go and interview Catherine tomorrow. I have much work to do; I am also trying to wrap up my case. We have identified the dead man in Agadir who went under the name of Roberto Palermo, as the bande, I think you call gang member. He is Réne Munroe. Remember the man and women we had the little encounter with at la Gazelle, who was dressed as a German officer? He stated his patron was Réne Munroe. This was the dead bande in la Medina Palace. The little bande was named Andre. We think Andre was supposed to kill Catherine and Réne. The plan was that Maxine would go for an early walk and Réne would come to the room and kill Catherine. However, Catherine was the one who woke up early and took a walk and when Réne came to the room, he found Maxine. They were discussing how to finish the job.

"Meanwhile, Mike had set it up with le Roi to have Andre to come in and kill Réne and Catherine. Andre, who had never seen Catherine but knew she was a blond, mistakenly killed Maxine instead. We are going to raid Andre's apartment at four tomorrow morning, hoping that will lead us to Mike."

"Why Mike? I was under the impression that he and Catherine were partners. Why kill her?"

"We don't know yet. We can only speculate that Mike has joined with le Roi to take over the full ownership of the un Bordel de Bonheur and la Villa Marrakech. A part we have not connected is the attorney from London, who has been seen from time to time with Mike and le Roi. We now know who le Roi is. He is an Arabian by the name of Ali bin Samad.

We received most of this information from one of our men. Remember at the killing of the uncover agent at la Gazelle, the man in the red fez? Also, Albert the detective? Albert was in the bande and was le Roi's right-hand man; we received most of this information through Albert. That is all I can tell you at this point, and I know that it will not go any further. I now must go, for I have to be up early, about one-thirty, to assemble the forces to pull the raid off."

After Louie left, Paulette and Jeff lay in bed discussing the turn of events.

"Go with me early in the morning so we can arrive at Villa Marrakech a little before seven. We may catch Catherine before she hears any news. I am sure Louie and his people will be at 13913-B Boulevard de Santi looking for Mike."

"Jeff, it will take a good thirty minutes to get to the Villa Marrakech. We should be up at five-thirty to dress, get breakfast if we are going to be at Villa Marrakech by seven."

The alarm clock woke Jeff up. He leaned over and kissed Paulette and said, "Let's postpone sex until this day is ended."

At fifteen minutes to seven, Jeff was ringing the doorbell at Villa Marrakech. He continued pressing the buzzer for about fifteen minutes until the housekeeper appeared.

"Mademoiselle Ledbetter just awoke and will not see anyone this early."

"Remember us? We went to Agadir to see her but she had departed before we arrived. I have important business, and I have been from here to Agadir and back. I know it is early, but I am tired, too. It would be much less trouble to allow us in to see her now."

"Follow me and I do hope that this is important."

The housekeeper led the couple to the rear of the Villa to a garden by the pool. The sun was up over the snow-topped Atlas Mountains, the air was fresh, and the scene was beautiful and peaceful. That peace would be shattered in a very short time.

"Mademoiselle Ledbetter, this lady and gentlemen have been here a number of times trying to talk to you. They say that it is urgent."

Catherine was seated at a round table near the pool. She looked up and said, "What is so urgent that you must encroach on my privacy at this early hour of the morning?"

I think I will try to get her off balance and come right to the point.

"Good morning. My name is Jeff Stewart. I am from New Orleans, and this is my interpreter Paulette. Please pardon us Mary Alice, for being so early, but it is important."

Catherine dropped her head for a moment, and then looked up at Jeff, as if she was a little girl who had been caught with her hand in the cookie jar.

"I am glad, I have been expecting something like this to happen."

"First, Mary Alice, let me tell you of some things you may have misunderstood. Your father did not steal your money. Your grandfather's attorney, Clifford Barnett, was the person who took it. He has been caught and all but a few thousand dollars has been recovered. He has disappeared and we believe Mike Martel has also disappeared. We know that Mike tried to set you up to be killed in Agadir. Maxine was supposed to be taking a walk while you were being killed. But since you were the one to get up early, when Réne Munroe came in, Andre killed the two of them."

"Why would Mike do this to me? I trusted him. He ran the un Bordel de Bonheur. After about a month, I have been there only two times. He even lived on my property without paying. I don't understand it. My father must have disowned me for not trusting him or talking to him about the money."

"No, Mary Alice, your father loves you. He hired me to find you. I have spent a lot of time trying to find you, in Casablanca, Erfoud out in the desert, the trip to Agadir yesterday and of course, Marrakech. With or without your permission, I must call your father to let him know I have found you. He will fly here immediately after I call. For his sake and yours, also, I wish you would greet him. He loves you very much."

"Yes, I miss my father and I want to see him and tell him how sorry I am about the way I treated him. My life has changed, resulting from a person I have met."

"Yes, I know the person you are speaking of. Louie Bennard has become my friend and was helping me find you. He didn't know who you were until last night, when he and I were at Paulette's apartment together. He is the one who told me about Mike. I believe Mike is heavily involved with a gang here in Morocco. Louie told me last night to tell you he loves you and wants to know you as Mary Alice Bakker. May I use your telephone to call Louie's office? I'll leave a message for him to call you and I would also like to speak with him. Now, I want to call your father and hopefully you will speak with him?"

"Yes, yes. Please make both calls. I will tell Camille to bring some fresh coffee and pastre."

Chapter Twenty-Five

Jeff asked the operator to place an overseas telephone call to Marshall Bakker.

"Hello, Marshall Bakker here."

"Marshall, it's Jeff."

"Oh, Jeff, I hope you have some good news."

"I have Marshall. There is someone I want you to speak to."

Jeff handed the telephone to Mary Alice, as he took Paulette's hand and they walked out of the house to the Fiat. They drove back to la Réfugier Hotel in silence.

Entering the room, Jeff just flopped into a chair, "Jeff, is there something wrong?"

"No, Paulette. I am just exhausted. I guess from the excitement of the chase and now that I have caught the prey, I am emotionally drained."

"My English is good, but I have a hard time understanding some of your American phrases. I don't think you are drained; let nature take it's course."

She moved over to the chair clasped his hands and pulled him up. She unbuttoned his shirt and began rubbing his chest, then unbuttoned his trousers, pulled his body to hers and started rubbing and squeezing his buttocks. His emotions were not drained, after all. He unbuttoned the three buttons on Paulette's dress and pulled it over her head. Next, he removed her slip. Pulling her close he reached behind her back and unsnapped her bra, letting it fall to the floor. She stood there looking beautiful in nothing but her panties. Finally, he put his fingers inside, sliding the panties down over her buttocks to her ankles. There she stood, "naked as a jay bird," as a true southerner would say. His eyes met hers and he lowered them slowly down to her firm rounded breasts, flat smooth belly, continuing down to...WOW, what happened here? Her pubic hair was trimmed in the shape of a heart.

"I did it last night after you went to sleep, especially for you."

He gently placed her on the bed and ran his hand down to the heart shaped hairs and nature took its course.

They lay there holding each other, exhausted, emotionally and physically, when the loud ringing of the telephone snapped them back to reality.

"Hello, Jeff Stewart here."

"Jeff, Louie. I have just spoken with Cath, uh, I mean Mary Alice. She talked to her father, and he is on the way here. I have also been busy. We have wrapped up le Royaume de Sang. Mary Alice wants you and Paulette and myself to come to Villa Marrakech this afternoon. She wants to say thank you to you two, and I have some news for you. It is now twelve, can you meet us there at two o'clock?"

"Yes, Louie we will be there."

When they arrived at Villa Marakech, Louie was already there. After they were seated Louie said. "First, let me bring you up to date on the case we have just completed. Clifford Barnett, the American attorney, who stole money from Mary Alice and numerous other clients, has been arrested in England and will be returned to New Orleans to stand trial.

"Mike Martel had worked for Barnett in New Orleans, and was paid handsomely to encourage Mary Alice to come to Morocco on this adventure. Mike was a thrill-seeker who was easily swayed toward a life of crime. What he didn't realize was, there is no room for error when dealing with foreign gangs. He lost his life because he botched the job he was sent to Agadir to perform.

"Maxine Wensel was a victim of her own making. She and Mike had a long-standing affair. Because she didn't have the willpower to refuse Mike anything, she agreed to go along with his scheme to murder Mary Alice and it ended up costing her her life.

"Réne Munroe is dead. His partner, Vincent Catola is behind bars, along with Andre, Albert, the detective, and Ali bin Samad.

"We located Mr. and Mrs. Palermo's son, Roberto. He had been robbed, beaten and had his uniform stolen. He has been reunited with his parents at a hospital here in Marrakech.

"That sums up the investigation of the bad guys.

"Now, I'll fill you in on the saga of three people who were joined together by fate; an unhappy young woman, who made some foolish decisions, but was fortunate to be reunited with the father who loves her, while falling in love with a man who adores her; a detective from a foreign land, who found adventure, love and friendship while solving his client's case; a lonely and bitter man, who after the tragic loss of a loved one, was fortunate to find another love to share his life with.

"And let's not forget Paulette, who went above and beyond her duties as an interpreter, and found a new life in the process.

"Well, enough of this. Now, let's eat, drink and be merry."

Mary Alice came over to Jeff and said; "Dad said for you to stay until he arrived, he should be here the day after tomorrow."

"Fine. Paulette and I will be leaving. I'll call each day to see when your father gets here and you have my hotel number if you need to reach me."

"Jeff, I'll have Camille clear out Mike's belongings and clean the place up by tonight, if you want to stay here. There's a telephone you may use, it's in my name and charged to my residence."

"Thank you Mary Alice, that would be nice."

On the way to the hotel Jeff said to Paulette, "I'll have about two days as soon as I move my belongings over. Let's go to Agadir and see what we missed the last time."

"Sure, let's go and let nature take its course."

Three days later, Jeff was seated by the window of the aircraft waiting for the plane to taxi down the runway for take-off. Louie, Mary Alice and Marshall Bakker had come to see him off. *Now, where is Paulette? She said she would be here to see the plane take off. Oh, well, gone and forgotten.*

The plane taxied out to the end of the runway and made its turn to line up for take-off. Looking out the window, Jeff saw the little Fiat by the fence with Paulette standing on top waving a red shawl. She waved until he could not see anything but a speck.

He adjusted the seat to the reclining position, laid his head back, wiped away a couple of tears and closed his eyes.

How in the hell, did a poor country boy from a farm in south Alabama get here?

About the Author

Olmond M. Hall is the author of two novels, Mansion on the Hill, a humorous muder mystery. Road to Marrakech a sizzling story of mystery, sex and murder in the intriguing cities of New Orleans, Casablanca and Marrakech. He lives with his wife Mary Ann in Marion Landing near Ocala, Florida.

Printed in the USA
CPSIA information can be obtained
at www.ICGtesting.com
LVHW042038071223
765879LV00030B/135

9 780595 181278